Also by Ingrid Bengis
Combat in the Erogenous Zone

Ingrid Bengis

I Have Come Here
to Be Alone

• • •

SIMON AND SCHUSTER
NEW YORK

Library of Congress Cataloging in Publication Data

Bengis, Ingrid.
I have come here to be alone.

I. Title.
PZ4.B4588Iag   [PS3552.E543]   813'.5'4   76-22610
ISBN 0-671-22330-5

Acknowledgments

To Nancy Seif, for helping me to understand Lola.

To Barbara and Bill, for stoking, maintaining and dampening the fires, whichever was required.

To Danny, for being an invisible part of the process, a standard.

To Ellen Halloran, for listening, over and over again, at the oddest hours.

To Ellen Hovde, for giving me a joyous scene and a letter.

To Genny and Gianni, for feeding me, talking with me, understanding more quickly than I did, and just being around.

To Alfonso, for living through it.

To Jonathan, for the moment of decision.

To Steve, for believing that I'm better than I really am.

To Wendy, for more than I can say.

To my parents, Lilly, and Lori Hutchinson, a family

Man survives earthquakes, epidemics, the horrors of disease and all the agonies of the soul. But for all time his most tormenting tragedy has been, is, and will be—the tragedy of the bedroom.

TOLSTOY
From *Reminiscences of Tolstoy, Chekhov and Andreyev,* by Maxim Gorky

I Have Come Here
to Be Alone

Part One

I HAVE COME here to be alone, to think about something, although I am not sure what. Stefan is gone and I no longer know the truth about anything. Stefan is gone. I keep having to remind myself of that. It is cold on the island. Last week, for the first time in anyone's memory, it snowed here, here in the land of mythic clarity, where everything is supposed to be sharp and lucid, dry, cloudless and calm. Stefan is gone and I am left to the Greeks. All week the wind has been weeping and wailing like Greek women in mourning, whipping themselves into a frenzied dementia that only subsides when they sleep. The sound lives in my bones, a dark fever which files my nerves to extinction. I have nightmares which I don't remember, but I wake up with my muscles marshaled for combat, my heart tossing like a single-masted sailboat wrenched free of its anchor, becalmed somewhere in the pale sea of the interior, with no wind to fill the sails and no new mooring to hold it in place.

I am very tired even though I slept this afternoon. I slept because of the sunshine. There were two rectangular patches of it shining on the walls, and through the high narrow windows above the door, I could see that the sky was blue. So I dragged a chair out onto the terrace and huddled there with my coat on while the wind mangled my mind. Then I came back in and stared at the sunlight on the walls again. Cold sunlight. Untouchable sunlight. Finally I crawled into bed, feeling angry at the sunshine, waiting for the night.

It is strange how the mind works to analyze some things as constructive and other things as useless. If I sit in the house and stare at the walls, that is useless; if I put the chair out on the terrace and stare at the sun, I am being constructive . . . I am catching some sun. There are millions of people who trek thousands of miles across oceans every winter to do that, but if I were to tell them that I spend hours staring at two patches of sunlight on bare white walls, they would think I was crazy. It will be two months before the sun really comes out and it gets warm again, two months before I can say that I am spending a wonderful time in Greece soaking up the sun.

•

I say to myself that beginnings don't matter, that the end is irrelevant. I say that what counts is going on from here, the past is past and all that. But each day I sift over the old moments, trying to find the moment when something struck bottom, looking for the decisive clue, parading each gesture, each conversation, each frame of our life together, stopping and examining and splicing together, trying to find something coherent, trying to nab the crucial second when everything finally failed. I have wound the film backward and forward, stared at single frames for an hour, and let my bouzouki record with the long scratch in it jar for ten minutes before giving the needle a nudge. But still nothing makes sense.

I have come here to be alone. I have come to start from scratch.

•

The wind has gotten worse. It has been blowing for days. I have to get out of the house. There is a cafe fifty yards away, but I can't go there anymore. The village idiot who has a large thick tongue and wears pants held up with string sits in the cafe all day long. His name is Demetrios. He is in love with me. He is very fat and his hair looks as if it had been cut with a pair of sheep shears. His eyes are crossed. One pupil seems much larger than the other. He chatters to me in a garbled Greek which I can hardly understand, and since I do not laugh at him or say anything nasty, he thinks I love him too. He sits in the cafe, waiting for me and waiting for Christos. Christos is ten. When Christos comes home from school, he plays cards with Demetrios in the cafe. Christos always wins. Someday Christos will be a sirtaki boy. He knows the sirtaki steps perfectly and can slap his heel, leap to the floor, pick up a glass of retsina with his teeth and drink it in one gulp. He never smiles. There is a frightening, cold concentration about him. He can sit for hours copying map after map of Asia. He can stare right through me. I have never been afraid of a ten-year-old before.

Sometimes Demetrios' mother comes into the cafe. She buttons up his jacket for him, strokes his hair, pulls her shawl back up around her head and goes away. The other day Demetrios was playing with Christos in front of the cafe and dropped a stone on Christos' head so that Christos was knocked unconscious. Now Christos has a bandage around his head.

Yesterday was the last time I went to the cafe. Demetrios came to the house in the afternoon. He stood in front of the door blinking lopsidedly at me. "*Gramma*," he said. "*Echete gramma.*" And smiled his idiot's smile, with one eye seeming to grow large in the light of the doorway.

"What?" I said. "What?"

"*Gramma gramma gramma gramma gramma gramma gramma*," he repeated, his voice rising to a shriek as spit drooled out of his mouth.

"I don't understand you idiot," I yelled, inexplicably raging. Then I burst into tears.

Demetrios put his fat hand on my face and wobbled his thick

17

tongue, murmuring soft sounds in my ear. Then he pulled at my hand until I followed him up to the cafe, loose as a dumb sheep being led to slaughter.

Inside the cafe, Thalassa and old Vasilios and Christos were clustered around the postman with his battered goatskin bag, drinking ouzo. He handed me a letter. The idiot boy started to dance with joy, but then he tripped over his own legs, fell and started to cry. His eyes were rolling. Vasilios reached out his cane and poked the idiot boy in the side. The idiot boy lay down in a corner and did not get back up. He made no more noise.

I ordered a cup of coffee and opened the letter. Thalassa and Vasilios fought over the stamp. I gave it to Christos who pasted it on top of Pakistan.

The letter was from Arnold. He wrote that his friend Karen, who had spent the winter in one of the Cretan caves, had just killed herself with a little pearl-handled nail file she used to carry around for self-protection when she was living on Crete. Karen had red hair, graduated from Simmons and wanted to write a novel about life in the Cretan caves. A Greek who wasn't quite clear on the theories of American female emancipation apparently thought that she was fair game and raped her while she was going to the village to buy eggs. Then she took a plane back to America. Six months later she killed herself. Arnold had no idea why. Neither did I.

I tried to remember Karen's face, to focus on her features, to think about the conversation we had had when she came to spend a day with me on the island just before going on to Crete. Nothing came back to me. She had been passing through, another visitor, another American. Now suddenly, I felt obliged to remember what she had said, obliged to inflate her human presence. But it was too late. The memory had evaporated.

While I was reading the letter from Arnold, the idiot boy stood up, came over and began breathing down my neck and stroking my arm. Spit drooled out of his mouth and dripped on

18

my hand. It made my skin crawl. I was afraid that I was going to scream or else hit him. Old Vasilios, who also spends most of his time in the cafe, saw the expression on my face and roared with laughter, pulling his mustache and raising his eyebrows. I cannot tell the idiot boy to keep his hands off me.

So I will not go back to the cafe.

•

"Dear Stefan. I am at the house on the island. Solitude inspires me. I know I promised not to write, but . . ."

"Dear Bill. This is a picture of my house. I drew it. The house overlooks the sea and has vaulted ceilings. It was renovated from an earthquake ruin. You have been a good friend for many years and I know that I can count on you. Will you please call Stefan when you are in Austria, just to see how he's doing. I know things are over between us, but . . ."

"Dear Mother and Dad. I am very happy here. The island is beautiful. And the people have been exceptionally kind. The mule driver and his wife invited me to dinner. Also the pope (that's what they call the Greek Orthodox priests) invited me over to his house because his son is the lame plumber who helped build the house and the priest is looking for someone his son can marry. I seem to be the newest prospect. I know you think it's about time I settled down. I am getting used to Stefan's absence. There is no need to be dramatic about it. It wasn't such a tragedy. My life is *not* ruined. I disagree with your evaluation of things. I am not being unreasonable. Your last letter sounded depressed. Why?"

"Dear Marge. I can't figure out what I'm doing here. It all seems an insane fantasy. I cannot acquire a taste for ouzo. I keep telling myself that nothing affects me. I would like to . . ."

"Dear Stefan."

·

I go for a walk, down into the village. I buy onions and tomatoes and eggs. When I start back to the house, the sun is already sinking on one side of the island and a full moon is rising
on the other. I stand on the terrace until it gets dark. The clouds
are thick and greenish in the moonlight, like sails wrenched from
their masts in a storm. The mules are braying near the house,
and on the road I can hear one of the mule drivers shouting,
"Delop, delop, delop," in a permanently angry but resigned tone
of voice. I know that the stick is prodding the mule's flank, already raw and bleeding and covered with sores. In the moonlight
I can see the volcano in the bay, humped and ugly, like a large
wart on the face of the Aegean. One day the volcano will erupt
or another earthquake will blow me to smithereens if I have not
evaporated into steam by then. I have estimated the possibilities.
In all likelihood, old Vasilios' house will fall on top of mine and
mine will then slide into the sea. The thought is strangely intoxi-
cating, as if it could happen tomorrow, and I could wake up two
days from now to read about it in the newspapers and discuss it
with my friends.

When I go back into the house, I discover that one of the
cats has stolen my dinner. It was a wedge of goat cheese I put out
on the sill to keep fresh, and now I will have to wait until next
week when the boat comes with food from the mainland. I blame
Lawrence Durrell, Henry Miller and Nikos Kazantzakis. They're
the ones who lured me here in the first place.

I thought I was a loner and discovered it was a lie. I thought
I wanted to paint landscapes, develop my own photographs, dig
for artifacts, write travel pieces, be independent. Those were lies
too, or rather the kind of deceptions which seem to give momentary balance to the fits, starts and fizzles of my life.

In a way it is true that I'm suited to island living. Islands are for people whose characters tend to disintegrate. There have to be boundaries somewhere. On the island I cannot wake up in the middle of the night, put a knapsack on my back and take off for Tanzania on an impulse. Impulses have to wait for the boat, and by then they've fossilized. I have very few impulses these days though. Except . . .

I have come here to be alone.

•   •   •

Today Hans, who has spent the last two years buying up the ruins of houses that were destroyed or partially destroyed during the last earthquake, has come back to Panaghios from Athens. I am taking care of his house for him, rent free. The last time he was here, I went with him and Ioannis the plumber to look at ruins. In the rubble above our village, we found a doll with a broken head, small shoes, pots and pans, the remnants of a dress, scraps of unidentifiable metal. In one house there was an old man with a thick yellow mustache lying in bed surrounded by his belongings: six icons, three crosses, and a garishly painted doll with her hand dangling into a pan filled with fly-specked feta cheese and tomatoes soaked in olive oil. The old man's son had agreed to sell their house to Hans, and Hans wanted to go to the notary immediately. At the door the man's wife stopped him, brandishing an armful of radishes in front of his face. She screamed that her husband was a drunk and crazy, that he had sold the house for a tenth of its worth. Hans was silent. On the way back to the village, Ioannis said he had nothing to worry about. It was in the nature of women to scream, and in the nature of men to ignore it.

All that evening, Ioannis talked about making a killing in real estate, using the English words he had learned from Hans. And still Hans said nothing.

I decided against going on any more expeditions.

•

Hans has tried to persuade me to buy one of his houses. "As an investment," he says. "Before it's too late. Besides, what's three hundred dollars for a house? Nothing." But the ghosts and the old man and the doll with the broken head; I cannot. Besides, all I have is three hundred dollars. So instead of buying a house, I watch as, one after another, the skeletons are fleshed out.

Someday, Hans says, tourists from France, Switzerland, England, Germany, Holland and Italy will come to Panaghios to live in these houses. An international colony. No, he says, reconsidering: not from Germany. The villagers laugh and say that Hans is "loco." Hans works, Ioannis works, Michaelis the mason works, Andreas the mule driver works. One by one the houses are restored. The others stare out at the sea like blind ghosts.

Tonight I am cooking dinner for all of them. They sit in the living room, Michaelis with his black curls, his round pretty child's face, his blue-and-white-striped work suit that is too tight across his chest; Ioannis with his raised shoe and cane beside him, his mustache covering most of his upper lip. His small teeth, like baby's teeth, are overlapped by large gums.

"I have brought you something from Switzerland," Hans says to Ioannis. It is a small plastic sack. Ioannis looks at it for a long time, not understanding what it is. Hans laughs and says, "It's sneezing powder." For a moment Ioannis stares at the packet in awe. He is addicted to practical jokes. Then he whoops, tries to leap up, trips over his cane and calls for a toast.

Hans brings out a decanter of grappa, and I bring out glasses. When the toast has been made, Hans rummages in a box filled with stockings and plates and oranges, and comes up with a bouzouki record he has bought in Athens. He puts it on the turntable, and the song of Zorba tears through the room. Michaelis looks at Ioannis, Ioannis looks at Hans and I look at all of them. Wordlessly Hans rolls up the reed mats on the floor and begins to dance. He is clumsy, tripping over his own feet and waving his arms in the air. He leaps, swirls, lands on the floor with his legs collapsing under him like a rag doll, picks himself up and leaps again. Michaelis watches. Then he too stands up and, bearlike, taps his foot against the floor as if testing its durability. Then he claps his hands together, throws back his head, yelps and jumps into the air.

At first they dance separately, moving toward each other, then gripping each other around the neck. It is a long time before Ioannis rises and limps along beside them, tapping his stick on the floor. Andreas arrives at the door while the music is playing. He has two mules with him, loaded down with barrels and crates. He ties up the mules, walks in, picks up a used glass from the table, fills it twice with grappa, downing both glasses, wipes his thick mustache and joins them. He dances to the old Cretan song as if he has been taking lessons at Arthur Murray's, gliding waltzlike across the floor, absorbed in himself and the music, trying out studied intricacies on the red clay floor.

Once I try to join them, but instantly all of their absorption in the dance itself vanishes and they are watching me. I stop and retreat to the sidelines. Then suddenly, as if by some prearranged signal, the four of them sweep past my chair and thunder onto the tabletop, crushing two glasses that stand in their way. Hans stoops for a bottle of grappa, pours several glasses, letting most of it splash down on the floor, and throws the glasses against the opposite wall, where they splinter and fall to the floor, leaving the pale yellow liquid staining the curved white walls.

It is late when Andreas, Ioannis and Michaelis leave. Hans stays in the living room. The music is still playing. He kisses me goodnight, and I go up to my room, turn on the heater, hold my hands close to the red electric coils and open up the bed. The sheets are cold, and I wake up several times during the night. Each time I hear the sound of the bouzouki turned up loud, and the thump of Hans dancing alone, until, close to the dawn, the dancing stops and I hear the new sound of Albinoni's Adagio, slow and sad, played over and over again. I get out of bed and stand for a long time on the cold floor, taking a small perverse pleasure in my own discomfort. Then I walk downstairs.

Hans is lying on the floor with his legs tangled around the wire of the electric heater, which has tipped over on its side. The orange light blazing across his face makes him look like some fiery apparition just pulled from the flames.

I sit in the room, listening to the Adagio until the sun comes up. I am trying to "evaluate" something. What I want to know is, Do I prefer dancing or not dancing? Do I prefer having Stefan or thinking about having Stefan? Do I prefer Zorba or the Adagio?

The answer is both. Almost always the answer is both.

• • •

"To Lola," my father said. "To my daughter." And he threw the champagne glass across the room. The glass splintered. There was pale liquid on the white walls. My mother flinched. Champagne glasses like that cost twenty dollars apiece. She said they would pay the Martinos for the champagne glasses. My father said that fun was fun, and why didn't she know how to have fun? She said fun was fun and that was fine, but what about not having twenty dollars apiece for champagne glasses? He said he would win it back tomorrow, didn't she know that he always won it back? She said, "But what if you don't?"

He said, "But I do."

She said, "Playing bridge isn't a life."

He said, "Neither is worrying, and being miserable."

He delivered a case of champagne to the Martinos the next morning. He put hundred dollar bills down on the table, bid four no trump and lost. He came home smiling, took my mother in his arms and said that tomorrow he would win enough to buy her a fur coat. In New York. In the middle of July. A fur coat. Alone in their apartment, she cried until her eyes shriveled.

What I want to know is, Which side am I on?

And what's brave?

"*W*OULD YOU SAY that you had an unhappy childhood?"

"I don't remember."

"Nothing?"

"No, nothing. Except things that didn't happen."

"Didn't happen?"

"Yes, I imagined them."

"And what did you imagine?"

"That I was born with a clubfoot. That I knew how to fly. That my grandfather told me the secret of when he was going to die. That I was invisible."

"I see. Can you tell me more about these things?"

"I can't. I don't know how to talk."

"But you are talking."

"That's different. I'm not saying anything."

"You're saying a great deal."

"Perhaps. But it's still not anything."

"Would you like to make an appointment for next week?"

"I think so. I'm not sure."

"How is this time?"

"This time. Anytime. It's all the same."

•

I want to be able to remember everything. But I remember almost nothing. Just occasional gleams and flashes. And huge holes in between, like craters of the moon. I fall into the holes and can't climb out. Sometimes a fragment of memory takes possession of my mind, holding it with the intensity of authentic revelation, but then it disappears to make way for another vision that is equally consuming. But I must know. Otherwise nothing will ever make sense.

When I talk about the things I remember, my mother often says, "No, you remember wrong, Lola. It happened this way . . . ," and then she tells me a story of something which I remember not at all.

Another thing she says is that psychiatrists always blame the parents, that they make children hate their parents. I don't know. We'll see.

•

As for the clubfoot, that definitely was my imagination. What really happened was that I was born upside down. My friend Leta says that when you're born upside down your head isn't pressed into shape the way other people's are, that you're born with a free head. An intrauterine act of defiance? Of acrobatic showmanship? The refusal to be ordinary? To me it seems there's just relief that you managed to make it at all.

The result was that I came out with one crooked leg.

"She's deformed," my mother sobbed, staring at it.

"She's not deformed," the nurse said. "She's perfectly fine, a beautiful child."

"No, she's deformed," Mother insisted and cried for a long time, from nervousness and exhaustion and an untamed, unchanneled imagination, which had no place to go but straight back into the fevered corners of her mind.

Dr. Jenness agreed to put my leg in a brace for six weeks, so that it would be perfectly straight, not a wobble or a wiggle or an unnecessary curve to be seen anywhere at all, not a toe turned inward or a muscle edged toward introspection.

27

Still, when I was older and stood before the mirror with my feet together, the classic three triangles, one from ankle to lower calf, another from upper calf to knee, and the third between knee and thigh, were not absolutely clearcut triangles. I had to strain at the knees in order to fix the middle one in place.

One day I said to my mother, "Was I born with a clubfoot?"

"How ridiculous," she said. "Where did you ever get such an idea?"

"From my imagination."

•

I am a baby. It is August. The air throughout the city is swollen as a woman in labor, damp as the womb from which I have only recently exited. I have prickly heat, red spots in the crooks of my elbows and the creases of my neck, spots that make me feel as if I am oozing fat. I wave my fists in the air. I am whale blubber. I scream. And scream. I will not stop screaming. My mother decides that she is much too nervous to take care of a baby. She decides that I should have a nurse. She interviews dozens of women, peering into their faces, looking perhaps for some mirror of herself, grown wholesome, though, and fearless. The faces come and go. A new nurse is introduced. She bends over my crib. "It is bad for the child to sleep on her stomach," she says. "All the doctors recommend keeping them on their backs when they sleep. It aids digestion and breathing." I am turned over on my back.

Eventually the nurse leaves. A new nurse comes. She bends over the crib and says, "The child would be more comfortable if she slept on her stomach. It's the most natural position for a child." I am switched over to my stomach. Like a chicken on a rotisserie, I am turned, basted from time to time, but never pronounced done. My mother listens with the ears of anxiety to each new nurse, craving the right answers. In between times, she gives

28

me her breasts. I cling to her and am happy. When she pulls away, I scream. Devastated, she retreats to her own bed. It is three o'clock in the afternoon. She turns from her stomach to her back, from her back to her stomach. She has nightmares. In them, I always turn out badly, deformed somehow. Racked with indecision, she waits, anticipating the consequences. Sometimes she calls my father to ask him if he wants chicken or steak for dinner. When he says, "Either is fine," she grows rigid with apprehension. "But which would you prefer?" she says.

"Really, Sonja, I don't care. I have a customer here now, and . . ."

There is a flood of Russian words between them, and Mother puts down the phone. She goes back to bed. What if she makes the wrong choice? What if the steak is overcooked, or the skin of the chicken not crisp enough? Maybe she should buy a rotisserie. She returns to her nightmares in which the chicken is never done, but instead keeps turning and turning until it is burnt and charred. That's what would happen. If she took her eyes off it, it would burn. She determines not to fall asleep, to lie awake and listen for any signs of restlessness from my crib. The nurse brings her afternoon tea. Mother's eyes are like the eyes of a shy wild animal, terrified of being trapped. She puts her head back on the pillows, sits up to sip the tea, leans back on the pillows again. She is exhausted. She sleeps fitfully, then gets up to dress. My father is coming home. She chooses a black dress. Basic black. It is always elegant, always appropriate. She looks at herself in the mirror. Thirty-seven, and just having her first child. But the war, the Nazis . . . everything. The chicken turns slowly in her mind. She sees the tear in her stockings from when my father had the motorcycle accident in Israel. After that, she refused to ride his motorcycle. It was crazy, she said, what with the Arabs shooting down from the hills. And besides, Israel was home. She didn't want to be a gypsy anymore, even if Daddy was the dashingest man on the Continent. "In America there is gold on the street.

Or better, diamonds," Daddy says. So they go on, with the Nazis stampeding behind them every step of the way, with fragments of their family drifting in the air above Eastern Europe. They go to India, to South Africa, to Cuba, and wait two years for their immigration papers. Daddy gambles for a living until the papers come through. By the time they board the boat for America, Mother is pregnant. I am her gift to America, born in Manhattan, born in the summertime.

That is when my father throws the champagne glasses across the room. Not our champagne glasses. I am launched . . . like the *Queen Elizabeth*, without a country to rule.

•

It was the nurse's day off. Mama took me to the park. She dressed me up in white shoes and a white dress and a white hat. She always dressed me up to go to the park. The cherry trees with their twisted trunks were blooming on the mall; the big kids were playing stickball. In the playground, there wasn't a swing or a seesaw empty. I kept complaining it was hot and trying to take my coat off. Mama was afraid I would catch cold. "Keep your coat on, Lola," she said. "How many times do I have to tell you?"

She held my hand tightly until, from the top of the hill, I spotted the river. It was far away, but it was somewhere to go. I pulled away from Mama and ran. I ran all the way down the hill with my legs churning, my body ahead of my legs, feeling like I was falling, falling, falling. The hat was sliding back on my head; the elastic under my chin was getting tighter. I tried to hold on to the hat and keep my balance at the same time. I wanted to rip off the hat and step on it. I hated hats and coats and shoes and dresses. But with Mama along, I didn't dare throw away the hat. So all the way down the hill I held on to it, feeling a moment's vertigo and then getting my balance back. It was like flying. When the ground leveled off, I was overwhelmed with pride. I hadn't fallen. I had flown through the air. I had almost fallen, but not. It was daring and dangerous. There had been a second when I thought . . . when my heart skipped, but then I didn't fall. I was breathless. And I had the hat.

Mama was still at the top of the hill when I reached the bottom. I skipped through the tunnel yelling, "My name is Lola. My name is Lola. The biggest. And the best . . ." The tunnel answered back, best, best, best. It was dark in the tunnel and cooler than outside. The sun made an arc of light at its edge. And on the other side was the river, the dank musky river with its eddies and swirls, where the fishermen stood with their tin cans filled with dough, dipping their lines into the water and waiting patiently for the eels that rhumba'd on their lines and then were thrown back. I loved to watch the eels dancing in the air like that, loved the silent slowness of the fishermen, loved the way they rolled the dough between their fingers. A tugboat plowed through the water leaving deep furrows in it. I waved furiously at the captain. He waved back. I jumped up and down, clapping my hands and shouting, "He sees me. He sees me."

Mama was coming through the tunnel. "Watch out," she called. Why was she always spoiling things? I tore the hat off my head and ran to the water fountain. A boy was standing there on tiptoes, drinking. He was concentrating very hard on getting all the water into his mouth. His head was turned sideways. He just kept drinking and drinking and drinking. I hopped up and down, first on one foot, then on the other.

"Hey," I yelled at him. "Hurry up."

He looked at me sideways. Water shot up into his nose. He shook his head, wiped his nose with the back of his hand and glared at me. "Dummy," he said.

"Don't call me dummy, you're a dummy," I said back, fury rising up in me like the water in the river when the tugboat went by.

"That's what I called you, dummy," he said.

My white shoe swung back and forward. I kicked him in the leg. He yelped. Water squirted into my face and onto my coat. I shrieked. He shrieked. Mama came running. Another mama came running. Both mamas held on to us and apologized to each other.

When the other mama was gone, she said, "I can't even have a quiet day in the park with you. I'm taking you home."

All the way home she held tightly on to my hand. And put the hat back on my head.

But I *did* fly down that hill. And that boy *was* a dummy.

•

At night, though, there was sometimes another mama who came to me, a mama with centuries of mamas in her blood. She wore perfume, Arpege, which filled the whole room. She wore dresses, always black, which were elegant, dazzling. There was one with a deep V neck and a narrow waist and panels of stiff crepe, which fanned out around her like a dozen mountains settling into her lap. Her skin was very white and her breasts showed above the V of the dress. Wide-mouthed, with perfect teeth, she had on clear red lipstick, a sea of color in which I drowned. The tips of her fingers were red too. Across my eyes and my cheeks and my hair, those fingers and that mouth wandered, always hesitant, never quite committing themselves to themselves . . . her voice silvered, faraway, like the upper reaches of the stratosphere, a region both wonderful and mysterious, which could never be attained. It was her smile, though, that devastated me. It came from I don't know where, perhaps from some deep, unexplored tunnel inside of her, where pools of warmth collected, undisturbed by the light, and then rose up slowly, finding a crevice here, a lazy spot there, moving always up, basking in patches of sunlight, preparing itself for its entry into the world. There was something so pure about that smile, as if she had never smiled before, had kept it stored away and was just bringing it out for the first time. She smiled and it was the first day of creation.

•

"Tell me a story," I beg. "The one about how you escaped from Russia."

She tells me the story. Every night it is the same story, the same dark, lost adventure, about how, when she was twelve, she and her mother and father and sisters tried to flee Russia in the middle of the night. They were stopped, arrested and kept in jail until Grandpa bribed one of the guards with the diamonds he'd saved from his jewelry business. They left everything behind except the few diamonds which Grandpa took during an ellipsis when the Whites were in power. Grandpa made arrangements for a traveling caravan to bring them to the border while he went ahead to settle things in Turkey. They were to stay with the caravan as long as necessary, pretending they were part of a circus act, until it was possible for someone to take them across the Dnieper River. But their connection failed; they were picked up again and thrown back in jail. Another month. Mother and her youngest sister were separated from the rest of the family. Finally, another guard was bribed, but this time the bribe included getting them to the river, getting someone to take them across. At last they arrived. In the middle of the night, they were rowed across the river in separate boats, Mother and her youngest sister together.

What I remember of the story is the image of her absolutely alone in a rowboat, rowing across the moonlit river with the current dragging her downstream, with nothing but fear in her possession, a twelve-year-old child whose strength no one had ever believed in . . . the frail one in the family, spending her days lying in a hammock . . . pulling the oars now until she reaches land.

33

When she finishes the story, she sings me a Russian lullaby, the same one every time. Sometimes I beg her to sing it twice. SPEEMLADYENITSMOYPREKRASSNYEBYOOSH-KYBAYOU . . . I don't know what the words mean, but they make me ache for her. The high clarity of her voice, the cadence of the music, the smell of her perfume and her smile, all blend inside of me, settling there long after she tiptoes out of the room and kisses me goodnight, long after I grow into a difficult child, a difficult woman, long, long, long.

•

She is pregnant. She walks with me to the park and tells me. "Lola," she says, "how would you like a brother for Christmas?"

I look at her, at her eyes, her stomach, her feet and then my own feet.

"No," I shout. "No, no, no," and run away from her, down to the river and away from her, away from a brother, away from her solemn eyes.

She doesn't even try to follow me at first. I walk alone along the river and then head inland where I crouch on a patch of grass and cry and probe the anatomy of a worm with a stick.

A brother. What kind of a Christmas present is that?

When she comes to get me, she stands in front of me with her hands crossed over her belly. I glare at the place until she grows embarrassed and says, "Now stop it. It won't be terrible like you think. It will be nice. You can help me take care of it."

"I won't."

"Yes, you will," she says, trying to make her voice lighter and failing.

I point to her belly. "That's where it will come from, isn't it?"

"Yes," she says.

"And you'll get fat."

"Not fat," she says. "But big."

"Fat," I say. "Fat and ugly."

Then I run away again and walk home after escaping her. I go up in the elevator alone and crawl into the closet with her beaver coat. I wrap it around me and sit on the floor of the closet. Then I close the door.

After a while, she comes looking for me. She sits down on the floor of the closet and holds me in her lap. She rocks me in her arms. I almost start to cry but then I don't. I almost punch her in the stomach. But then I don't do that either. I almost let her rock me. But then I make myself stiff. She rocks and I refuse to yield.

In the bathtub, when the nurse leaves me alone, I start to cry again. By the time the nurse comes back, she can't tell the difference between the tears and the bathwater. She wraps the big towel around me. I pull it over my head. From inside the towel, I can't see anything.

"I'm invisible," I say.

"Oh," she says, from very far away in the world outside the towel.

"Yes," I say and stumble out of the bathroom.

•

"Did you brush your teeth?" Mama says. I say yes. But the answer is no. I stand on a stool in the bathroom and stare at my face in the mirror. I squash my nose against the glass and look at myself cross-eyed. When I breathe close up, the mirror gets foggy and I can't see myself anymore. I try looking at my profile. I turn sideways to look. Even when I strain my eyes all the way around, it is impossible. Three-quarters is the best I can do, and even then, darts of light shoot through my eyes from the strain. Sometimes I just close my eyes and press harder and harder on my eyelids until I can see yellow and black diamonds inside my eyes. Then I open them and wait for the diamonds to disappear.

Other times I hold the toothbrush in my hand and make wild circular motions in the air with it. Then I climb off the stool and make even wilder circular motions, getting my arms going until I think maybe I'll fly across the room. The toothbrush never enters my mouth. It is easier to say yes than to say no, though. Besides, no one can tell the difference. Just to be sure, I always wet the brush before I go out of the bathroom.

Mama says, "I'll show you how to run the water in the tub for your bath." She turns the handle on one side; a cloud of steam rises up in the air. She turns the handle on the other side. Cold, clear water spurts out. She holds my hand under the tap. Cold water chases down my fingers. Then she turns both handles together. The water comes booming and crashing down. It is warm. I can't tell the difference between it and my skin. I shudder with the thrill of it. She watches me while I turn the water on, both taps full blast.

"All right," she says. "Now when the water comes up to here . . . ," she marks the tub with her finger, "turn the tap off." She holds my hand in hers as she turns off the taps and then turns them on again.

She leaves me alone in the bathroom. I put my finger up against the spigot so water sprays all over the wall and bright colors flash through the air. Drops skid across the paint. The floor is wet all around the tub. I watch the water creep up and up and up. It just keeps creeping up all around. It doesn't start in one place and finish in another. It just gets higher. I sit on the floor, put my chin on the edge of the tub and stare at it. I make whirls in the water with my finger.

After a while I get tired of watching the water and walk out of the bathroom. I go into my room and draw whirls on a piece of colored paper with a blue crayon.

The bathtub floods over and drips into the downstairs neighbors' apartment. When I come back into the bathroom with

Mama, the whole place is like a small lake. The white hexagonal floor tiles wobble underwater. Mama is angry. But she lets me try again. A dozen tries. A dozen floods. Mama gives up and runs the water herself.

●

She promised. Even though she says she didn't, I know she did. And when I said so, my father said, "Don't say 'she.' Who's she? That's your mother, not she."

"All right," I said. "Mother promised."

"How many times have I told you," he said, "that it's impolite to talk about your mother that way?"

"What way? All I'm saying is, MOTHER PROMISED."

"I don't see what you're getting so worked up about. You can go to the zoo another day."

"She promised today."

"You're acting like a baby. Stop the nonsense."

"But why?"

"Because I say so."

"That's not a reason. Give me a reason. Tell me why."

"The reason is that I'm your father. That's all. And if you can't behave . . ."

I cried for three hours. The rule is, don't wish for anything. Except I wish they were dead, so they couldn't make promises they don't keep.

●

What I really want to know about is the hexagons. And the blood. The bathroom tiles were in the shape of hexagons. The sidewalks around Central Park are blocked out in hexagons. But why should thinking about the hexagons make me sick? Why should I have to go and look for them, day in and day out? It's an

37

obsession. They were in a dream once. But I don't remember anything else about the dream. Just that hexagons were in it. There's another dream I remember. About the doctor. He came and touched a needle to my arm, but I didn't feel it go in. NO. IT DIDN'T GO IN. But it made me crazy afterward. And he made scratches in my arm with his nails. And put spikes in my body. Once I heard someone tell about a belt they have in a museum in France. It's an iron belt, and it has sharp teeth in it. It's to protect women. But what does that have to do with the hexagons? And the second dream wasn't even my dream. It was Antonia's. She's ten. She told me the dream and said her father said it was silly, even though it kept her awake all night. I don't think it's silly.

BUT WHAT ABOUT THE HEXAGONS?

The doctor wasn't Dr. Jenness. It was another doctor. Who had a mustache. The thin kind. And brilliantine in his hair. But I don't know a doctor like that.

And what about the hexagons?

•

Mama lied to me. The thing didn't arrive for Christmas, like she said. Instead, for Christmas, I got tonsillitis. All through December I had a sore throat. Mama wouldn't let me take a bath anymore; instead she gave me alcohol rubdowns and talked to Dr. Jenness on the phone. I hated the smell of the alcohol, the cold, goosebumps feeling I had after the washcloth passed over my skin. In the bathtub I was an adventurer on my own, exploring beneath the water, my hair waving like a mermaid's when I held my nose and dunked backward. Sometimes I pulled the muscles of my belly together so there was a tight round ball sticking out in the middle of it. Pulling my belly in like that pulled water up inside of me at the same time. When I pushed out, the water squirted out. It was a little bit like peeing, but it felt different. It felt nice, and sometimes I would spend a long time in the tub pulling water in and letting it out of me. If I didn't push it all out, though, when I climbed out of the tub a stream of water would roll down my legs. I was always afraid the nurse would see it dripping on the bathmat and think I was peeing.

Now though, with Mother giving me alcohol rubs, there was no pushing or pulling. She was brisk about it. The washcloth was rough. There was no time to luxuriate. There was just, "Stand still. Don't keep wriggling around." I pressed my legs together and wouldn't let her put the washcloth between them.

"Will you let me wash your pee pee?" Mama said.

I shook my head no.

"All right then, do it yourself."

I was embarrassed, but I took the washcloth and swiped at myself fast.

"That's not washing," Mama said. "If you don't do it right, I'll have to do it."

"I couldn't stand having her look at me like that, so this time I took three swipes, moved the washcloth down and scrubbed hard at my knees.

Mama sighed. "I guess I'll just have to settle for a dirty child," she said.

She dumped the water out and dried me while I stood there shivering. She didn't even give me the towel to hide in. I couldn't say I was invisible. She took the towel away when I was dry, poured powder over me and helped me put my feet into pajamas. Then she looked at my throat.

"It's still red," she said. "I'm going to call Dr. Jenness in the morning again. I want him to look at you."

I didn't want Dr. Jenness to look at me. I didn't want to be sick. So in the morning I jumped around and said, "See, I'm not sick." Mama wanted to look at my throat again, but I wouldn't let her. She asked me how it felt and I said fine. It didn't though. It hurt.

"I just want to see it," she said. "Don't be a baby."

39

I backed away from her. She was trying to trap me. "Leave me alone," I yelled. "Leave me alone."

Leave me alone. Leave me alone. Whenever she was worried, that's what I said. Until she did. And I was even madder.

After a week, my sore throat hadn't improved. Dr. Jenness gave me an appointment. But first Dr. Barnett had to do my chart. I hated Dr. Barnett. She wore orthopedic shoes, tailored tweed suits and tortoiseshell glasses. She had a German accent and was very efficient. Every time she asked me a question I was so frightened that my throat would block and I couldn't answer.

"Don't make such a fuss," she said, while I sat imprisoned in my silence.

"I want my mama," I said.

She looked at me with what I thought was contempt.

"Well, right now you can't have your mama," she said. "You can't always have what you want."

I could feel the tears starting to come, but I held them back. She would say I was a baby. Why did she seem so mad all the time, like I was bad for being scared of her. Why wouldn't she smile? Why . . . I was in a cold sweat from just having to stay in the room with her.

"All right," she said finally. "Go to your mama. See Dr. Jenness first and then we'll come back to this."

Mama was in the waiting room. "My poor baby," she said. "Your face is all white. What did she do?"

I shook my head. "Nothing," I whispered.

She tried to take me in her arms, but I wouldn't come. Instead I fled back into the children's waiting room, where I sat scratching at my arms and legs until Dr. Jenness came.

"Well, how are you, young lady?" he said.

"I'm fine," I said, licking the blood from my finger where I had scratched at a scab. Daddy always said I should stop scratching like that. "Only monkeys scratch," he said. "It's bad manners." But I couldn't stop. I couldn't stop even if it was the worst manners in the world, couldn't stop even if Mama said I would have scars. "You'll have scars for life," she said. But I still scratched.

Dr. Jenness took me into his office. I liked him. He was fat and wore glasses and a bow tie. He was always wearing gray suits. He joked a lot with me, saying things like, "Well, what do you know, you still have a heart and eyes and a mouth. Pretty good ones at that. I bet you talk a blue streak at home. Your mama tells me all about it. How about now? Let me see that tongue of yours?" All the time, he would keep on talking, trying to make me relax. "Now breathe deep," he would say. "You can do better than that. A really deep breath this time. As deep as you can. Again. Again. Why you're quite a girl. I like those deep breaths you take. Why not give me one more?"

Then he put his wooden spoon down my throat. "Say ah," he said.

"Ah," I answered.

"Louder."

"Ah," I said again, putting all of my energy into the syllable.

"Wonderful," he said. And lifted me down off the examining table. Then he gave me a lollipop and told me to wait in the children's waiting room, while he talked to my mother.

Dr. Jenness told Mama my tonsils were inflamed, but he would prefer not to operate. "Take her to the mountains for a few weeks," he said. "The fresh air will be good for her."

When we were leaving, I felt happy. I really *was* sick. Not because Mama said so. That would show stinking old Dr. Barnett. That would show her.

I held Mama's hand and skipped on the street and made funny faces until she told me to stop being silly.

"Quiet down," she said. "You're sick."

Still, inside myself, I could jump for joy.

•

41

Mama's belly was very big. She sat out on the porch of the hotel while Daddy skied. He got a tiny pair of skis for me and took me over to a small hill where he taught me to walk around on them. Then he went off to ski by himself. I was infatuated with the crystalline light on the snow, with the birdlike prints my skis made on its flat white surface. I fell down a few times. The snow was very soft. A cloud of it blew into my face like fairy dust. When the cloud disappeared, my face was wet and stinging. I got up and walked again. The next time I fell, I took a handful of snow and put it in my mouth, feeling it disappear fast, leaving just coldness in my teeth. When I fell again, the snow wasn't so soft. My leg hurt. I was alone on the hill. There was no one to hear me crying.

Mama had gone inside the guest house, so she didn't see me fall, even though I was only a short way from her. But the guest house looked very far away to me, all the way at the top of the hill. It no longer seemed like a hill; it was a mountain. I tried to climb up it, but it was so steep I kept stumbling. I got up again and stumbled again. I was so cold. And where was my mama? Why wouldn't she come? I felt terribly alone. For the first time I was really on my own. I stopped crying. I was too scared to even cry. Everything hurt, everything was white, everything was cold. There was nothing to mark the boundaries of the world. It just went on and on and on.

Mama came back out on the porch a few minutes after I reached the top.

"Your clothes are soaked," she said. "Come inside and change. Well, how did you like it?"

"Good," I said. "It was good." But I didn't say anything about being afraid or about the world that now, suddenly, occupied the space all around her.

•

Francine had long blond hair. She tied it back with a ribbon and worked at the guest house, in the dining room. Whenever she saw me, she would smile and say, "Hi, how are you doing
today?" And I would smile back. She knew my name, and said it
like it made her happy. She brought me orange juice in bed. She
talked about skiing and said I would be all better by the time we
left. Sometimes she asked me what I was going to do when I got
back to New York and my throat was fine again, so I told her a
story about going to the park, or feeding the seals, or sliding down
snowbanks on the street, or flying. It took a few days before I told
her about flying. She didn't act like I was making it up. She believed me. She asked me where I flew to.

I'd never thought about that before, but instantly I answered,
"Albany."

"Albany," she said. "Why, what's in Albany?"

I was stuck, unsure now of what to say. There was a dark
place in my mind that moved around like black water.

"My father," I finally said.

"Oh," she said. "Why, I thought your father was here."

"He is," I said, feeling as if I were on the edge of a precipice. "But a lot of the time he's not." I had the strange
sensation that I was giving away a secret, even though no one had
ever said it was a secret. She must have noticed that I was uncomfortable, because she just said, "Well, that's interesting," and
changed the subject to prune juice, which I hated.

Whenever I was out of bed, I wanted to be near her. Even
when she was with her boyfriend I managed to play close by. I
couldn't bear to have her out of my sight. When she came in
with my orange juice, I begged her to tell me an extra story. I
pretended to be feeling very sick.

Gradually, she stopped sounding so happy when she said my
name. I think she must have said something to my mother, because one day Mother said she knew I liked Francine a lot, but

43

Francine had a life of her own, and wouldn't it be better if I played with the other children, instead of . . .

I ran away from her and for three days wouldn't let Francine bring me my orange juice. I refused to eat. I starved myself and grew feverish. She hated me. That was why she stopped working in the children's dining room after Mama talked to me. She didn't want to see me anymore. So she went to work in the grown-ups' dining room. With my mother and father. I was frantic with love and fear: what I later came to call "holy terror."

One day, when some new girl was serving us in the dining room, I jumped up from my chair, knocked over the tray and ran out of the room. I went straight into the grown-ups' dining room. Francine was serving dinner to some people who were sitting in a corner. I ran to my parents' table.

"I won't eat there," I said. "That new girl is mean. I want to eat with you."

"Lola," my mother said, "would you please go back and eat with the other children? We can discuss this afterward."

"No," I said. "I won't."

"I'm warning you, Lola," my father said.

"No," I said again, trying to hold my ground but frightened by the expression on my father's face. Out of the corner of my eye I could see Francine, moving between the tables. I was afraid of my father, but I loved Francine more. I didn't move.

My father got up from the table. He came over and took my hand. "Come on. You're not having any dinner. You're going up to your room."

"No," I yelled, and this time my voice rose to a wail. I tried to pull away from him, but he held on to me even tighter. "Lola, no scenes," he said. His voice was very strict and angry. I yanked away from him and threw myself on the floor screaming.

For a moment everything stopped. Mother put her hands over her face. People from the other tables turned to stare. I lay on the floor kicking and yelling while my father tried to grab hold

44

of me. At last he succeeded. He dragged me out of the dining room and took me up to my room. Then he took off his belt.

"It's time you learned to behave, young lady," he said. And whacked me across the behind. The belt stung. I yelped. "Don't you ever do something like that again," he said. "Do you understand me? Never. Your mother and I intend to eat dinner in peace. If you behave like a spoiled brat, I'll have to treat you like one." He put his belt back on again and stood there while I put on my pajamas. I was still furious, but beneath the fury was a terrible ache of fear, aloneness, helplessness. I climbed into bed.

He turned off the light. "Good night, Lola," he said. The words sounded like a death sentence. Then he walked out of the room.

A few days later, Francine left. Mother said it was because she was getting married and moving to Ohio, but then she added, "and probably because you were a pest."

I was heartbroken. And believed her.

•

I watched my father pack for the trips to Albany. He took his best pajamas, the silk ones with the blue-on-blue stripes, and his special King's Men Shaving Lotion. Once there was a carefully wrapped package with a curled ribbon around it tucked under his shirts. But before he left, he swung me around the bedroom until the room swam and nothing existed in it for me except the warm, rough worsted of his jacket, the cool smoothness of his face.

"One of these days, princess," he said, "I'm going to trade you in for a pair of no-eyed twins." That made me sad, I don't know why, but when he pointed to his cheek, I kissed again the just-shaved face and watched as he disappeared into the elevator.

Maps meant nothing to me. I didn't know where Albany was. But when I went down to Riverside Drive with the new nurse and stood by the river railing, I decided that since it was far away, it must be right across, there on the opposite side of the river. Whenever he was gone, I watched the water and wondered about the lure of that farther shore, watched and wondered and thought about Albany, strange, mysterious Albany. Sometimes I kept my eye on the bridge in the distance, believing that I might be able to spot him at the precise moment when he started across in his shiny blue Lincoln with the spare tire on the back, see him as he began the trip home.

I missed him terribly, missed his craggy blond eyebrows and his blue eyes, missed his shaving lotion. Sometimes, when he was away, I went into his bathroom, unstoppered a bottle of Old Spice and dabbed a drop on my nose. Then I sat on the edge of the bathtub sniffing air now saturated with the smell. It was a secret between myself and myself. No one could see the shaving lotion on my nose, and walking around the house in the privacy of my own world, I could sniff as often as I pleased, wrinkling up my nose to catch an extra whiff, the scent of him and his presence locked into my nostrils for hours, like a genie released from the bottle.

At other times, when he was away on "Business" (I tried repeating the word over and over to myself until it sounded like a bumblebee buzzing around in my mind), I would sit on his side of the bed and look at the small framed sepia photograph on his night table. The photograph was of two young women, two young men and a middle-aged couple. The young people were in their twenties, and even though their features varied, their faces all had the same quality of gentle intensity. The women's hair was all finger-waved; the men wore suits and ties. No one was smiling.

Once when my father was away, I asked Mother about the photograph. "Who are those people?" I said.

"Your father's family," my mother said.

"Where are they?" I said.

"They're dead," she said.

Dead? Like grandpa. Dead. "All of them?" I said.

"Yes," she said. "But you mustn't talk to your father about it. It makes him sad."

I went back into the bedroom again to look at the picture. One of the men looked like my father. Maybe he was my father. Alone in the room, I tried talking to him, tried asking him what was sad.

Once, when he came back from a trip, he said to me, "You know, Lola, you look just like my younger sister. She was a fine woman. You would have liked her."

I wanted to ask him about her but didn't dare, and besides, right after he said that, he started talking to Mother in Russian. I strained after the words, wanting to understand. But it was all blurry, and I couldn't even tell where one word started and another one ended.

In the middle of the conversation, the tone of their voices changed. Mother's ran around in circles, like a rat in a cage. Daddy's got louder and louder. And all the time, the words went back and forth between them, the unknown Russian words. Watching their faces, I became part of a silent movie, with only my father's eyebrows, my mother's red fingernails and pale smile to direct me. Maybe they were fighting about Mother's spending too much money on the charge account. Maybe about the maid. Maybe afterward Daddy would go to Albany again. Maybe . . . my mind trembled under the onslaught of its own imaginings.

"Why are you fighting?" I said, desperate to stop the war of images inside of me.

"Lola, go to your room," my father said.

"Lola, we're not fighting," my mother said.

"Please," I said. "Please tell me." My own voice had shrunk to a whisper.

"Did you hear me?" my father shouted. "Go to your room. Now."

He almost never shouted. What was it? What was it? I started saying the alphabet to myself very fast to drown out any

47

other thoughts, but the alphabet kept turning into whatwasit-whatwasitwhatwasit.

I didn't go to my room. I went to theirs. I sat on the bed and looked at the photograph again, at the girls especially. I didn't know which was the youngest. But none of them looked like me. And just as with Mommy and Daddy, if they had something to say, it was in a language I didn't know. Never never would they explain themselves. I sat on the bed and cried.

•

Mara Palevsky walked in the door. She was wearing a hat that dipped down low over her eyes and a dress that dipped down low in front. She was very suntanned even though it was winter. "Darling," she said to my father. Her voice was very husky. Daddy took her in his arms and kissed her, a long kiss. Then she said, "Darling, it's wonderful to see you."

I was stunned. My father was kissing another lady. Suddenly my stomach buckled. I wanted to run away, but instead I moved closer to my mother . . . just at the moment that she moved away from me and toward Mara.

"Darling, it's been ages," Mara said to Mother, kissing her too. But it was different. I knew it was different.

While my father walked with Mara into the living room, I grabbed hold of my mother's hand. "Aren't you jealous?" I said insistently.

"Don't be silly," she said. "Of course not. What's to be jealous about?" I could see, though, that even under her rouge, she was blushing.

•

Mother went to the hospital on February twentieth, and by morning the baby was born. My father wandered around the house muttering to himself, as if he couldn't believe it, "A boy, a

48

son, a boy." Lunch and dinner were lost in the web of his amazement, while I went to sleep and dreamt about an orphanage where children were fed to the seals.

The next morning, the new nurse took me on an expedition to buy a present for Mama and the new baby, even though I never said I wanted to buy a present. We rode the double-decker bus down Riverside Drive. I sat on the top deck, watching the park sway below me. When the bus stopped on Fifth Avenue, we got out.

"Where are we going?" I asked the nurse.

"To Bonwit's," she said.

Bonwit's. Bonwit's. I strained to remember. Oh. The blouse Mara Palevsky gave me came from Bonwit's. She said she always did her shopping at Bonwit's, she always found the best things there. Thinking about it made me sick. I didn't want to go there, even though a part of me was magnetized by it. It had become a special place, one which had passed from the farthest outposts of my imagination to the inner circle of places that had a macabre fascination, like the stores with pictures of naked ladies in the windows, like the butcher shop. Bonwit's was shrouded in my illusions and my fears.

Through the doors of the inner sanctum we went, into a private world of perfume and clicking high heels and whitewashed faces absorbed in the contemplation of scarves and jewelry. I held on to the nurse's hand as we plowed our way through to the elevator in the back. I wanted to go to the floor where you could buy pen sets, but the nurse said pen sets were for men and Mama would like a nightgown better. The elevator was stuffed with bodies, perfumed bodies, all the odors competing with each other for the small bit of airy space above our heads. I squirmed the whole time the elevator was moving. Finally the door opened to our floor. We stood in the middle of "lingerie," in the middle of bras, panties, girdles, and a nightmarish assortment of other restrainers.

We turned the corner bound for nightgowns. But suddenly the nurse stopped. Over by the nightgown counter, surrounded by acres of delicate material were Mara and my father. Both of them were laughing. Mara held up one of the nightgowns. Daddy held his head sideways and looked at her. She turned around once, and then tossed it back on the counter. They were completely absorbed in each other. I stood there, suspended between perfect knowledge and perfect denial.

"You know," the nurse said brightly, "why don't we keep what we're getting a secret? And not even tell your father. I think a pen set might be nice."

I looked at the nurse for a moment. Then I ran, past the counters with their bright faces, past the ladies in their elegant clothes, past the salesgirls with their well-groomed good looks. The elevator door was just closing, but I squeezed myself in next to a heavy woman who squashed the breath out of me. I ran down to the street. But I didn't know where to go, so I just stood there, remembering how Daddy had kissed Mara that day. When the nurse came out of the store, she didn't say a word. She just squeezed my hand and took me home.

That night my father didn't come home for supper. I ate jelly beans and listened to Tallulah Bankhead on the radio, noticing how husky her voice was, how deep her "darlings." I finally went to sleep, and sometime very late Daddy came in, kissed me on the forehead and whispered, "You've got a brother now, princess." I pretended I was still asleep until he left the room.

He carried a box from Bonwit's under his arm when we went to the hospital together in the morning. The baby was in a separate room. We could look at him through a glass. To me he looked like a skinny frog. But mother looked happy, really happy. She was wearing a simple sheer white nightgown and her hair was tied back with a blue ribbon. Her face had lost its look of strain and her stomach was gone. My father sat down next to her on the bed, holding her hand, and then he picked up the box which he had put on the floor next to the bed.

"I bought you seven nightgowns," he said. "One for each day of the week, and one for each child we're going to have, with Lola's permission, of course."

My stomach contracted and I looked down at the floor. She hugged Daddy gently and began to open up the box. Seven beribboned, beruffled nightgowns. She held them up one by one with a solemn look creeping into her eyes. She laughed, a thin, forced laugh, and said, "They're beautiful, really beautiful. I thought you had simpler tastes, but they are beautiful, they really are." Her voice faltered. She buried her head in Daddy's shoulder and started to cry. He rocked her back and forth saying, "There, baby, there. Everything's fine. Everything's just fine now."

I went to the bathroom, sat on the seat and cried, washed my face and came back to the room. I gave her the pen set, which she said was beautiful, really beautiful, just what she'd said about the nightgowns. I could tell she wasn't paying attention.

Daddy sat on the bed and had me sit on his lap. He put his arms around both of us.

"Well, what do you think, princess?" he said. "What do you think of your mother and this present she's given us?"

"Wonderful," I said. But I couldn't look at either of them.

•

I never saw Mother wear any of the beribboned nightgowns. She didn't say anything when I wouldn't wear the blouse Mara gave me. My father didn't seem to notice.

I HAVE NOT COME to the island for my pleasure but because once, I was happy here, and I want to know what went wrong. I have never found it easy to face the obvious. What went wrong? I can proceed no further than the question. Sometimes I catch the edge of a thing out of the corner of my eye, remember a phrase like, "You suffer beautifully, but you don't know how to be happy." The words ring like buckshot against tin cans.

When was it that I started to live across him?

When was it that he told me he couldn't accept that sort of thing, couldn't understand why women needed to do it, why women had no independent lives of their own, why women's lives took their forms from the men they loved?

One day he showed me a letter from his wife in which she said that women should live together instead of with men because women understood what it meant to belong to someone.

He thought I was different. More independent. It did not occur to him that I was just more afraid. Or that, despite everything, there was still a part of me that wished to be conquered, wished to lose that will I had struggled so painstakingly to construct.

The point was that he never wanted to influence me or to try to mold me.

And that I wanted someone who would have the capacity to do exactly that.

•

I go into the kitchen. I peel the potatoes. I heat up the water. I chop the potatoes into eighths. I draw the outer skin off the onions, down to the thin inner skin. My eyes are tearing. It seems that my eyes are always tearing. Everything seems to bring on a flood. Memories. The wind. A pile of dishes in the sink. A mosquito trapped inside of the house at night. Albinoni's Adagio. Everything makes me cry. Everything has a raw edge. Not capitalism or imperialism or feminism or nationalism or communism. Sometimes I think that we will smother under the weight of our ideas, under the power of our imaginations to sabotage even what our imaginations have created. Of course it is also true that half the world cannot afford to do things this way. Half the world is starving. Is this then, necessarily, a luxury?

A slit in the fish's belly. Blood on my hands. The knife scraping out the guts of the fish, scraping against bone finally until there isn't a trace of either blood or guts anymore. The flame turned down to low. The cup filled with lemon and an egg, beaten together. The fish disintegrating in the boiling water, bits of flesh falling off the bones. The water turning yellow from the egg and lemon.

The mail has arrived. The package of letters from Stefan. Two months ago he wrote, "I want to stop living in the past. I have to make a life for myself. I will send you back all of your letters. Perhaps they will help . . ."

That was when I came here, after that letter. But the package has followed me . . . forwarded, finally, from New York.

The postman wears a tie and a woolen vest over his white shirt, the same gray woolen vest that everyone wears. When I came back to the island, he hugged me. He said, "We must have some ouzo together. To celebrate."

53

"How have you been?" I asked.

"As well as I could," he said. What he meant was that the regime had not been harassing him, that he had been safe.

It has been five years since the colonels took over, five years since that afternoon when all of the phone lines were cut, all of the telecommunications stopped, the military music playing on and on through the whole night, five years since Stefan and I sat in the house turning the dial of the tiny pocket radio from one end to the other, quickly at first and then ever so slowly, in the hope that maybe somewhere along the line, in between all of that martial music, a voice would come through to tell us what was going on.

And then finally, after midnight, Radio Belgrade announcing, "There is a news blackout in Athens today. Sources say a military coup has taken place. Leaders of the coup have not yet been identified. The capitol is ringed by tanks. All communications have been severed."

We lay silently for a long time after that. When he touched me it was with a flat hand. Something strange and impersonal about it . . . particularly after the day at the beach.

"What are you doing?" I asked finally.

"I have a friend who's a blind sculptor. I'm trying to figure out what it must feel like. So I can start to paint you."

I was suddenly afraid. I thought: I will not model for him . . . ever.

•

Now, five years later, the enormous signs are still all over the streets of Athens. *21 apriliou 1967*. Something unbearably cruel and ironic about it. The phoenix and the faceless soldier with his bayonet: Andreas, Ioannis, Michaelis.

The islands are always the same . . . no matter who is in power. Ioannis with his hands raised, his palms facing outward.

54

The twenty-first of April. Memorialized in the Greek calendar. That day, we were happy. Even despite the coup. Even despite the blind sculptor. Despite everything, we were happy. But it is the coup that is immortalized. It is the coup they are referring to in all of those giant banners. They are not referring to Stefan and me, though every time I walk down the street in Athens, every time I mail a letter, every time I walk into a store, I am thrown back, over and over again, to April 21, 1967.

It is the postman who said, even before we drank the ouzo, "But where is your friend?"

"We are not together anymore. I am alone this time."

And the postman said nothing more. But he did not look directly into my eyes as he had during those days in the past.

•

The letters are neatly stacked on the bed, laid out on the spread, which Stefan and I bought five years ago. Maroon and orange stripes. It was the only thing we owned in common, that bedspread.

Sometime today I will have to untie the packets. He was always neat. Every envelope is still there, every letter in its own envelope. I am sure they are arranged according to date. While my letters, the ones he wrote to me, are piled up in boxes somewhere, at my parents' house, at a friend's house, in my apartment in New York, I can't even remember anymore. Somehow it has become impossible for me to focus on where the letters are. I do not want to remember. I want to remember.

"*Ma petite*," he said. I was never petite. And yet, it was true.

The letters are lying face up on the bed.

What was it I was thinking . . .

That I have been conspiring, that I have been all these years conspiring . . .

There are things I flinch away from. I approach them sideways, backward, from any direction, hoping that I will finally get to them. Five years, and still, now, it is just as it always was, right back where I started, as if no time had elapsed at all, trying not to flinch, but flinching all the same, trying to know and thinking, I don't want to know I don't want to know.

The fish soup is ready. The plate is on the table. The table is set for three. Because I own three heavy, beautiful plates and three beautiful glasses from Venice, so the table is always set for three. I eat alone.

The letters are on the bed.

All these years I have been conspiring against myself.

•

It was the beginning of March when I came up the island road behind him. He was standing at a portable easel, facing the whitewashed walls of the village, oblivious to anyone, his head turned slightly sideways, as if he were listening to the exact tones emanating from the walls, drawing them out by the very act of his attention. There was nothing of interest in front of him. This was not one of those streets ordinarily inhabited by artists. Nothing picturesque here. No boats. No fishermen. No long view of the village. No cove with turquoise water lapping up against the rocks. Just a white wall. Or rather, two white walls, rising up on either side of him, covered with lichen, ten feet high, curving up toward the outer edge of the village, toward and beyond the house I was renting. There were piles of mule dung along the path, a saturated sky above, a dark shadow from the afternoon sun slanting along the edge of the wall and making a narrow stripe across the path. From down in the village I could hear the sound of the donkey man with his baskets of tiropita, shouting in his singsong voice. The palette was like a field of irises, golden buff, apricot, deep violet, dusty rose. In one hand he held a paintbrush, in the other a cigarette, which had burned down almost to his fingers.

56

He squinted, dragged on the cigarette, crushed it under his feet, mixed a fragile, rich blue, put down the brush and picked up a palette knife, applying color with the knife. There was none of the cramped, awkward gesture of the amateur in his stroke, none of the inattentive sweep that went into supposedly abstract versions of the local landscape. It was the stroke of someone absolutely in control of his materials, absolutely in control of his vision.

I watched him for ten minutes, as the color expanded on the canvas, layer upon layer building up a strangely gentle and compelling luminosity.

"When you're finished, would you like to come to my house for tea?"

He looked up. His expression did not change.

"Where do you live?" he asked.

I pointed up the path to the blue door beyond the edge of his canvas.

"There."

He nodded and picked up the watch balanced on the edge of his easel box. There was a narrow band of pale skin around his right wrist, unselfconsciously exposed and oddly vulnerable. The skin under his bathing suit would be the same color.

"Five-thirty," he said. "Maybe six."

His accent wasn't American, as I'd assumed it would be. It was German. I compensated for a quick inner recoil by assigning to him all those qualities a German was not supposed to have.

. . .

Stefan dances like someone who has never danced with a woman before. He holds me at arm's length. He does not dance like a German. He does not dance like a man in complete control of his stroke, in complete control of his vision. I think of the pale wrist. He is afraid of me. He trembles when we dance. I will not be able to tell him anything. He will not be, cannot be, what I need.

When we walk back to the house, up the same path where earlier in the day he had been painting, I say to him, "I just want to be friends. I don't want anything else."

He has not asked for anything else. He hasn't, it seems, dared to suggest anything beyond a cup of tea. Even the dancing was my suggestion.

I want the words to be a sign of my independence. I know he will take them that way. What I also know is that they are, in reality, a sign of my fear.

Should he have been expected, already, to know that too?

•

My father danced with continental elegance. The Mountain Club was having an affair. Large round tables surrounded by eight folding chairs. A revolving silver ball hanging from the ceiling throwing off sparks of light against the walls and the faces of the dancers, a constantly shifting chiaroscuro. Harry, the bartender, is surrounded by polished sets of glasses, red wallpaper, a leather-cushioned bar. He can mix the drinks and look into the bar mirror at the same time, can record what is going on at every instant: who needs fresh drinks, who is balanced between friendliness and aggression and should, therefore, be unobtrusively watched, whose hand brushes against whose shoulder or rests on a seat seeming to touch no portion of the anatomy, advancing only in the middle of a conversational gesture, as if touching only lent emphasis to a story or joke.

My father is talking to Joan Maslow. "Do I get the next cha-cha?" he says. She laughs and doesn't answer. Her husband, Rick, says, "Sure, go ahead, Joan." And then to my father, "Take good care of my wife. No monkey business." Rick Maslow makes room for Mother and me at his table. "Sit down," he says. "Make yourselves comfortable. Anything to drink?"

Mother orders Coke and I ask for grenadine. Rick is surprised. "No liquor?" he says.

"I fall asleep. And Lola is only fifteen," Mother says.

"Fifteen! You mean fifteen going on twenty-five! Would you like to dance?" he asks Mother.

"No thank you," she says. "But Lola loves to dance."

"How about it, Lola," Rick says and leads me out onto the dance floor.

The cha-cha has changed into a fox-trot. Rick puts his arm around my waist. I put my hand on his shoulder and he holds my other hand. My palms are sweating. After the second dance, he moves my hand in toward him, holding it up against the edge of my breast. His other hand advances along my waist. He is several inches shorter than I am. I can feel his breath on my neck. His palms are sweating, too.

We pass my father with Joan in his arms. "How you doing, puss?" he says.

"Fine," I say. And we both move on.

When the music stops, Rick says, "Want to try another?"

"Sure," I say. My father is far away, on the other side of the room.

This time, he holds me very close. "You're some kid, Lola," he says. "I like the way you dance."

The silver ball spins on the ceiling.

"Well, I'm enjoying myself," I say. "I really am."

The truth is that I'm not. Rick is sweating through his shirt now. I can feel the bulge of him against me. I'm scared, but I can't show it, because he would think I was a kid. I try to hold myself away from him, with my muscles stiffening. I look for my father, but can't find him. The more I hold myself away from Rick, the tighter he holds on to me.

Suddenly I panic. I can't get away from him. I don't know what to do. I try to keep the bottom half of my body apart from him, but I'm afraid people will notice me dancing with my behind sticking out. His hand slips below my waist, pressing me toward him. My knees are starting to wobble. I can feel a burning between my legs. I want to yell at him, "Let go of me. Let go of me." But I can't.

Then the music stops. Rick and I are standing apart again. I don't look at him. I look instead for my father again. When I turn back to Rick, I catch him staring at my breasts. I want to cry without knowing why.

My father appears alongside of us. "Mind if I cut in on you and my daughter?" he says.

"My pleasure," Rick says. And hands me over to my father.

"Why so sad, puss?" my father says.

"Nothing," I say.

My father does not tremble when he dances. His palms do not sweat. He holds me at arm's length.

"You move too much," he says. "You should dance with your feet, not with your body."

I think of Rick Maslow and shiver. Maybe it was because I dance with my body.

I smile at my father and don't answer.

•

"The trouble with all of this, though, is that it's not true."

"Not true?"

"Yes. That's the way I remember it. But my memory is wrong. And when it's not wrong, it's incomplete. When I was little, my mother told me the story about the boy who cried wolf. He told lies all of the time. And then when he told the truth, no one believed him."

"So you have not been telling the truth. And these things

did not happen. And when you do tell the truth, I won't believe you?"

"I don't know what to believe myself. That's the worst part. According to my father, Rick Maslow would never say a thing like 'Lola, you're some kid,' and he never let anyone dance with me more than once. According to my father, it was Mara who brought the nightgowns. They were a gift from Mara. According to my mother . . . I don't know. I don't know and I don't understand. I'm sick of it all. I want things to be simple, but they refuse to be simple. I want to remember. But I can't. I want for the world to stop being like some merry-go-round with the colors changing and the people changing and everything being stretched out of shape, becoming grotesque. That's what it is: it's grotesque. Inside my mind, there's a steel door, and whenever I take a stroll in there, the door snaps shut and I'm trapped. For the rest of my life, trapped inside of my own head. And everyone else trapped inside of theirs . . . wondering, what did I do wrong, whose fault is it, maybe he wasn't doing what I thought, maybe I just overreacted to nothing, maybe I made the whole thing up! IT WAS ALL IN MY HEAD. What an awful phrase."

"It's all right," he said. "It doesn't matter whether it's true for someone else or not. What I'm interested in is what's true for you. I believe you."

"You believe me?"

"Yes, I believe you."

Suddenly I was crying, the way children cry. "You're crazy," I said, turning my head away.

He laughed. "Maybe so," he said.

The hour was up.

Part Two

*T*HE HARBOR below the cliffs is like a conch shell, the horn of Thursday morning's boat rising up from the inner side of the island's crescent, a low sound, an animal moan. I dread the moment when that horn sounds. It penetrates the walls of my house, reaching deep into my dreams like a minesweeper dragging along the floor of my subconscious, touching off a thousand tiny time bombs of association. The explosions are simultaneous: live images, noisily overlapping emotions leading like a series of fuses to different times in my life, different stages of the person I have been. And all of the memories come hurtling forward in full battle dress, a mob scene clashing violently over my history.

I cannot bring myself to think about Stefan. I must but I cannot. Cannot, cannot, cannot.

The minesweeper along the floor of my unconscious.

•

There are almond blossoms and seeds in the buckets Lola brings up from the well now, boiled in with her morning coffee. It is two weeks since she has come from Panaghios to Mithra. In the evening they walk down along the high road, the anemones in the terraced fields around them backlit with a fiery inner translucency by the lowering sun, the lichen mustard bright against the grays and drab greens of the rocks, forming a rim of color that curves with the downward slope of the hill.

65

They sit in a taverna on a small beach at the outer edge of town. He drinks ouzo from a finger-high glass. She drinks retsina. Between them are tiny plates of chopped octopus soaked in olive oil, above them, octopi drying on a line that stretches across the small painted metal tables and chairs of the taverna. The sun shines through the octopus skins, flaring like transparent bats lifting their wings in the wind. Two fishing boats are pulled up onto the sand, their yellow and turquoise and purple stripes painted along the gunwales like crayoned childrens' drawings.

The sun descends slowly, then plunges onto the mast of a tall ship, speared there until the mast itself seems to dissolve in a quick flare of obliterating light. Stefan reaches for Lola's hand. She flinches but does not pull away. Her acquiescence seems almost a matter of form.

He drops her hand. The farther off islands move closer, then recede, as the air thins into evening. She thinks of his shyness and his pride, then reaches for him again. It is the maximum that her will can accomplish. The air shivers as it slips into the belly of night. The priest who has been sitting in the corner gets up to leave. Then the Swede carrying his empty sketch pad goes. In the silence Stefan remembers the first time he saw Lola, sitting out on the pier, one hand slowly rubbing the back of her neck with a kind of controlled yet exaggerated passion . . . the gesture of a woman without other resources. He looks at her now out of the corner of his eye. She is staring straight ahead of her, bare tanned legs stretched out and crossed at the ankles where her sandal straps become a tangle. Her back is very low in the chair. A parody of relaxation.

In a moment she is sitting up straight.

"Would you mind if we went and had something to eat?" she says.

"Fine," he says, letting go of her hand again.

She does not look at him, but when he stands up he can see that the expression in her eyes is one of fear.

• • •

Crowds blow in and out of the narrow doors like balloons carried by the meltemi. The fisherman Stratus twice brings retsina to their table. The second time he stumbles and grips Lola's bare shoulder to steady himself, though when he has become steady, his hand remains there. Stefan is staring at Stratus' hand as if hypnotized. He knows how it is for the fishermen who come to the restaurant alone to drink and eat, whose wives do not come with them, except after church on Sunday. He knows how they eye the foreign women in their short skirts and halters, offering retsina until it is easy in a moment of friendship to lay a hand on a shoulder, put an arm around a waist, touch skin, bare skin, as if it does not matter, does not count a bit, as if it has no power to stun the senses, which among their own women are ordered into submission.

Stefan exchanges glances with Lola, his glance acknowledging the familiarity of a problem, hers conveying something more which he does not quite understand. She seems to expect him to do something, though he does not know what to do. He has not yet developed that sense of possessiveness about her and her body which would make her so much of an extension of him that her experiences would begin to feel like his own. He does not like Stratus, does not like what he is doing. But that is her concern, not his.

Suddenly she stands up, pushing Stratus' hand away. Her eyes are blazing. "Don't touch me, do you hear?" she says in a voice filled with controlled menace. "Don't you ever dare to touch me." Stratus does not understand the words, but he does understand her expression and her tone of voice. He has never seen a foreign woman react like that. It jolts him into a blend of confusion and shame that almost instantly transforms itself into

67

a kind of humiliated fury. There is nothing he can do now except preserve it.

Stefan is surprised by her reaction. He would have expected her to be used to that by now, to regard it as something commonplace, even slightly comic. He remembers her flinching in the taverna. He does not understand. The depth of her fury now seems disproportionate and, in a strange way, also archaic.

Lola looks away from Stefan and walks over to the stove where Chrysula keeps her pots of food, alongside a counter covered with freshly slaughtered baby lamb, goat cheese, turtle steak and red snapper. Chrysula's thick black hair fans out around her head. She reminds Lola of Saraghina dancing on an Italian beach while Fellini catches each coy undulation of her hips. But Chrysula is not a seductress, she is closer to a gypsy saint, but with the same power to make children sit raptly on the shore clapping and shouting, "more more more."

Lola and Chrysula talk for a moment and then Chrysula calls out something to Stratus in Greek which Stefan cannot understand, though Stratus immediately moves back to his seat in a corner and does not offer them any more retsina. Chrysula hugs Lola and pats her on the back. Lola smiles.

When she comes back to the table, she has with her a bowl filled with fish soup. "Chrysula always takes care of me," she says with an edge in her voice, though she moves so quickly to telling him about how, during the month of February when she had no money, Chrysula always made sure that she ate, always put extra fish in her soup, that he is not at all certain whether or not the edge has anything to do with him. He feels suddenly as if he is on dangerous ground, as if he does not know Lola at all.

Glancing sideways he can see now that Stratus is standing at the four tables the Americans have pushed together. He has brought them a bottle of retsina. There is a brief argument over who should pay, but then Stratus pays, as he always does, and the Americans ask him to join them, as they always do. His hand is on the bare inner elbow of a new Swedish girl, who does not seem to mind. She smiles at him and Stefan hears her say something about "getting to know the country, getting to know the people."

A boy at the table, who is wearing an army jacket, says, "I don't even *read* the newspapers anymore. I'm sick of problems. I just want to have a good time."

"But you can't 'just have a good time,'" says another American, who is very fat and is wearing a white muslin Greek shirt with puffy sleeves.

"What do you think I'm doing?"

"I don't know. Do you?"

"No. But I'm drinking retsina until I find out."

Another boy, who has been sketching everyone at the table, says, "America is going down the drain. Soon there'll be nothing left. Except sludge. All the good people are here. Or else in Canada. You can hear the storm troopers getting ready in Washington. Fascists. Every last one of them is a fascist."

The girl with him, who is also wearing an army jacket, says, "Absolutely. Jim is absolutely right. Just imagine. This time *we're* the Nazis."

Stratus nudges her. "Retsina," he says, pouring it into her glass. Half of it spills on the plastic tablecloth, but no one seems to mind. One of Chrysula's daughters mops it up. She laughs too.

"It's all talk," Lola says. "Armchair outrage. They're contemptuous of all the American tourists who come off the cruise boats with their money and their suitcases, but they're not so different from them as they think. They carry knapsacks filled with travelers' checks. They talk about politics and art and change. And spend their money on dope instead of souvenirs."

He has not expected this high moral tone coming from her. Privately he agrees, but it surprises him to hear Americans scorning other Americans, though he has seen it happen often. One would expect them to defend each other, particularly since everyone else criticizes them. He remembers that, before she approached him on the high road, he had seen her here in the restaurant and had noticed that, although she sometimes talked to the Americans, there was always a kind of withheld aloofness about her, as if to guarantee that she would remain unapproachable, as if the boundaries had to be very firmly delineated, as if she was afraid that without the firmness they would cease to exist at all.

"Don't you consider yourself an American?" he asks.

"Yes," she says. "But that doesn't mean I have to like everything we do. Anyway, my parents came from Europe during the war. I'm a Russian Jew." She stares at him very hard when she says that, as if she expects him to balk at it, as if she is challenging him.

"I know," he says.

That disarms her. "What do you mean you know?" she asks.

"You look like what you are," he says.

Privately, before they met, he had already named her "la petite Russienne," even though she was not at all petite and more Jewish than Russian. But it was too soon to tell her that, so he said instead, "I have nothing against the Jews, you know."

Instantly she flares up. "Did I say you did?"

"No," he says, smiling to himself at her vehemence. "But it's what you think."

"Already you think you know what I think," she says.

"Some of it. There are a lot of things I don't know."

There is something very earnest in his voice, as if he expects that after a time he will know everything.

"No one ever knows everything," she says, feeling as if a wave is crashing over her head, a wave that she does not know whether or not she can ride.

"That's true," he says and shifts the subject slightly, seeing that he has scared her and wondering why.

"It bothers you that I am Austrian," he says. She does not answer him at first, but when she does, the answer is like a punch.

"My father's whole family was killed by the Nazis."

70

"Do you think that I am a Nazi?"

"You are Austrian. That's enough."

"But not all Austrians were Nazis."

"Not all. But too many."

"I was a Nazi," he says.

He can see that she is ready to jump up from her seat and leave, that she remains only by sheer force of will.

"Yes," he says quietly. "When I was ten. My father was killed on the Russian front. The Nazi soldiers came into our school and said that we would have to make our contribution to the war effort. He said that from then on we would be helping to dig trenches. The next day my mother took me into the mountains with her. She didn't want me working with the Nazis. Neither did I. I hated the idea of digging trenches. I just wanted to make drawings. So she kept me there with her in the mountains. We had practically no money. Then she was in a motorcycle accident and lost her leg. Life became very difficult. So after a while I was brought back to the school and I dug the trenches. So you see . . . in a way it is true . . . I was a Nazi or at least I helped the Nazis. Even though I was a child. There are many Nazis still in Austria, you know. Many Nazis still in power. Of course, they are no longer Nazis, or that at least is what they say, and few people comment on it. No one wishes to remember."

It is difficult for her, listening to him. At one moment she sees him as a caricature of himself, as a child with his arm raised saying "*Sieg Heil.*" At the next, she sees him sitting in the mountains with his mother, a sketchbook on his knees. Her sense of morality being very precise, it is hard to reconcile the one image with the other, and even harder to reconcile either of them with the image of her father's family being herded into camps and never coming back, being herded by sweet snub-nosed young soldiers who looked as if they had no desire to harm anyone, as if they too enjoyed drawing and sat with their mothers in the mountains.

71

She does not want to talk anymore. She is tired of talking. What is there to say anyway? Everything you say only makes things more obscure, more confusing.

Over at the Americans' table, she hears one of the boys saying, "Man, I gotta piss. I really gotta piss." Stratus is getting another bottle of retsina. She feels a sudden desire to do something light-headed, something frivolous.

"How would you like to join them?" she says to Stefan.

The question startles him.

"Join them?" he says.

"Yes," she says. "Once in a while they're not so bad."

He is confused by this. First of all, no one has asked them to join. Second of all, she does not like these people. Third of all, they are in the middle of a conversation. But he decides not to question her, for already she has stood up and walked over to the table where the Americans are sitting. What he does not know is that she has never done this before, gone over to people without being asked. He assumes that it is an American thing, that Americans just go over to each other without being asked. In Europe, things are more formal. Perhaps it had something to do with . . . perhaps he should not have said anything about . . . But there was nothing to be done about it. And besides, he did not want to avoid . . .

He waits at the table, expecting her to call him over. When she does not, he feels a sudden surge of anger toward her. If she did not like what he was saying, all she had to do was tell him. But this walking away as if it was nothing . . . this . . . Some perverse desire not to let her get away with that makes him break all of his own rules of behavior. He stands up and walks over to the table where she is standing now, with her back toward him. It is some minutes before she even notices him. When she does, her face contracts suddenly, and she looks away.

"Who's your friend?" the boy in the army jacket asks.

"He's Austrian," she says.

Again he feels angry. She is being unjust, more unjust than these Americans for whom she feels so much contempt.

"Stefan," he says sharply. "My name is Stefan."

"Pull up a chair, Stefan," the boy with the puffy sleeves says. "I'm Peter. This is Marty." He points to the boy in the army jacket who says, not to anyone in particular, "Well, it's no skin off my nose. Not for a minute," and pours himself another glass of retsina.

"And that's Mim." Mim nods and leans against Lola's shoulder for a second. Then she says to Marty, "Oh come off it, will you? Just come off it."

The boy with the sketch pad does not lift his head and is not introduced.

No one seems to know the Swedish girl's name. She lights a match and allows it to burn almost down to her fingers before she lights her cigarillo.

Marty pours Lola a glass of retsina. She swallows it and lifts her hand to her neck. There is a line going all around her neck just below her chin, where the skin of her throat darkens.

She needs a bath, Stefan thinks. She definitely needs a bath.

• • •

There are nine of them now, on their way to a *festa* on the other side of the island, crammed into Costas' taxi, a 1948 Dodge that was a gift from his American father-in-law.

Marty wants to do the bargaining. Costas says it will be one hundred drachmas, both ways. Marty says, "One hundred drachmas! Man, you're crazy. We're not paying any hundred drachmas."

"That's cheap," Costas says.

73

Marty offers fifty. Costas sticks at a hundred. Marty offers sixty. Costas still sticks at a hundred. Marty offers seventy. Still a hundred.

"Man, what kind of bargaining is that?" Marty finally yells.

Stratus, who is swaying alongside of the taxi, says that he'll talk to Costas. "*Then birazzi. Then birazzi.* No important." He keeps tapping Marty on the shoulder or grabbing him by the arm until Marty finally tells him to "shut up for Christ's sake and let me pay what I damn please." Stratus swings and misses. Peter holds on to Marty. Costas leans casually against his taxi, insisting that one hundred drachmas is not much, since he will stay with them the whole night if necessary on the other side of the island. He will make sure they get back at any hour. He swears by the cross around his neck.

They pile into the taxi while the moon rides high in the sky and they swim in a pale sea of retsina.

Lola wants to know if they can bring Nina along. Costas fiercely says no. Ever since their marriage he has been saying no. It is not right, he says, for his wife to go to cafes, to go out at night. None of the Greek women do if they are respectable. She should learn from the Greek women. A year ago their first child was born and Costas got his taxi. On Sundays he drives around the island with Nina and the baby Antonïo, named after his father. The rest of the week Nina stays home, remembering that Costas courted her in a way that American boys never had, that he was a fisherman doing "real work," that he had, and still has, a dramatic chiseled face which implies more strength than she has ever known, even though he is no longer a fisherman.

Costas drives fast; he takes the turns at a clip, yelling at the people who are on the road with their donkeys, telling them to get out of the way. A girl, who seems to have appeared out of nowhere sometime between the moment when they left Chrysula's and the time they reached Costas' taxi, announces that her name is Michel.

Jim sits in Mim's lap with Marty on top of him. The Swedish girl is wedged in between Stratus and Peter, who is holding Michel. Lola has edged herself up against the door, bracing herself on the armrest and seeming to reject the idea of sitting on anyone's lap. Stefan is alone in the front seat with Costas because "you can't have more than two in the front," as Costas says. *"Polizia,"* he says gravely. "Police."

The sea seems to rise along with them as they ride the crests of the hills. The taxi jolts from side to side. In the moonlight, the tiny roadside churches with their whitewashed walls and high whitewashed crosses are islands floating from cliff to cliff. Every time they pass a church, Stratus and Costas cross themselves and Costas sometimes kisses the cross around his neck.

There are flowers everywhere in the niches set up for the worship of the virgin, though fewer icons than usual. Tourists have taken them for souvenirs.

"Retsina, retsina," Stratus shouts in between crossing himself. Stefan is the only one who does not drink. He is quite sure that hours from now it will not be Costas driving the taxi, but him. He sits stiffly, watching Lola through the rear view mirror. She does not look at him. Instead she stares out the window and, once in a while, takes a swig from the bottle of retsina.

•

The taxi stops in front of a church. The Mousouris family is inside. Outside, the priest is helping to carve the lamb, which has been roasting on a spit. The sound of a sartouni, the ancient traditional instrument of Greece, comes from inside the church, the music twisting and curving in Oriental cadences that are never heard inside the bouzouki-saturated cafes of the town.

The beach gleams in the moonlight. Someone moves in the shadow of the grape arbor. Lola recognizes Eleftherios walking out of the door. He greets them formally, politely. "Would you like to join us?" he says in a voice that is less an invitation than an attempt to remove the awkwardness created by their having come in the first place.

"Sure," Marty says.

Peter says, "We thought it was a *festa*. We thought . . ." He does not know what else to say.

"You are welcome to our celebration," Eleftherios says.

Costas has not gotten out of the taxi. He sits low behind the steering wheel saying nothing. Stratus is swaying along the edge of the shore.

"It's their feast day," Stefan whispers to Lola. "It's their private feast day. We can't go in."

"Well, there's not much else we can do now," she says. "If we leave, they'll feel they insulted us. If we stay, we're insulting them."

"Nice church you got here," Marty says. "This your church?"

"It is from my family," Eleftherios says, trying to smile but instead seeming even graver than before. "Well, please come."

They follow Eleftherios into the church, trying not to look at each other.

"That's what we wanted, wasn't it," Mim mutters. "To go to a *festa* where there wouldn't be any tourists."

"Big joke," Jim whispers, trying to figure out where to put his sketch pad, since he has a feeling that bringing the sketch pad in with him would be almost as bad as bringing a camera.

"I don't see what the big deal is about," Marty says.

"The only thing that's a big deal is that you don't see what the big deal is," Peter says. "So why don't you keep your ideas to yourself?"

"You hear that?" Marty says. "We've got Socrates the philosopher along with us."

"This is a church," Stefan says pointedly.

"Yeah?" Marty says.

76

Stefan says nothing.

"You know, Marty," Michel says, "it's the same as a synagogue."

"I gotcha," Marty says. "A synagogue. A fucking Greek synagogue. And they're celebrating Passover."

Inside the church, a long wooden trestle table fills up almost three-quarters of the low-ceilinged room, which is so small that it seems more like a vault. There are two wooden benches on either side of the table. Everyone is sitting close together, children on their mothers' laps: a human string of beads, uniform in style, on the verge of being broken and scattered. The table is cluttered with plates, edged as closely together as the people; feta and kaseri and mykoniatico cheeses, olives, tomatoes, fish, lamb, chicken, pastitsio, souvlaki on skewers, yoghurt, country-style salad, enormous loaves of bread and fresh-churned butter. The men are all close-shaven, their mustaches clipped and trimmed, blue suits carefully brushed, hair with the sharp clear lines of a same day's haircut, the women wearing embroidered traditional skirts and blouses which, in their innocent designs, speak a language known only to the initiated. The sartouni does not stop playing when the Americans file in through the low door of the church; the conversation does not altogether stop, though it shifts and drops like a slow-rolling wave passing around a reef; no one jumps up and leaves the room; there are no bursts of angry protest. Yet in a way everything does stop. The room becomes like an egg that has been pierced at both ends and the insides sucked out. The shell is the same, but there is nothing in it. Everyone is gone; the spirit of the tribe has been coaxed out of its body and has left to take part in some other invisible ceremony.

Stefan sees Aristides, who has a cataract in one eye and sells him cigarettes, pencils and paper, sitting at the far end of the table next to the boy who runs errands for Theodoris' restaurant, bringing dessert back to the restaurant from the *zacharoplasteion*

77

every time foreigners ask to have baklava and Nescafe in the same place where they have just finished eating meat. Toward the center of the table, there is a woman wearing a traditional black shawl. Stefan recognizes her from the bakery, though he has seen her only in the dimness of the bakery's back room where, at five every morning, she stands in the rising white dust kneading loaves of white and black bread, passing them on to the baker who will put them into the oven. On either side of her sit two giants, twins. Only now does he realize that they are brothers, never having seen them together before. They both drive mules and he has always thought they were one. Now it appears that they are two, and that both of them are the bakery woman's sons.

Lola sees the vegetable man whose vegetables are never fresh. He is sitting opposite the bakery woman, and two seats down from her is the woman who rents rooms in the house at the top of the hill: all month masons have been working there, and the house has become an ongoing series of additions—an extra room, an extra balcony, an extra shuttered window—a process which, it is clear, has been repeated several times, so that the house has come to look like a railroad timetable indicating increases in service from one year to the next. Beside her is another woman whom Lola passes each day on her way to the yoghurt store; always she sits in front of her house, seeming never to change positions, knitting a seemingly endless white sweater.

Each of them recognizes someone else. Some recognize three or four. Marty says, in something close to a whisper, "Hey, isn't that the guy who told us about the American chicks in that whorehouse in Piraeus?" He points to a small man squeezed in between two larger ones.

Suddenly Lola understands something about the island that she has never quite known before. All of these people, who have existed for her as random flashes of life moving in and out of the periphery of her vision like strangers on a city street, are not strangers to each other at all. They are permanently linked, like the members of a secretly constituted gang which in public expresses only a nodding acquaintance, but in private shares a bond more complex than anything the outside world might imagine.

To be friendly, generous, welcoming is their second nature. To be ingrown, hidden, insular, is their first. The churches are untouched by foreigners; the weddings are untouched; the deaths untouched, the family feuds untouched, the births untouched, all the family relations untouched. Everything that counts in their lives is untouched, everything that would make them come together to celebrate a name day in this church on the far side of the island where no one ever goes.

"Please sit down," Eleftherios says. Then, almost as if it were a jointly agreed upon act of obedience, spaces open up between the bodies which moments ago seemed to be sitting as close together as possible. There are quick small cries rising up from all sides. "*Kali spera! Kali spera! Ti kanis? Kala? Kalosuarrisite! Kalosuarrisite! Yasu fili mu. Yasu! Yasu! Yasu!*" Cries repeated over and over again, like the chirping of a roomful of birds, all of it in the same cadence, the same tone of voice, a ritual of welcome and simulated delight, which is their best protection against invasion by the strangers.

Stefan is standing beside Lola, who is consenting to be with him for the first time since she walked away from the table at Chrysula's. No longer is he the Austrian outsider; they have both become "the foreigners," the strangers, the intruders. What then separated them now joins them. They sit next to each other at the table, without speaking. The vegetable man sits next to Stefan. Michel is beside Lola.

The music rises up again. Hands reach out to serve them food, urging them to take some of the lamb, some of the salad, chicken, bread, take everything, you are our guests, welcome, eat, please eat, you must eat. In the rush to make sure that they will not feel unwelcome, it is almost, but not quite, forgotten that they are the strangers.

Gradually the music begins to draw dancers from the table over to the small corner where the sartouni player is sitting. At first only the men dance in the cramped space, a slow hasapiko, but by the time there is nothing left on the plates but traces of olive oil, the women too have begun to enter the small circles that form and break with ritual regularity. Never before have the foreigners seen women dancing. The sartouni is no longer playing familiar music but instead has switched to something more intricate, which makes different claims upon the dancers. Slow, grave, complex, the women move without any of the men's daring, but instead with a stately elegance that reaches back through generations of accumulated memories. Their hands are joined, their chins raised; two women have even unbound their hair. It is a dance so intimate, so private, despite the fact that the dancers scarcely touch each other, that Lola holds her breath as if she has stumbled on some forbidden ritual. The tension among the dancers builds as their muscles are drawn to the limits of an absolute inner restraint.

There is silence in the room. The dance becomes slower and slower, seeming on the verge of stopping altogether and yet maintaining that high almost suspended rhythm. Then the music begins to slide away, as if it has been completely absorbed into the dancers. The group dissolves back toward the tables; the voices escalate again, and the music becomes faster and more joyous. Stefan puts his arm around Lola's shoulder. She stiffens, then half relaxes and leans in toward him. He can feel the tautness that remains in the muscles of her back, the struggle between opposing tendencies that is contained in her every movement, at once guarded and expansive. He reaches out for a section of pear that has just been placed on the table but is halted in mid-gesture by a stinging blow on the back of his head. Instinctively he reaches to cover himself, but already Stratus has begun to pummel his back, shouting over and over again, "*Schweinhund! Schweinhund!* You no touch. You no touch."

In an instant the vegetable man and the twins have leaped out of their seats and grabbed Stratus' arms to hold him back. Stefan is shaking. Eleftherios is talking to Stratus in a voice filled with low fury, while Stratus struggles to free himself from the grip of the three men and continues to shout in Greek until the men finally let go of his arms. He lifts his eyes to the ceiling of the church and waves his arms in the air. Eleftherios flushes and nods his head. The men who have been holding Stratus smile nervously, then look over at Stefan and Lola. The women's faces are frozen.

"Eleftheri," Lola says. "Why did he *do* that? What for, just tell me what for?" Her voice is trembling.

Eleftherios does not look at her when he answers. "Because the man put his arm around you."

"But what is wrong with that?"

"It is because . . . he says it is because this is a church. It is a holy place."

Lola looks at Stratus. In his eyes there is an expression of spiteful contempt and avenged pleasure, the remnants of what remained unexpressed hours ago in the restaurant. He spits on the ground, sneers at her and then suddenly bursts out with another volley of words. This time many of the women shake their heads in agreement.

"What did he say?" Lola asks.

"I cannot tell you."

"Oh for Christ's . . . I mean for cripes' sake . . . you might as well say. This is ridiculous."

"I don't think you will want to know."

"I'm not that delicate, Eleftheri. If Stratus can try to beat someone up, we might as well know what it is all about."

Costas has been standing in the doorway all along. Now he says, "Stratus said that you can do any dirty thing you want in your own country . . . but not here, and not in church."

"Dirty? I don't understand what's dirty about putting your arm around someone."

Costas shrugs. "I didn't say it, he did. Ask him."

"I think we should go," Stefan says to Lola. "We should go right away." He stands up from the table, nods his head briefly at everyone and walks toward the door. His face is very pale. Lola follows him, not nodding at anyone or smiling, though she can see that Stratus is now standing with his arms folded across his chest, a smug smile on his face, the laws of retribution fulfilled. There is a slow shuffle of movement among the Americans as they shift in their seats, some of them starting to stand up, others unwilling to move. Peter is the first to follow them out, saying to Eleftherios, "I'm sorry, I'm terribly sorry." Marty glares at him, then mutters grimly, "Sorry, everyone's sorry. Nothing to be sorry for. Just a bum party that's all. A bum party."

The others do not speak or look at anyone. They file slowly out of the church. No one tries to stop them. Costas is the last one out. He makes the sign of the cross as he leaves. Then he turns back toward the church and gives Stratus a quick, quiet salute. Stratus salutes him back. A slow smile spreads through the church.

• • •

"Where are you going?" Costas asks. "To her place or yours?"

"I am going to mine and she is going to hers," Stefan says.

Costas laughs. "Stratus upset you, eh?"

"No. I'm just going home and she's going home."

"It's all right," Lola whispers. "If you want to come over for coffee, you can."

"No."

"I want you to come," she says.

"I said no. Maybe some other time, but not tonight."

"Why are you so upset about it? It is nothing to get so upset about."

"Yes it is. It's something to get very upset about."

"Because you are Catholic?"

"Because I am a human being."

Costas stops the taxi at Stefan's place first, idling the motor. "You still have time to change your mind," he says.

"No thanks," Stefan says. And climbs out of the taxi. Lola climbs out after him. She reaches up and brushes her mouth against his, then climbs back in.

"First fuck is at the altar," Marty says. "Like the good old days. Hoorah for the first fuck." He lifts the bottle of retsina to his mouth, drains it except for one last sip and reaches forward to give it to Costas. "On me," he says. "Drink's on me. Think I'll walk from here. Want to walk." He stumbles as he gets out of the taxi. Costas grins at him and drives off. It is the fifteenth of March.

*S*HE STANDS OUT in the bleached bone-white courtyard staring at the lemon trees with their painted white trunks. "We can be friends. Of course we can be friends." She repeats it over and over again to herself. But the fear is like a lock inside of her that won't release. There are contractions in her stomach. She tells herself that it is all self-created, this terror at the core of things, this certainty that to be approached is to be devastated. She tries running her hands slowly across her face and down her throat and over her breasts, tries it in an attempt at preparation, as if by getting used to her own hands and imagining them as his, the strangeness will be obliterated, the nightmares will be obliterated, and things will be simple.

Sweet and decent, sweet and decent, sweet and decent. She says the words to herself while touching her own face. She even tries kissing the back of her hands in the search for some kind of familiarity. She stuffs her mind with contemporary tales, people doing it for fun, people just . . . It is mortifying to her that she has never done it for anything but love, or what she thought was love, even though that was so often and so intolerably misplaced. Because she made it so important, it has now become impossible. Her worldliness is a sham. Love, or the belief in it, has been the only thing strong enough to knock out the fear, the pounding fear of she didn't know what, even though it was instantly replaced with another kind of fear: the terror of being torn from herself, the terror of being violated, replaced in an instant transmogrification by the terror of being abandoned, the terror of losing that contact which, once made, could not be severed.

What she wants is to be casual, flippant, easygoing, for things to take on some natural rhythm of growth and change and development. Not for all of it to have this fitful, panicky quality, this simultaneous desire to just plunge in and let whatever happens happen, and the desire to hold everything back until you're sure absolutely sure that there won't be any damage. But who can ever be sure that there won't be any damage? Where has there ever been such a guarantee? She feels a sudden yearning for the rituals of courtship, antique courtship in which each gesture was ensured its absolute weight, everything had time to sink in, the sight of a face or an ankle, the effects of a conversation, the thousand and one slowly removed shields that kept people from inundating each other so quickly that it almost became obliterating. She does not want to lose herself again, anymore. It is not freedom that she wants really; she wants not to be afraid of love, or even of intimacy, of its power to throw everything into some frightening relief that destroys utterly her sense of the true proportion of things.

With him there will be no risk like that, she thinks. He is not really the type for me to lose myself in. We could be friends, maybe friendly lovers. It wouldn't be a passion like the other times. It would be more mature. And yet, every time she thinks of being touched, there is this flinching away, this involuntary withdrawal into herself, as if her body transmits signals of its lack of preparedness to her, as if her brain can concoct any tolerance whatsoever, and her body can construct none.

She pours herself a glass of retsina. It has been three years since the last time. But it's like riding a bicycle; you don't forget. Maybe there's some shyness in the beginning. Maybe you're tight inside. But that goes away. You'll remember, she says to herself. And the fear that sends her scuttling back into herself, that will go away. It *will* go away, she insists. Her breathing has become shallow, throat closing up.

Suddenly she is crying. She cannot stop. She sits on the whitewashed wall and sobs until her eyes ache. Everything is a delayed reaction. But how long can delayed reactions go on? Can you finally cry this year over what happened ten years ago? And when will you cry over what happened today? How long must everything be postponed?

She doesn't know what she is crying about. The hexagons are spinning in her mind, a mass of them moving in upon her like the black and yellow diamonds that form when you press slowly against your eyelids. There is sunlight on Riverside Drive, bushes surrounding the mall, the sun sinking onto the mast of a tall ship . . . no, not the Hudson, the Mediterranean, no, not the Mediterranean, the Aegean, the Aegean Sea. "It is far away, it is very far away." And anyway, when she went to look for the place in the park, it didn't even exist.

She cries until she is exhausted. And then goes into the house still holding the bottle of retsina. She lies awake on the bed saying over and over again, "Sweet and decent. Sweet and decent. Sweet and decent."

• • •

She avoids him altogether now. When she does see him, her face grows blank with a kind of guarded fury, something almost random in its intensity and beyond any reasonable comprehension. It is as if she is looking for a reason to spite him.

Once, on the high road, she stops near where he is working and stands in resolute silence behind him for almost half an hour. She is not there out of curiosity or interest or for pleasure. It is an act of will, of defiance, a test of his ability to tolerate her presence while he is in the midst of working. She is waiting for the moment when he will ask her to leave. He doesn't. She wants the triumph of being the one who can stand there, in silent domination, the longest. He wants her to know that, at the very least, he has enough staying power to resist being juggled.

It is a matter of simple endurance, like the game played among children trying to outstare each other. Ultimately, she wishes to grate him . . . either into submission or irritation, he is not sure which.

He concentrates his own will upon the canvas, forcing himself to continue painting, though each brushstroke is an intensification of risk. It is like appearing before a hanging judge who cares nothing for the loopholes of evasion. It angers him to see himself giving in to this, painting for the sake of her approval rather than his own, though it is not exactly a matter of approval. It is more a matter of pitting himself against himself in an effort to make real for her the person he is within the work. He is completely unused to this. Ordinarily, he will not tolerate anyone's watching him while he is working. It is a sealed world, defined by its intimacies. And yet, he *is* letting her watch: he is not telling her to go, as she expects.

In the space of half an hour he smokes and puts out half a pack of cigarettes, discarding a few after several puffs. The curve of hills in the distance becomes the imagined curve of her body from breast to belly. The walls of the alley move off into purple shadows.

He stops for five minutes. She has moved far enough behind him that he cannot see her without turning around. He does not turn around.

He is tired of the game, the war of wills in which his strengths are all passive. His sketch pad is on the ground next to him. There is a letter from his wife on top of it, weighted down with a stone. He feels a sudden perverse urge to push the stone aside with his foot. He is certain that she would notice. That would take care of it. His wife's handwriting is large and clear, the return address almost bold. He imagines the instant collapse of

Lola's defiance. And yet, he is not angry enough at her to do that. He senses that the defiance is a paper-thin wall between herself and herself. Besides, this war of wills between them now is not a matter of ultimate consequences; his wife's letter is.

She has followed his eyes to the sketch pad though, and moves forward suddenly, bending as she says, "I'd like to see your sketch pad." The same note of simulated innocence and ultimate challenge is in her voice: the willful effort to make him refuse. His hand trembles slightly. But he does not say anything.

She picks up the envelope first and glances at it.

"I see," she says after a moment. "Her name is Marianna. Your wife, I assume?"

"Yes," he says.

"Strong handwriting. Well, I'm glad you told me." She forces herself to look at him, as if to prove that the letter has had no effect on her, but she is not strong enough for the effort. There is a struggle on her face, a wavering as she tries to reestablish the control which in an instant has slipped from her eyes, her mouth, her jaw. First one gets away and then another; the eye muscles are strained into submission, but the mouth trembles; the mouth is halted but the jaw stiffens. Again the fury comes into her face, though now it is of a different kind: fury at her inability to master herself.

He looks away from her, out of a sudden sense of embarrassment. Dominate everybody, he thinks . . . except herself. He feels a wild surge of protectiveness toward her, something which cuts through him viscerally.

"The painting is not as good as the last one," she says coldly, turning away from him. "It is rather conventional, in fact."

"Thank you," he says.

"You're welcome."

She turns away from him and walks up the road to her house. Even her walk is controlled now; she moves from the knees rather than the hips. When she has rounded the curve in the road, he lights another cigarette. She has forgotten to look at the sketch pad.

He picks up the letter from Marianna and puts it in his pocket. In two months they will meet each other in Athens "to discuss things." Her letter is consciously light. She asks only which islands he would prefer, how the work is going, whether the trip has been good. Have you met anyone to talk to?

He stands smoking until he has finished the pack. His brushes remain in place. The canvas is untouched. He tosses away the cigarette package and gathers together his things. It occurs to him that Lola has succeeded in outstaring him.

•   •   •

On Sunday, he walks all the way across the island, twelve kilometers, to the beach. She is there alone with Marty. He sits on the other side of the beach, watching them unfold a picnic: feta and tomatoes, bread and retsina. They kick around a beach ball. Once she kicks it toward him, and he suspects that it is only a matter of misplaced aim that it misses him and rolls by. When she rushes past him to retrieve it, he says hello but she doesn't answer.

They stop playing, race each other into the water and come back to the beach. She laughs loudly and often, her gestures stylized and self-conscious. After an hour, she seems to have run out of energy. She keeps walking down to the water and coming back again without going in.

Then there is a change. The large gestures stop. She sits with her legs crossed, her body tense, leaning toward Marty and listening. Occasionally, she brushes her hair back from her face and asks a question. He keeps shaking his head, building up a sand castle and repeatedly leveling it. He only rarely looks up at her while he talks. Every once in a while he glances around him in a sudden panic, as if trying to make sure that no one is watching him, though there are very few people on the beach besides Stefan, and none of them has Stefan's interest in the conversation. Once he looks over at Stefan and his manner instantly becomes stilted. His back stiffens and he makes a quick joke at which Lola doesn't laugh, though in a moment his face is serious again and he is absorbed in their conversation.

Stefan swims once, but the water seems annoyingly warm even though it is only March. The irritation grows in him at his own obstinacy in staying there in the first place, at his persistence in concentrating on the two of them rather than on something else. She most certainly is aware of his watching them, and it gives her a power over him, though now even that is gone, and she seems to have forgotten him entirely. He walks along the rocks finally, restless, frustrated, vaguely disappointed. When he comes back they are gone.

• • •

It is three o'clock in the morning when she knocks on his door. "Stefan, are you there?" she stage whispers. He has gone to bed only an hour ago, after writing a long letter to Marianna, and is still half awake, lying on the narrow cot in his pajamas.

He comes to the door. "Of course I'm here," he says. "Where do you think I would be?"

She ignores the question. "Do you want to go swimming?" she asks.

He looks at his watch and then at her. She is wearing a bathrobe, loosely tied, and underneath it, a bikini.

"You're drunk," he says. "You should go home to bed."

"What does that have to do with swimming? I'm not asking you to go naked. See . . . I have mine on." She takes off the bathrobe. In the moonlight her skin is even darker than during the day.

"Cover yourself up," he says. "It's too cold to go swimming at night."

"No, it's not. It's warm at night. Because of the phosphorus."

"What phosphorus?"

"The phosphorus in the *water*."

"What does phosphorus have to do with the water being warm?"

"Well, it's light isn't it?"

He stares at her and laughs, remembering now that the water was too warm earlier in the day, remembering Marty.

"You should go home to Marty," he says and realizes instantly that he has made a mistake. She flinches visibly.

"That was cruel," she says, sounding not at all drunk anymore.

"I'm sorry," he says, thinking that it is impossible to adapt to her constant changes of mood. If he responds to her coldness by being cold himself, she is offended. If he tries being warm, she attacks his vulnerability.

"I don't understand what you want of me," he says.

"Nothing."

"Well, obviously you want something, otherwise you wouldn't be standing here. It's just that I can't keep up with your expectations."

"Go inside, Stefan, and get your bathing suit. Please."

"I'm not going swimming with you, Lola. But I'll walk you back to the house, if that's what you want. Is it what you want?"

"I suppose," she says. She looks exhausted now, and on the verge of tears. "Marty, by the way, isn't at all like what you think he's like."

"Forget it. I shouldn't have said anything. I told you I was sorry."

"But it's important, Stefan."

"Look, I have no idea what he's like."

"He's . . ."

"Please . . ."

"All right."

When he comes back out of the house, she is sitting on the stones with her bathrobe spread out underneath her, as if prepared for another picnic. "There's something I want to tell you," she says.

"What?"

"Sit down."

"Why can't you stand up?"

"Because it's not something you say standing up."

"You can say anything standing up." He is getting impatient with her. He does not like these dramatic ruses, midnight expeditions, drunken encounters. He is tired of being manipulated like an adolescent.

"There was only one sentence I wanted to say," she says, standing up unsteadily.

"What was it?"

"I wanted to say that you shouldn't bother with me unless you're serious."

He looks at her face, highlighted now by lines of tension. He wants to ask her to come in, to stay, but doesn't dare. He senses obscurely that it would give her an excuse to turn on him again, that there is some kind of restraint required of him that goes beyond the mere formalities of waiting, though he still suspects that it may yet be part of a game.

"Did you think I would?" he asks.

"Of course you would," she says. Her voice is stripped now of its earlier coyness. It is very clear, almost harsh. "Go back to bed, Stefan," she says. "I can walk home myself."

He sees that she means what she is saying, that the entire visit has been a cushion for that one sentence, that she has exhausted her energies with the effort of saying it.

She picks up her bathrobe from the stones and stands for a moment in her bikini before putting it on. "The bathing suit wasn't to tempt you," she says. "Because I'm scared to death of you. I'm really scared to death."

She ties the knot on her bathrobe slowly, carefully. "Goodnight, Stefan," she says, emphasizing the Stefan.

"Goodnight, Lola," he says, and watches her walk away.

When she is gone, he sits in his room looking at the letter he has just written to Marianna. All he can think is that things are not going to be simple, not simple at all. Marianna is alone in the house. She has been alone for weeks.

"Yes, I have someone to talk to," he thinks. "Yes, Marianna, I do."

•   •   •

"Tell me about your wife," she says.

He is sitting on a pillow on the blue floor near the courtyard window of her house. There is a charcoal brazier in the center of the floor, an army blanket on her bed. It is cold, damp, a wintry day in the middle of spring.

"Why do you want to know?" he says.

"I don't know why I want to know. I just do."

It's a kind of self-punishment the question. "Why do I want to know?" Perhaps because of the jolt created by that sudden increment of interest that rose up in her during the moment of discovery that he had a wife, rose up right alongside of her fear. It nags at her to have felt that. She cannot dismiss it, or dispose of it, or transform it. The very second that he acquired a wife, he became more valuable to her. The thought sickens her. And now, like a patient probing an aching tooth, she pursues the question, "What is she like? Tell me about her."

"I don't want to tell you," he says.

93

"Why not?"

"Because it is wrong."

"Wrong? What is wrong with it?"

"It's voyeuristic. It's using her somehow."

"No it's not."

"Yes it is. She's a person too. She's entitled to a certain . . . I don't know exactly what . . . a certain privacy. My relationship with her has to do with me and with her, not with me and you. I don't want to take advantage."

The seriousness which she demanded of him before now frightens her, particularly when it is applied to someone else. He approaches everything with this kind of thoughtful integrity: it is not something he summons up merely for her benefit. To talk about his wife is, for him, to betray her. To make him talk will bind him to her in a different way, in a pact created by the temporary forfeiture of his sense of honor. She wants to cry again. Why this wish to bind him dishonorably? Why this need to hoard up things to be used, sometime in the future when she will require them, against him? Why this certainty that she must have weapons? She persists. "Tell me. It is a part of your life, that's all. An important part. How can you be serious and conceal something like that from me?"

"I am not concealing it," he says. "You know she exists."

"Do you love her?"

He is silent.

She feels a quick, wild urge to punish him, to break his will. "Do you love her?" she repeats.

He knows that whatever he says now will be wrong. If he claims to love her, then Lola will want to know why he is with her now. If he claims not to love her, then Lola will want to know why he doesn't divorce her. Her rigidity again, her sense of absolute moral imperatives, used not as a humane standard but, rather, as a weapon to diminish everything imperfect.

94

"In a way, yes," he says, regretting that he has committed himself even this much.

"How can you love someone 'in a way'?"

"If you've lived with a woman for over five years, there is bound to be something between you. We've shared a life, that's all. I don't know if you'd call it love or not. I don't even know if I'd call it love."

"You know what I mean," she says angrily, trying to resist that near-to-irresistible feeling of respect for him that grows inside of her faster than her capacity to destroy it.

"No, I don't," he says.

"Well, forget it then," she says, getting up from the floor where she has been sitting. "I'm getting some water from the well. I'll be back."

In her absence he surveys the small room, sparse as Van Gogh's hospital room at St. Rémy where he once spent five days painting and repainting the images drawn up from his imagination by that austere scene. A blue floor, a cot, a window, an armload of books, a notebook on a yellow desk, a kitchen bare of anything perishable, without a refrigerator even, just a small two-burner stove. And then the enclosed whitewashed courtyard with the almond tree in the center, the lemon grove beginning outside of its walls and extending to the upper stone wall edged by cypresses. He does not know why she has come here in the first place, or what she wants of him, why she tries to break him down inch by inch and seems to care for him only at the moments when she fails. Why must everything be a test of his limits. It is this that fascinates and disturbs him . . . the sense that in her most destructive moments, she wishes to find something indestructible.

Nonetheless, it is a dangerous game, a very dangerous game. You flatter yourself, Stefan, he thinks. You flatter yourself a great deal.

She comes back into the room carrying a bucket filled with

95

water, sets it down, and before she has stood up to face him says, "You want to fuck me, don't you?"

He does not move from where he is sitting. "I thought you said I shouldn't bother with you unless I was serious."

By now she is looking directly at him, her face accusatory. It is obvious that she has not expected him to say that, and she turns suddenly scarlet.

"Oh yes," she says. "I'd forgotten about that."

"You'd forgotten?"

"Yes. You know, sometimes I say things . . ."

"Sometimes you say things?"

"Yes. For Christ's sake, you don't have to be the Grand Inquisitor, do you?"

"I'm sorry," he says. "I have just one more question, though."

"What is it?"

"Why do you call it 'fucking'?"

"It's just a word," she says. "Like any other word. What's wrong with it?"

"Nothing, I suppose," he says. "But you don't carry it off very well. You make it sound like a six-year-old proving he knows how to talk dirty."

"Fucking isn't dirty," she says.

"I didn't say it was. You did."

"I did? I did not."

"That was the way you made it sound."

"Oh shut up," she says. "I bet you talk that way to your wife, too. Holier than thou all the time. Mr. Wisdom and Purity."

"Did I say that?"

"Say what?"

"Say that I was Mr. Wisdom and Purity."

"No you didn't. But you act that way."

"I see," he says, thinking that of all the things she has said, this is perhaps the only one she really believes, and thinking as well that if she does believe it, she will punish him for it.

96

"So tell me about your wife," she says again, harshly now.

"No."

"Well then, there's no reason for you to stay."

"Would you like for me to leave?"

"For God's sake, Stefan. You're so literal. So serious and so literal. I'm going to get some water."

"You already got it," he says.

"Oh." She sits down on the floor, seeming to have run out of words. "I don't want to talk anymore," she says.

"We don't have to," he says. "Would you like for me to make some coffee?"

Her legs are crossed, her knees raised up under her chin, her head tucked down. He can see nothing of her except a dark head of hair, bare knees, bare calves and bare feet.

"Go ahead," she says. Her voice is very soft, almost inaudible. He walks out of the room and into the kitchen. On the small shelf above the stove is a tin of instant Greek Nescafe. He looks around for a pot. There is only one, and it has the remains of the morning's boiled milk still in it. He finds a scrub brush which looks new and unused, pours some water into the pot and heats up enough to clean it out. There is more than one day's boiled milk in it, he thinks. She probably uses the pot over and over again for the same thing and never washes it. His own sense of cleanliness being acute, the sight of the dirty pot makes him vaguely nauseous. When he has scrubbed it thoroughly, he heats up some more water for the Nescafe. There is sugar in a paper bag on the shelf and powdered cream in another small tin. He finds two plastic cups and brings them back into the room.

She is still sitting on the floor in the same position as when he left her.

"Coffee?" he says. "Cream and sugar?"

"Yes," she mumbles without lifting her head. "Two sugars, a lot of cream."

She reaches out her hand for the cup, and he gives it to her.

97

"I don't understand why you're nice to me," she says. "It makes me sick."

"Makes you sick?"

"Yes, I get nauseous from it."

"Are you nauseous now?"

"A little bit. But I'll get over it."

They drink the coffee in complete silence. When he has finished, he says, "Well, I suppose I should go now."

"Yes," she says. "I suppose you should."

She walks him through the courtyard, past the lemon trees and out to the high wall surrounding the property, but doesn't open the outer door.

When she speaks, her voice is so low that he can hardly hear her.

"Would you like to stay?" she says.

He doesn't answer immediately. He is not certain whether or not this too is intended as a way of punishing him, and just as uncertain over whether or not she wants him to answer yes or no.

"Do you want me to?" he says.

"Yes," she says.

"Then I will."

"But you have to promise something."

"What?"

"That you won't touch me. Can you do that?"

He is not at all sure that he can. Nor is he sure what lengths she is prepared to go to in order to prove that he can't.

"I'm not sure," he says. "I can't say that it will be easy. But I'll try."

"Everyone always says yes and then they don't," she says.

"Everyone?"

"Yes," she says. "It's something I've always wanted, but it's never happened."

"Maybe you didn't really want it," he says.

"Maybe not. But I think I did. I think I at least wanted to try. They didn't even try.

"Were there many?"

"Enough," she says. "I don't want to talk about it. I have a nightgown for myself. But you'll have to sleep in your clothes. It's all right if you just wear your underwear."

"You're sure you want me to?" he says.

"I'm sure," she says. This time she looks directly at him. There is a peculiar kind of determination in her face, like a child trying to be brave enough to enter the room in which it has just had a nightmare.

He thinks that this is not a game. Though as yet, he doesn't understand exactly what it is.

"All right," he says. And walks behind her back toward the house.

SHE LIES on her back with her arms pressed against her sides, her palms flat against the mattress. He lies near her but not touching, on his stomach, his arms drawn in underneath him. She does not say a word. She hardly seems to be breathing. She does not move. He waits for her. She still does not move. At first, he can hardly see her in the darkness; then he can see her profile, the sheet pulled up almost to her collarbone. She tells him nothing, nothing of desire, nothing of fear, nothing of anger or tenderness or distance or familiarity, nothing of will or abandonment, nothing pure and nothing vulgar. Nothing. Nothing at all. It is like waiting for a photographic print to surface from developing paper and take form, as if she does not exist and is waiting to exist, though she does not know who she will be. It is as if she could as easily kill him as love him. He lies there and is afraid of her.

He does not have a watch. He does not know what time it is. He does not know whether or not she has fallen asleep, whether she is waiting for him, whether in the morning she will be contemptuous of him for doing as she has asked. He wants to say something to her and cannot. He does not know what to say. Do you want to make love? Do you want me to touch you? Do you want me to stay? What do you want? Are you even awake?

At first there is the strain of holding himself back. Then there is the wondering whether she simply wishes to be conquered, to be taken. His mind swings from one perception to the other, like a monkey swinging through treetops. Except it is dark, and he does not know where the branches are. There is nothing now. Just an absolute stillness.

He rises up on one elbow to see if she is awake. Her eyes are open. She is staring straight in front of her. She does not even acknowledge him. Suddenly he wants to scream at her or shake her, to say, for God's sake at least tell me what is going on. But he doesn't.

Instead he gets up out of bed and goes to the window to smoke a cigarette. He comes back. Her eyes are still open. He lies down near her again. And waits. Still she does not move. This is enough, he thinks. An hour, two hours, who knows how long, but it is long enough. The complete absence of explanations has left him without resources. He feels as if he is traveling through pure space, in which time has ceased to have any meaning.

He counts: sheep, sable brushes, villages where he has painted, and stops counting. Finally he says, "Lola, are you okay?"

"Yes, I'm fine," she says. Her voice is very calm. He expected it to be strained. He knows even less now than he knew before.

There is nothing at all to mark the night, except its absence of event, its chilling distance: the waiting for he doesn't know what. For some calamity? Some act of violence? Repeatedly he is frightened. He begins to doze off and wakes up terrified, certain that in his sleep he will touch her and trigger some torrent of fury and fear. His eyes are burning. There is a cramp in his right leg. The bed is too narrow for both of them not to touch. He gets up and walks around the room.

Her eyes are closed when he looks at her again. "Lola?" he whispers. She does not answer. He feels betrayed. There is no reward for his having proven he could do it: no gratitude, no reassurance, no final capitulation. Nothing. How could she fall asleep? How could she?

He gets into bed again, smokes a cigarette in bed, feeling a great fury at her. And something about sitting out on the steps of his house all night while his mother screamed inside, and no explanations for it ever, nothing but a silence afterward, and not knowing what was going on.

There is the sound of a rooster down in the town, echoed back in the hills.

He gets up for the last time and puts on his clothes.

Lola does not move. She does not say anything. He walks home in silence.

• • •

On the second night she asks him to come back again and falls asleep again and he goes home at dawn again. On the third night it is the same. He does not understand why she asks him to stay, nor why he agrees: all he understands is that some hidden and imperative process is taking place which she refuses to explain, some healing or repairing with which he is being asked to cooperate, with which he is cooperating, perhaps out of nothing more than a strange intrigue. The difficulty is that he is not sure whether or not Lola is to be trusted. He does not know whether, in the long run, she will turn gentle or cruel.

On the fourth night, after an hour has passed (on the second night he brings his watch to protect himself against that escalation of anticipation and fear that could transform a thought into a nightmare within an instant of unclocked time), she turns over very slowly until she is lying on her stomach with her head on his chest. The bed is so narrow that a single half-turn leaves her stretched full length against him.

"I can hear your heartbeat," she whispers and kisses his breastbone. This time he is the one who does not move. He is not sure how much or how little she wants, though he knows that in her own mind there is some very precise mechanism that controls the movement of events. She lies there quietly for a full minute and then spreads her arms around him so that her hands slip under his back meeting at his spine.

"Stefan," she says.

"Yes, Lola."

"Would you mind if we made love?" Her voice is barely audible, almost childish, and trembling.

"No, I wouldn't mind," he says, feeling that if he holds his breath any longer he will suffocate. He puts his arms around her and begins to rub her back. He has never seen a woman tremble so much, each muscle stiffening and relaxing as it is touched. When he moves to kiss her mouth, her teeth are chattering, and he tastes salt in the hollows of her eyes. He lifts the sheet and tries to cover her with it, but she pulls it away and turns over on her back, separate from him again. Then she begins to cry in earnest.

"I can't stand it," she sobs. "I just can't stand it anymore."

He is not sure what it is that she can't stand. "Do you want me to stop?" he says.

"No," she says. "For God's sake, don't stop. Please don't stop."

He has never experienced anything this slow, this painful. It is like making love with a virgin who at any moment might bolt with fear. At first, she seems to be simply allowing herself to be touched. She initiates nothing; it is almost as if being touched is more than she can endure.

Then gradually she begins to move. She does not move with just her arms or her legs or her mouth; somehow her entire body shades off into the curve of an embrace which even at its most assertive seems shy, hesitant, fragile.

Her toes trace his, moving from arch to heel to ankle bone to calf, to the inner edges of his thigh. Her elbow slides against his belly, her mouth against his collarbone, all the while trembling. Then suddenly, as he is kissing her breasts, she stiffens, her breath catches and she freezes. He enters her, but it is too late. She has lost and regained herself already. She is a spectator now, a quiet spectator.

He had not expected that. It takes him utterly by surprise. He would have thought that she would be slower, that he would have to wait for her to catch up. He slips the pillow out from under her head and moves to slide it under her pelvis, but she shakes her head in refusal. With his hands under her, he feels her body lift and shift, as if his weight on top of her is nothing at all. She is being helpful, cooperative, but not passionate. For a moment he ceases to care. He moves quickly, deeply—and explodes.

In the darkness he lies on top of her, breathing long and slow.

"Was it good for you?" he asks.

"I was too fast," she says. "But yes it was fine." There is a trace of disappointment in her voice.

"You should have told me," he says.

"I don't like to talk when I'm making love."

He remembers suddenly the way she said "everyone" that first night. Again he is confused: the woman of experience and the virgin contradict each other.

"Do you want for me to stay here?" he asks, feeling that nothing is to be taken for granted.

"I'm not sure," she says. "I'm not sure if I can take so much at once."

"Shall I leave now?"

"No. Stay for a while at least. Can I have a cigarette?"

He has never seen her smoke before. He gets up to look for the cigarettes. She watches him walk from one end of the room to the other. "I like your body," she says. "It's beautiful."

He does not answer. He comes back and lights her cigarette. Her face is illuminated by the flare. He is surprised by it: her voice sounds calmer, happier than her face, which is still drawn and tense. Her eyes are bare, rinsed; she turns her head away and refuses to look at him.

He climbs in beside her and puts one arm around her. In the darkness and silence they smoke together. Her body again seems stiff.

Suddenly she says, "Stefan."

"Yes," he says.

"You won't mind if I ask for you to leave, will you?"

"No" he says, though it isn't true.

"I'm sorry. I can't . . ."

She does not finish the sentence. He gets out of bed again, dresses, pulls the sheet over her. She kisses him lightly, innocently, like a child kissing a parent good night.

He closes the door and leaves her lying there alone.

They have known each other for three weeks.

THE DAYS SPREAD OUT like a Japanese fan on which have been drawn the familiar patterns of the ordinary . . . opening and broadening when she joins him for dinner at Chrysula's, a swim on the far side of the island, an evening in the cafe with the Americans of whom she is no longer contemptuous, narrowing into solitude while he paints and she reads (rereads, she says) Dostoevsky's *The Gambler, Tender Is the Night, Under the Volcano* and *The Stranger*, all at the same time, with apparent disregard for the clash of psychic imagery which must result in her mind from the collision of so many and such intense visions of the world. She has even begun Engels' *The Origin of the Family*, though this she seems to pursue more out of conscience than instinct. When she is not reading, she sits alone in the cafe watching people or sketching them with a meticulous attention to detail.

The world subtly begins recoloring itself in her eyes, and whereas before she often remained aloof and skeptical, she now rushes with a quickening enthusiasm into conversation after conversation, tilting forward into that semimystical universe of political transfiguration which the Americans refer to as "the necessity for social change."

Still she will not allow him to stay through the night and evades him when he asks why, but there is no cruelty in her face now, just an odd-angled slant of bewilderment. He accepts the rules of her privacy, of whatever the war is with herself, thinking that in time . . .

One morning she takes a bus with the Americans over to a small village in the hills. He stays behind to paint, but the work has a stiffness and lethargy to it which he cannot seem to surmount. He thinks of Franz's letter . . . "In technique, yes your work has become more subtle, yet there has been no real growth, no reaching beyond the surface you mastered years ago. I say this as your friend . . ."

It is true, he thinks. The day is hot, the air shimmering already in the anticipation of summer. He strips off his shirt, forces himself to concentrate, but cannot. He is plagued by a sense of disharmony. The canvas is developed in its parts, yet the parts seem separate, distracted. He cannot find the core of what he wishes to express. It is as if the center of gravity of the painting is missing, and he has no feeling for what ought to be there. Just something that is missing. There is no way of camouflaging that in a painting: what is absent reveals itself as acutely as what is present. The analyst in Zurich who commented on the "paths leading into the canvas, ending in blind alleys, paths inward . . ." Well, there was never any way of knowing where things might lead.

In the village up in the hills Lola is probably having Greek coffee and yoghurt with honey . . . and the Americans are being pompous . . . though maybe not . . . She has begun to insist now that he is wrong about that, that they are not pompous at all, as if her national pride has somehow been aroused by his comments, and she feels obliged to defend what otherwise she herself would find indefensible.

He calculates. It would not take him so long to walk to the village. Two hours perhaps, and then they could walk back together. Maybe they are already on the road. They had planned to walk back, and even if they don't, there is only a single road, and the bus will have to pass him. He folds the easel, straps the canvas to it and attaches the whole of it to his back like a knapsack complete with belt.

In his room he rereads the letter from Marianna and the one from Franz, Franz's first, with its observations about his work and its disconcerting paragraph at the end, in which the tone abruptly changes. "Of course I am your friend, you know that, don't you? I am saying these things because, well, because I think that you should be aware of them. And of course it *is* true that you take Marianna for granted, and that she is not to be taken for granted. The whole business with *la jeune fille* was damaging to her. She is not the way she was. We can talk about that when you come home. You are not, though, I hope, planning to see any more of *la jeune fille*. It would be best, I think, for both of you. Anyway, I hear she is planning to be married. I repeat, of course, again as your friend, that I do believe this would be best . . . and in the interests of all concerned. Well, of course, Stefan, you know how I feel. You do know. In all friendship, I feel obliged to tell you what I think. I will spend the evening with Marianna tonight and will try, though I cannot promise anything, to smooth things over. We shall see. In time perhaps the entire affair will be forgotten. Franz."

And alongside of that, the letter from Marianna, scattered throughout with the edges of her fears, snatched back before they tumble fully into articulation. "It has been so long since we spent any time together; sometimes I feel as if we are not married at all, as if we have remained the friends we were six years ago in Switzerland, each of us coming and going, pretending to a casualness that doesn't exist. Perhaps this trip will be a help. We need to talk. You know as well as I that we do." And then, the very last sentence, an indulgence for which she probably, even now, is unable to forgive herself, "Do you love me, Stefan, tell me, do you love me?"

He lies on the bed for half an hour thinking about *la jeune fille*, who only a month ago had been planning to meet him here. There was nothing to be done about it, he thinks, nothing at all. It happened because it had to happen and because the work was going downhill, his life going downhill, his marriage, though when had it ever really been uphill? A friendship, all along, for five years, it had been a friendship, with assumed loyalty as its cornerstone. Though now even that is gone. And at any rate, it is useless to pretend . . .

He takes a shower, empties a package of Maggi mushroom soup powder into a pot, mixes it with water, heats it up and eats it for lunch with a slice of *mavro* from the bakery.

Then he walks across the island to meet Lola.

•

They have not started back yet. He finds them sitting in the cafe, which is all, besides the church, that the town consists of. He hears their voices before he can see them, the air so clear that sound travels through it completely unsaturated.

One voice rises emphatically above the others, but he does not know to whom it belongs. "Well, but the Palestinian Arabs *do* have a right to their land, as I see it, and the Israeli government, you must admit, has become part of the entire capitalist-imperialist world. If one cares to look at the problem historically . . ."

Then he hears a voice he does recognize, clipped, impatient. "I lived there," Lola says. "And things are not so simple as that. How can you judge as imperialist a country that is barely managing to survive, and which, in terms of socialism, anyway, is far more advanced than . . ."

By this time he has reached them. Lola's back is to him. She is sitting at a table with Marty, Peter, Mim and the voice he just heard, which belongs to Michel.

"Well, if it isn't our artist in residence," Marty says.

Lola turns in her chair. Her face wavers between pleasure and an unwillingness to seem affected. "Sit down," she says. "We were just discussing the Arab-Israeli question."

"And the Vietnam question, and the Algerian question, and the Negro question, and the question of the Indians in England, the Italians in Switzerland, the Indonesians in The Netherlands, the Americans in Latin America, on ad infinitum," Marty says. "What we were discussing was the downfall of the human race."

"Well, not quite," says Mim. "There are, after all, solutions."

"She calls starting a commune in Wisconsin a solution."

"You have to start somewhere," Mim insists.

"Yes, yes, we all know," Marty says irritably. "We indeed must start somewhere. The question though is where."

"The conversation always winds up in the same place," Lola says. "With no one knowing what to do and everyone getting upset and feeling helpless. If we cared as much as we claim to we wouldn't be sitting here. We'd be doing something. But instead, we just talk and drink retsina. Sometimes I wish it were the Spanish Civil War or World War II when at least you could tell who was good and who was evil."

She glances sideways at Stefan as she says this.

"It's always harder to know than one thinks," he says and gets up to ask for a limonada. It occurs to him that this obsession with "getting to the bottom of things" is a purely American phenomenon, as if they believed, with a kind of innocence that Europeans can no longer feel, that there must always *be* a bottom to things.

Spiro, the owner of the cafe, who knows America from when he was in the navy, comes out to urge them to stay for some ouzo. "I tell you good story," he says. " 'Bout the Brooklyn Navy Yard. You know where is Brooklyn?"

"Sure," Marty says. "Do you know where Flatbush is?"

"Flatbush? What is this a Flatbush?"

"It's where I'm from."

"Oh oh. Is a good place, America. Is good people, Americans."

"Terrific," Marty says. "The best."

"I have brother, he live in Astoria. You know Astoria?"

"In Queens, you mean?" Lola says.

"Astoria. Astoria. Yeah. Is someplace a New York. You know Forty-Second Street? I know Forty-Second Street good."

"Sure I know Forty-Second Street," Marty says. "You know that dirty book store on the right side of the street at Times Square, the one with the peephole next to the Apollo movie?"

"Oh for God's sake," Peter says. "He's starting again."

"Starting what?" Marty says, assuming an air of innocence.

"If you don't know by now, I can't tell you."

"You sure you no want ouzo?" Spiro says.

Everyone refuses. When Stefan comes back out, they pay the bill, which comes to fifteen drachmas, and leave half a drachma on the table.

Only Marty stays to take the bus back. He orders an ouzo and waves to them as they go. "Adieu, adieu," he says. "And off into the capitalist sunset."

•

That evening, when they reach the town, Lola and Stefan walk to the near beach for a swim. "Why did you do that?" Lola asks.

"Why did I do what?"

"Walk all the way to the village?"

"Because I wanted to see you," she says simply.

"You walked nine kilometers just because you wanted to see me?"

"Yes."

"I don't understand. I just don't understand."

For a long time she does not speak. When she does her voice is sad. "I've never been this happy," she says. "And I don't think I ever will be again."

He doesn't know what to answer. Why, if she is so happy, does she manage to sound so sad? And why should she not keep on being happy?

"You will be," he says.

"No," she says, looking at him closely. "No, I don't think so." There are the beginnings of tears in her eyes. "I'll race you to the beach," she says.

She runs off ahead of him, and he races after her with the thought of Marianna's letter flashing for the merest second through his mind.

Lola dives quickly into the sea, lavender now in the late afternoon sun, and swims out in a clear, precise crawl.

He dives in after her.

When they come out, she lies on a towel with her head turned away from him. He sits, watching the islands in the distance.

Suddenly she bolts upright and faces him. The warmth and traces of melancholy that were in her face have vanished altogether.

"If you loved me," she says, "would you get a divorce?"

He is thoroughly taken aback by the question. "A divorce?" he says. "How did you arrive at that?"

"How does one arrive at anything? Just answer the question instead of avoiding it."

"I'm not avoiding it. I'm just shocked that you asked it."

"That's your Aryan constitution . . . always expecting the expected."

"Lola, please," he says.

"Yes, yes, I know, please stop being . . . I know what you're going to say. You didn't like that, did you? Tell me the truth." Her voice is hard. Her eyes focused on some inner calculation, which is incomprehensible to him, as if she has proposed an arithmetic in which everything must add up perfectly or else be denied altogether.

"There is nothing to like or dislike," he says. "But tell me why I would get a divorce."

"I don't know," she says, her voice wavering, her face expressing her confusion.

"All right," he says, feeling suddenly, strangely trapped. "If you want to know, I'll tell you. The answer is no. No I wouldn't get a divorce."

"You don't even care enough to lie," she whispers. And jumps up to run into the water again.

When she comes back, she apologizes. "I don't know what got into me," she says. "I certainly was being silly. Besides, we don't even love each other." She phrases it as if it is a question.

He remembers, with something approaching an instant nostalgia, the moment, which already seems very far away, when she said, "I've never been this happy."

He does not answer her for quite some time. Then he says, "If it's what you want to hear, Lola, I love you."

She looks at him without saying a word, again sadly, though now with a different kind of sadness, something that is a cross between the sadness of memory and the sadness of anticipation.

"Oh," she says finally, very quietly. "Oh." And nothing more.

. . .

"Would you like me to tell you about Marianna?" he says.

"I thought you didn't want to."

"I didn't, but now I do, if you want me to. Things have changed."

She does not answer right away. They are sitting in the kitchen off the courtyard after dinner. She isn't sure if she wants to know now. She is afraid of knowing. She remembers how she felt at that moment demanding of him, "Tell me about your wife." Maybe, if he starts talking about her, the same thing, the same desire to smash everything, to exert some final and binding power over him, will come over her. Or else, if not that, then its opposite, which would be worse: sympathizing with her, understanding her, caring about her, becoming her ally, her defender. Not to have even the safety of hatred; that would be the worst of all. That would be impossible. It would tear everything to shreds. Marianna would begin making appearances in her dreams, sharing their bed, going with them everywhere, judging silently, and from a distance. No, I don't think I want to know, Lola thinks, I don't think I want to know.

"I don't think I would like it," she says. "But go ahead anyway."

"Why should I go ahead if you won't like it?"

"Because facts are facts. You can't pretend them away. She's part of your life, as you said."

"You don't have to be stoic about it," he says. "I'm not going to torture you, you know."

"Oh, of course you will," she says suddenly, angrily. "You will no matter what."

"What do you mean by that?"

"I mean it's built in," she says. "Built in to the situation."

"If it's built in," he says carefully, "then why are you here with me?"

"I don't know," she says, dropping her voice very low and looking away from him. "Would you mind if I have a cigarette?"

He strikes the match for her and cups his hand around it. There is something about the gesture that always tears through her: the way the light glows through his fingertips, that compelling yet contained luminosity. European men light matches differently; the match disappears altogether into the center of their palms, as if the light is coming from beneath the surface of their skins. With American men you are always conscious of something learned, conscious of the match, conscious of the cigarette, conscious of the effort. American awkwardness, she thinks, feeling a protective rush of national affection. European style. Oh well, yes, now what was it we were talking about, what was it before the cigarette? She doesn't want to remember, but can't help remembering. "If I knew," she says, "if I really knew, I probably wouldn't."

"Wouldn't?" he says.

"Wouldn't be here with you."

"You mean it's bad for you to be here with me."

"Stefan," she says, "don't be naive."

"I thought you were so happy," he says stubbornly, insisting on his refusal to understand.

"The one thing has nothing to do with the other," she says. "And you know it. If you want to tell me about her, tell me about her."

He begins to talk. He talks about their having gotten married when Marianna was offered a job in Switzerland and they had to choose between getting married and separating altogether. He talks about their having been friends, about his being a virgin at the age of twenty-six and her being frigid, about his fear of turning into a *bon bourgeois*, of life's becoming completely digestible, about what Franz has said of his painting, about *la jeune fille* and the ways in which he intentionally made things slide out of control, about Marianna's tolerance of everything he needed to do, even that.

He talks for a long time, almost two hours. But when he has finished talking, Lola feels as if she knows nothing more than what she knew before he began. These things cannot be told, she thinks. What is inside of them cannot be told. All that emerges is something that refuses to cohere: of things being fine and then not being fine, of the dissatisfactions that spread until they engulf the satisfactions, of something being missing, he doesn't know what, just something, because of course she is a very fine woman and always has been.

Lola realizes suddenly that the worst thing she had been able to imagine has happened: she has begun to care about Marianna. It is all the same anyway. For every woman somehow it remains the same. Always, in men, that desire for a change, that sudden looking elsewhere. And always, in women, that endurance, despite everything.

She wants to say to him, "But, Stefan, there is always something missing. Don't you *know* that?" but then he says, "Of course, you can't have everything, but this staleness, this feeling of not going anywhere, of being trapped in a life that you were never intended for, that can't be right, can it?"

She remembers his telling her that he wouldn't get a divorce. It was just this afternoon that he said it. And now, she could no longer even ask him to do it without being divided by the real life blood life interception of Marianna's image. "It can't be right, can it?" Well, if it can't be right, then why doesn't he leave of his own accord? Why is that so difficult for a man? They can neither stay with nor leave. That's the problem. One or the other. Do one or the other. Maybe these things are difficult for everyone, though, she thinks. But even if there's no love? Even if there's no love. It's not to be comprehended really . . . none of it . . . the way things become more and more entangled the more you struggle to disentangle them. And things go on until they can't go on. That's the way it is, or the way it seems to be, with almost everyone. Not with me, she thinks, thank God not with me. And wonders whether or not that is the truth.

"Would you like to sleep here tonight?" she asks.

His face is puzzled. "Why tonight?" he says.

"Because if you don't stay with me, she will."

The puzzlement leaves his face, and regret enters it. "I'm sorry," he says. "I shouldn't have told you."

"It doesn't matter," she says, feeling suddenly very tired, as if she has been listening intensely to a tape recording with a long blank in it, waiting for the significant word to emerge, the word that will free her from all doubt, but the word isn't there, and the doubt persists and the tape winds on and on and on with no end in sight, though at any moment, at any moment, the word might, just might . . . and then everything will be fine.

"I'm sleepy," she says.

"Do you want some tea before we go to bed?" he asks.

"No, nothing. There's nothing in the world that I want right now."

"Except?"

"I don't know. If I knew, then . . . well, then things would be different, wouldn't they?"

"I guess so. I don't know."

"Stefan?" she says.

"Yes."

"If you ever stop loving me, will you do me one favor?"

"Why should I stop loving you?"

"It can happen. It can always happen. Just promise."

"This is ridiculous. But yes, Lola, I'll promise."

"Promise you'll tell me. No matter what happens, promise you'll tell me."

He feels drained all at once. Why must everything be a drama? Why must beginnings always be signals launched in the direction of endings? Why can't it be possible to just let things be?

"All right," he says. "If that's what you want, I promise."

"And also, one more thing."

"What?" he says, feeling suddenly, inexplicably irritable.

"If I have any nightmares, wake me up. Promise that too."

"Yes, Lola," he says. "Yes, Lola, I'll wake you up."

• • •

In the morning, when he reaches out for her, she is not there. She is standing naked by the window with her back to him.

"Good morning," he says.

"Good morning," she says, without turning from the window. Her voice is not cheerful at all, but grave. He feels as if he is living in a sea of molasses from which it is impossible to extricate himself. He wanted to make love this morning, almost as a continuation of the dreamlike accidents of entanglement in the middle of the night . . . to make love, eat breakfast and paint. Not to discuss, analyze, explain or understand. Not to think about the crosscurrents in his desires.

The person she becomes in bed is a person she won't allow him to know at any other time. During the day, even when she is happy, it is covert and counterbalanced by a stubborn defensiveness. During the night, the labyrinthine system of checks and balances is abandoned altogether and always there is the sense that she is out on some precipice of herself, exquisite in its pleasures, nightmarish in its prospect of dependency upon pleasure itself.

The early morning light is crowding in upon the edges of her body.

"What's the matter?" he says and instantly regrets it. Now a discussion will be unavoidable. He will not be able to persuade her to abandon the exertions of an overly energized mind and simply come back to bed. He will not be able to paint.

"It's no good," she says. "I've decided to go back to my own island."

"What's no good?" he says. There is no way to turn back.

"Nothing is any good," she says. "You should go to Marianna and I should go to Panaghios. It's that simple. I don't want to make a drama out of it."

118

"Lola, I'm afraid it's too late for that. You already have made a drama out of it."

She turns around and faces him. "I have?" she says. "How?" The earnestness with which she asks the question disarms him. Of course, when she thinks about it, she always knows exactly what she is doing. Except it is impossible to know when she has thought about it. He has grown used to her anger, her stubbornness, even her fear, but not yet to her theatricality, which is at once innocent, vulnerable and calculated. He thinks that he is going to have to be cautious in what he says, that he will not be able to come out with, "Listen, Lola, I really do want to paint this morning."

"Never mind," he says. "It's not important."

"Yes it is. I want to know."

"Your wanting to know makes it even more of a drama."

"I'm sorry," she says, coming to sit beside him on the bed and leaning back so that she is lying across his stomach with her head turned toward him. "It's just that there are too many obstacles," she says. "Real obstacles, not obstacles that I've invented or dramatized. You said yourself that you don't have any intention of changing your relationship with Marianna and that you want to spend a few months with me and a few months alone and a few months in Austria. I don't think I want that kind of parceling out. And I know I don't want to be the instrument of your restored union with Marianna. I don't want to be the one who makes it easier to keep on going with her because I provide a comfortable supplement. Besides, you're going back to Austria. And I'm going back to America. It's as simple as that. I'm not so unsophisticated that I can imagine it to be something extraordinary. And it has a predictable, cliché ending."

"You leave out one thing," he says, thinking that he does not enjoy early morning conversations, but that she seems to have a special facility for leaping into discussions the way she leaps out of bed. By evening, she is quiet, thoughtful, often silent. By evening he is, perhaps, ready to talk. "We're not clichés, we're people," he says. "It doesn't matter how we met. It matters who we are. Situations can be clichés. Real people never, not unless you choose to see them that way. And if you choose to see them that way, choose to see *us* that way, what you're choosing is not to see anything at all."

"All right, Herr Professor," she says and laughs. "You know you do sound that way sometimes, as if you're repeating a lesson plan."

"Maybe so," he says. "But early in the morning is not my moment for philosophical originality."

"That sounds right," she says and runs her finger across his forehead. "But the facts still remain, Stefan." She rubs her forefinger against the space between his eyebrows, though a crease has formed between her own. "The house I had in Panaghios is waiting for me to come back. Houses, unlike people, stay right where they are. And there's nothing to hold me here. I don't want to put you in an impossible position."

Suddenly, he feels as if he is back in Switzerland, as if it is Marianna he is talking with, Marianna saying, "But there's no reason for me to stay here. I have a good job offer in Switzerland," and he saying, "Well, maybe we should get married." Women are always saying that they don't want to put you in a position, and then doing exactly that. He is being drawn into making a choice that he isn't ready to make, doesn't want to make. If he says that she should stay on the island for him, then he will be to blame if it doesn't work out, will have committed himself on a scale that is too literal and precise, that allows no time or space for those inner transformations to take place that would make it natural for him to pass from "I love you" to "I want to be where you are." Women assume that the two belong together, right away. But they don't, not really, at least not so early they don't. Of course, he *does* want to be where she is, but he doesn't like this intentionality, this being forced to take a stand in advance, to deny his own sense of the undercurrents of things and their evolution. Stay or go. Love me or leave me. But in a way she is right. Marianna is coming in a month. Why perpetuate something that will have to be dissolved so soon? Why not let go of it now?

She rolls over against him, from her back to her stomach, lying on his chest now with her face inches from his. The trouble is that he wants her, he wants her right now, and, wanting her, he cannot say to her, "Well, you're right."

"You act as if I'm made of glass," she says. "As if I'm breakable. I'm not that fragile, you know."

She swivels her body around again, so that she is lying flat on top of him, though he is still under the covers. She kisses him. The friction of the sheet between them, the pressure of her body and its elusiveness, even as she moves against him, make him forget altogether about Marianna and Panaghios. She slides upward, moving her body against his mouth until her knees have reached the upper edge of the covers and she is wrapped over and around him. Then she slides downward again, this time under the sheet and against him, never breaking the entirety of contact, the fluidity of motion.

"I'm not so fragile," she whispers again. And stays with him the whole way, not fragile at all and completely fragile, not withheld at all, just riding above him through the Greek morning while white light fills the courtyard, the room, and engulfs the bed, until finally he hears himself say, "I'll come with you," and she says, "Yes."

STEFAN TAKES OUT a hammer and nails and a strip of leather from his knapsack to fix the broken strap of Lola's carryall. He kneels on the deck surrounded by Greek women who are either fighting off seasickness or succumbing to it. The ship mounts the waves like a prize stud. The Aegean hisses through its teeth, froths, turns the whites of its eyes and yields. The Greek women, their bellies in revolt, vomit. When there is nothing left inside of them, they retch and press their white faces encased in black hoods against the warped and grimy deck.

The tears and wailing as the boat pulls out of the harbor, the caïques simultaneously loading and unloading passengers and baskets and wooden crates with rope, while the people going down the ramp push against those coming up the ramp in brief but impassioned skirmishes. Everyone shouting, pushing, directing, the first and second class passengers branching out to the left, the deck passengers being herded below. "No, I sorry sir, this way, this deck reserved second class." Said very firmly and with absolute authority.

Five knapsacks come on board, red and green knapsacks. One with an Australian flag, another with patches from Chamonix and Saint Moritz and Courmayeur and Kitzbühel, two with Peace Corps Ghana marked on them, one with the sleeping bag attached below, another with the sleeping bag attached above.

There is a bottleneck at the doorway to the lower deck. A box of tomatoes vanishes. A baby starts to cry. Piles of blankets are unfolded on the platform that stretches across the center of the hold. Picnics are unwrapped in the middle of the floor. Feta and bread and tomatoes and olives. Olive oil in jugs protected by woven baskets. Retsina. Families congregate on the blankets. Gray braids are untied. Old women in black stockings stretch out on the floor to sleep. Old men sit on the hard, slatted wooden benches along the edges of the hold. The bathroom door is open. The traffic is constant. The smell is pervasive.

Then the waves come. The women pray and vomit. The men finger their crosses. The picnics skid across the floor. The deckhands come in and look scornfully at the vomit, pretending to mop it up but instead spreading a thin coat of slime across the deck. After a while they abandon even that and make violent gestures with their arms at the women who are praying and vomiting. They point at the vomit. The women shake their heads with shame. The deckhands gesture violently again. The women pull out handkerchiefs and try to clean up, but again the retching overtakes them, and the handkerchiefs are quickly lifted from the floor to cover their mouths instead. The deckhands watch them with contempt. Soon the deckhands abandon the hold altogether. There are no windows to open. Salt spray fogs the glass.

Stefan stays in a corner, concentrating on repairing the carryall, trying to trim the edges of the leather properly while the boat heaves. A mother is sitting on the floor close to them. She is struggling with a baby who is screaming and choking on his own vomit. Another small girl is sitting next to her with the corners of her mouth turned down and her eyes welling up with tears, though she does not make a sound. The mother is preoccupied with the baby.

Lola offers to hold the child. The mother shakes her head up and down emphatically, pressing Lola's hand and saying over and over again, "*Kala kiria. Kala kiria. Efcharisto. Efcharisto parapoli.*" The little girl is very light, thin, small-boned. She looks at Lola solemnly, keeping her head back and away, as if to be sure that she can still keep track of where she is being taken and by whom, and whether her mother is still within sight. Her arms hold on tightly. Lola carries the child back to where Stefan is working on the carryall. He looks up. There is an expression on Lola's face that he has never seen before, a relation to the child that is permanent and visceral. It shocks and unnerves him.

The little girl has begun to cry. "Eh, little one," Lola says, rocking her back and forth. "Don't cry." Her hand slowly rubs the child's back. She kisses the edge of her hair where it wings back from her forehead.

"Do you want me to sing you a lullaby?" she says. "The one my mother always sang to me?" The little girl doesn't understand but watches her mouth as if there are giraffes and elephants coming out of it. Lola starts to sing in a very low voice, slightly melancholy, as if she is her own mother and her own child. Stefan is completely distracted and suddenly angry. He does not know why.

He tries again to concentrate on the bag, looking away from Lola, but even when he cannot see her, he hears her voice, singing over and over again the unfamiliar Russian words to the Greek child who is soothed finally and falls asleep.

Lola continues to hold the child in her lap, watching Stefan work on the bag. This is new to her, being taken care of by anyone, or even allowing it to happen. Always she has traveled deck class. Always she has had to pass the men standing in the doorways, pass their eyes. Never has she felt safe. Always she has seen the women watching her and pointing at her skirts saying, "Xeni, Xeni," though smiling broadly when they would notice that she noticed.

It is Stefan who has bought the tickets for this boat. Stefan who helped her pack things in two bags instead of eight, Stefan who got her down to the pier before the last horn sounded. His competence comes as a shock to her, though she has known it was there. She does not like to think about the pleasure of it. That would be to acknowledge that things had not been satisfactory before and that, even though she has always managed, managing was never quite enough. Still, she has been proud of managing. To enjoy letting someone else make the effort is alien to her, bewildering to her sensibilities.

It is true that she has gotten along before not by conquering crises but by pretending that they didn't exist, by arriving with half the luggage she started out with, by losing her passport and taking philosophically a two-week delay, and then, somewhere else, losing it again and waiting again, by not planning ahead simply because she knew she could not be depended upon to stick to her own schedules . . . free because she was constantly being bound by the immediate, spontaneous because her only way of dealing with the inevitable was by surrendering to it and transforming irritation into enthusiasm for the new experiences that resulted from the sudden clogging of her life's machinery. Leaning with the wind in the direction of emotional upheaval.

The zipper on her suitcase has been patched together with safety pins for over a year now.

She keeps thinking about the child in her lap, about the rush of tenderness that always comes over her when a child is involved, thinking that somehow, no matter how free your life becomes, there is something quick and instinctive about protecting a child, something about the fit of its body to yours, its head immediately moving to your breast, its weight in your arms. Something about the ache that comes over you. Something about the longing.

Suddenly she is very tired. There is a headache tunneling its way through her mind. The house in Panaghios with its single iron bed. Hans drinking grappa. The fiery light of the heater on his face. What will the village people think when she does not come back alone? Ioannis, the pope, Michaelis. Marianna only a month away. The days piling up like down, loose and spacious but beginning also to settle. I don't want it to be over, she thinks. I don't want to luxuriate in this and then have to let go. The thought is more painful than she ever expected it to be.

The child shifts in her arms and puts a thumb in its mouth.

"I finished the bag," Stefan says.

"Thank you," she says and feels that she could choke on the words. It is not easy, this pleasure in being helped.

"Do you want to sleep?" he says.

"Yes," she says.

He unrolls a blanket from his pack and lays it out on the floor while she returns the child to its mother. He watches her this time, feeling the same anxious irritation, only now it is worse.

He remembers a recurrent dream he has been having for the last five years. In it he is carrying a child on his back through the mountains. He tries to leave it with a peasant woman, but she refuses to accept it. He goes on, always carrying the child, always looking for a place to leave it, always finding no one who is willing to take it from him. Finally, walking through a desert, he unstraps the child from his back and sets it down on the ground. Then he picks it up again but notices that its skin feels strange. It feels like canvas. He touches its face and oil paint smears across the child's cheeks, blue oil paint. He looks into the child's eyes, and they are a mirror of his own. He straps the child to his back again and walks on. He does not try to leave it with anyone ever again.

He watches the mother smiling and thanking Lola. The two women hug each other. No matter how many times they drink retsina together or dance together, or talk about women together, or even talk about painting and politics together, this bond between Lola and the other woman is something he will never be able to share with another man, nor for that matter with another woman. It is a closed world, this world of women and children. But he does not want children, does not want that world of intimate exchanges. What he wants is something more elusive, or at least, it seems more elusive.

When Lola comes back, he has already unfolded her sleeping bag and is stretched out on the blanket. He covers her with the sleeping bag, kissing her once, but then keeps his head turned away from her, though they hold hands under the covers.

The Greek women continue to wail. The boat pitches forward.

*I*т is dawn when the ship slides into the crescent of water dividing the volcano from the island. In the violet light, the cliffs are vertical gashes, burnt umber, rose, scarlet, black, bronze and vermilion streaks of lava. The air is thin as ether, the sea gentle, milky, turquoise, the narrow passageways of the deck crystalline with salt. There is a white line stretching along the spine of the island, like the skeletal X ray of a prone giant, with clusters of cartilage around the vertebrae. By the time the boat has dropped its anchor, the clusters of cartilage have become villages, the line of white, scattered houses between each ridge. The air thickens with sunlight. There is a white zigzag moving from the water to the top of the cliffs, vanishing into the spreading zinc of the town. Black dots move along the zigzag in a slow, jerky procession. A collection of caïques fans out toward the big boat, their motors rupturing the stillness, which, in the first moments of arrival, had the consistency of embalming fluid. The crowds begin pressing toward the gangplank, obscuring now with their rapid, urgent movements that momentary glimpse into an almost prehistoric ferocity which preceded the arrival of the caïques.

Lola is leaning out over the railing, waving to the men in the small boats. "*Yasu, yasu,*" she shouts. The fishermen smile back vaguely. "There's Ioannis," she says, reaching for Stefan's arm. "And I can see Andreas on the dock."

"Weird-looking place, isn't it?" the Australian with the knapsack says to Stefan. "It reminds me of the opal mines back in Australia. I used to work down there. It was a nightmare." He stares out at the island. "Are you staying at the hotel?"

Stefan is trying to juggle his knapsack, the paintings and the suitcase that Lola abandoned in her rush to the railing. "No," he says. "My friend has a house."

"Her own house? Here?"

"She's taking care of it for someone."

"She's American, eh?"

"Yes."

"You're on vacation together?"

"Not exactly," Stefan says, thinking that there is a peculiar persistency·in the Australian's attempt to strike up a conversation in the middle of a debarkation.

"Well, I am," the Australian says. "Vacationing from the mines. For the rest of my life I hope. I picked the right place, didn't I? It should make me feel right at home. Why don't you tell me where this house is, the place where you'll be staying? Maybe I could drop in later on. For a drink and a chat. Something to pass the time."

"I don't think so," Stefan says and begins moving away. "Not right now."

The Australian watches him. They make a perfect pair. Spoiled American bitch and ramrod German. It really *is* like the mines here, he thinks.

And follows Stefan down the gangway.

•

"Thirty drachmas," Andreas says to the man in the straw hat and Bermuda shorts.

"Don't give it to him, John," his wife whispers. "Remember what they said in the guidebook. Start at half."

"Okay, boy. We'll pay fifteen. How's about that?"

"Thirty drachmas," Andreas says.

"Now, now," says John. "Let's be reasonable about this."

"Thirty drachmas," says Andreas.

Already several of the mules have started up the stairs, lurching awkwardly from side to side. Lola and Stefan are almost halfway up, with the Australian right behind them. Andreas has his eye on the other drivers. If the American takes too long, there won't be time to drive back down for another load. "Thirty drachmas," he repeats.

John too is watching the other mules. This fellow could probably stand here all day arguing over ten drachmas, and by then it will be time to come back to the boat.

"We're not made of money, you know," John says. "Not even Americans are made of money."

"Thirty drachmas," Andreas says, understanding only one word of the sentence.

"Okay," John says. "But understand something. It's not because we're rich. Because we're not rich."

This time Andreas understands nothing.

John is watching his group again. Some of them have already reached the top of the stairs. If he keeps this up, he'll lose more by trying to discuss things than by giving in. They'll never understand anyway. Besides, how often does a man get to take a trip to a place like this, still untouched by civilization? Once in a lifetime, if he's lucky. After thirty years of marriage.

"How about a picture first?" John says, pointing to his camera, and then to Bertie.

Andreas has already started to load the luggage onto one of the mules, tying it with rope to the mule's side. The mule stands dumbly in place, shifting its weight with the weight of the suitcases.

Andreas points to Bertie and then to himself, and makes a lifting motion with his hands toward the mule.

"I think he means the picture is okay," John says. "He'll put you on the mule first, though. Good idea, boy. Good idea."

Andreas lifts Bertie up, her weight heavy in his hands. There are a dozen pictures in his drawer at home of him holding the mule while Bertie or Ingeborg or Danielle sit smiling high above him. There is even one picture of a girl sitting on the mule wearing a bikini. The envelopes all had stamps from foreign countries on them, but he has given most of them away to Christos.

Bertie shifts in the saddle. "It's not very comfortable up here, John," she says.

"Wait a second while I focus," he says. "Pull your skirt down a little."

"I can hardly move around on this creature. John, look at this poor animal."

"I can't right now, Bertie. I'm trying to focus. Smile now. Okay boy, you smile too. That's fine. Get a little closer together. Smile like you're friends."

Andreas doesn't smile. He smooths his mustache and moves closer to the mule's head.

"How about putting your hand on his shoulder Bertie?" John says. "Okay. Here we go. Ready?"

"Ready," Bertie says.

In a flash, it is done.

"*Helas, helas. Delop. Delop,*" Andreas says, prodding the mule in its ribs. Slowly, the mule shifts from one foot to the other and begins staggering up the stairs.

Bertie watches Andreas, trying at the same time to keep her balance. It is awful sitting on these animals. Worse even than being on the boat. You feel like you're going to fall off any second. There are saddle sores on the mule's back. Andreas hits the mule again, this time around the mouth. Bertie notices that the mule's mouth is already torn and bleeding.

"Don't do that," she says to Andreas, reaching out her hand to intercept the stick. "Don't hit him."

Andreas ignores her. Every time it is the same thing. The tourists getting upset about the mule. Well, it's in the nature of mules not to want to move. And the way to make them move is to hit them. He pokes the mule in the ribs.

"Stop it, stop it, stop it. Oh please stop it," Bertie cries. "John, I can't stand it. Make him stop. Look at what this man is doing to the poor mule. I want to get off, John. I swear to you, I want to get off."

"Don't get off, Bertie. There's no other way to get up these stairs. Just close your eyes and hold on. It'll only be a few more minutes. There's nothing we can do about it now. These people aren't civilized. No respect for their animals. Abuse them all the time. Now, Bertie, stop crying. Will you please stop crying?"

At the top of the stairs, Bertie dismounts. There are still tears in her eyes and her face is pale. She avoids looking at Andreas. John gives him a dollar. Every place you go, he thinks, there's always some kind of suffering. "It's all over now," he says to Bertie. "It's all over. Just try to relax. Smile and relax."

Andreas starts down the steps again, hammering at the mule's flanks. Maybe there will be time for another trip after all. Sixty drachmas altogether. And maybe another sixty when the boat leaves this afternoon. And on Thursday the same thing.

"*Helas!*" he shouts. "*Helas!*" And beats the mule over its eyes.

•

"Which way are you going?" the Australian says.

"This way," Lola says, pointing down a narrow alleyway that leads off to the left of the town. "And you're going that way," she says, pointing in the other direction. "To the hotel. It's a terrible hotel, but the only one there is. The owner knows that most people won't come back anyway. Have a good trip," she says, picking up her suitcase.

"Yes, of course," the Australian says. "Of course I will." And stands at the crossroad, watching them go.

•

Hans, it seems, has rented Lola's house. She stands on the road arguing with him about it. He says that he is very sorry, but she did leave after all, and he wasn't sure when she would come back and . . .

"But I *said* I was just leaving for six weeks," Lola says.

"People always say things," Hans says. "I've learned not to believe what I hear."

"People may say things, but I don't happen to be one of them," Lola says. "I keep my word."

"How was I supposed to know that?" Hans says. "For all I know, you could have disappeared off the face of the earth with your foreign friend here. If you recall, by the way, you were simply using the house and not renting it. There was no agreement about making it a temporary way station for whoever might join you en route. Besides, this couple came while you were gone. They were on their honeymoon, and they needed a place to rent. Was I supposed to save the house for you based on an uncertainty?"

"What uncertainty?"

"I told you already. The uncertainty about when you were coming back."

"There was no uncertainty."

"To me there was."

"Lola," Stefan says. "There's no point in discussing it. If he's rented the house, he's rented the house. He's not going to tell them to move out just because we've arrived."

"There you are," Hans says. "Your eminently sensible friend agrees with me."

"I don't care if he agrees," Lola explodes. "It's still not fair."

"Fair, shmair. What's fair in life? Is it fair that Ioannis takes

133

a salary from me and then doesn't come to work? Is it fair that I had to stop playing the piano in order to support a family? Is it fair that I spend my time trying to reconstruct a house and then have to contend with a bunch of beatniks who want to come and go exactly as they please without any responsibilities whatsoever, because responsibilities are 'bourgeois'?"

"Since when did I say that I thought responsibilities were bourgeois?"

"Did I say you said it?"

"Well, that's what you're implying, Hans, for God's sake."

Hans pushes his blue cap back on his head and hitches his thumbs through the loops of his corduroys. He looks for a moment like an aging version of Hans Brinker with his silver skates. Except the skates have been replaced by a hemp bag for carrying groceries. "Look, Lola," he says. "Kids like you are a dime a dozen. Your parents put you through school, your parents give you an allowance, your parents finance your grand tour through Europe, your parents cover you for every mistake you make. You're free as the wind, at their expense. You don't know a damn thing about life, except what you think people ought to do for you."

"And where did you get *that* idea?" Lola says. "Because I'm living in Europe by myself? For your information, I was not born into money, and I am not rich, and my parents do not support me. I may look rich and act rich and sound rich, but I happen to come from a family that cultivated the fine art of appearances, no matter how bad things were. Complaints were considered bad form. It was called pride. Have you heard of it? I've worked at some very boring office jobs and carried some rather heavy trays. Which does not by any means constitute poverty. But I have been supporting myself since I was seventeen. And like most people in this world, I've worked for what I have. If *you* recall, the only reason I was able to afford your house in the first place was because I worked for you in exchange for the rent. You are not the only hard luck case in the world, you know . . . even though you may think it."

"Stop it, Lola," Stefan says. "Would you please stop it? None of this is necessary."

"Why should I stop it? He's so immersed in feeling sorry for himself that all he can think of is how easy other people have it. Well . . ."

"All right," Hans says. "All right already. Call off the American matriarch. No matter what you have to say, the house is occupied. You can take your things out of it whenever you please. I put them in the closet in the back. I'm sure the honeymooners will welcome you with open arms. Unlike myself, of course . . ."

"The hell with you," Lola says.

"I'm sure the feeling is mutual," Hans says. And tips his hat. And walks off.

•

It is Ioannis who finally finds them a house in the next village up from the town, near the cafe and just below the stone wall that divides the donkey path from the fragile shells and semi-shells of houses wavering on the edge of the cliff. The inside of the house is damp, like a cave, the newly plastered wall already sweating, bleeding through the whitewash like frescos fading faster than the artist can complete them. A whitewashed terrace leans out over the bay on one side and curves around to face the church at the crest of the hill on the other. It is impossible to see over the island's ridge to the other side, with its milder slope, its carefully terraced vineyard moving like waves, halted, each at its crest, en route to the sea. The houses are all built on the side of the cliffs that faces the volcano, as if the island people preferred to look out on what menaced them rather than see the fields they had plowed in defiance of the lava. The church is the dividing line, a white tower surveying the sharp and sudden drops of the

135

cliff's edge on one side, the sharply enclosed, hard-won fertility of the fields on the other. The house rests uneasily balanced between the island's two halves.

Thalassa comes to the house with sheets in one hand, her son Christos holding on to the other. There is nothing inside the house except two bare cots pushed up against the walls, a sink with cold running water, a hotplate, and a small metal table with one chair. Everyone from the village has gathered in a cluster on the road above the house to watch the foreigners move in.

"Padrimeni?" Thalassa asks, staring first at them and then at the cots. Lola hesitates. Ioannis, standing behind Thalassa, taps his finger wildly to his lips and rolls his eyes.

"Fiancata," Lola says finally. "Engaged." She begins to point to her ring finger but then remembers that, of course, she doesn't have a ring.

"Ah . . . fiancata . . . ne . . . fiancata," Thalassa says. But her voice halts over the unfamiliar word, and she hits her son on the head and orders him to leave. She shifts the sheets from one arm to the other but does not move to make the beds. Living together is supposed to be for people who are married. But lately, there have been Swedish girls and German girls . . . It is her husband's fault. He says just rent to the strangers and don't ask questions. But she is the one who will have to make the beds. She is the one who will have to confess in church this afternoon that she rents a house and makes the beds of foreigners living in sin.

She stands on the inner edge of the doorway, tugging at the back of her skirt as if her own hand were the hand of a small child drawing her back out of the room. Lola moves toward her. "I'll take the sheets," she says. "I don't mind."

Thalassa averts her eyes and gives Lola the sheets. *"Kali sperasas,"* she says, nodding her head, and flees out the door.

There is no closet, not even a shelf or a drawer. Stefan piles his painting supplies in one corner, and unpacks the well-worn but meticulously cared for pot, pan, plate and silverware which

136

he has been bringing with him on every expedition he has made over the last ten years. His belongings carry with them the aura of a near-to-absolute self-sufficiency, something so fine-webbed in its accumulation of detail that it seems, at times, to be constructed of groupings of objects arranged in a still life that Morandi might have painted: quiet, precisely shaded, unassertive, yet clear in its every relation of the part to the whole. He puts his toothbrush, soap, razor and shaving brush on the edge of the sink, creating a half-conscious grouping even in their arrangement. Lola looks at the sink for a long time, at the shaving brush and razor in particular. It is the old-fashioned kind of brush, like the one her father used to use, with a solid bone handle.

"Why aren't you unpacking?" Stefan says.

"I don't know. I think I just want to sit here for a while and watch you. I want to get used to the room."

"There isn't very much to get used to," he says.

"Oh yes," she says. She lies back on the unmade bed. The springs creak. She does not move. Her hands are folded behind her head, her elbows extending like wings growing out from her shoulders. Stefan takes out his two pairs of pants, his underwear, his two shirts, bathing suit and sweater and puts them in another small neat pile on the floor.

"Stefan," she says. "Will you come here for a minute?"

He walks over to the bed and sits down next to her. She reaches up and traces a line with her finger from his collarbone around the inside edge of the V of his shirt. "I'll try not to be so difficult anymore," she says. "I promise I'll try."

"I expect that you'll continue to be difficult, no matter what you try," he says, kissing the pale skin of her inner arm halfway between elbow and armpit. "All in all, though, so far I think it's been worth it."

"That's what I don't understand," she says. "Why it's been worth it for you. Or even why you decided to come here with me."

"Because I'm in love with you," he says.

"I know. That's what I don't understand."

"I don't either. All I know is that love changes people's lives. Including mine."

She flinches and closes her eyes. "But I don't love you," she says very softly. "I wish I did, but I don't."

"You wanted to come here with me, though," he says.

"I know. I don't understand that either."

"Don't worry about it."

"I do," she says and thinks that it is strange for him to be reassuring her now, when she should be the one to do the reassuring.

"Well," he says. "Then don't worry for the time being."

"All right," she says. The dividing line between loving and not loving is so thin anyway, like the thread of a spider web, visible only when the light and the dew combine to illuminate it. Touch it and it breaks, she thinks, and says, "I'll unpack the bedspread now."

"And the rest of your things?"

"Not right now. Maybe tomorrow."

"Because it still feels temporary?"

"Because it doesn't."

She pulls the maroon-and-orange spread out of her suitcase. Then she comes to stand in the middle of the room. "Come here again," she says. He comes. They stand facing each other, not touching. Then she puts her arms around him.

"Your eyes are so innocent," she says. "As if nothing had ever happened to you. Things will be all right, Stefan. Won't they?"

"I hope so," he says. And holds her until her breathing becomes even again.

•

They eat breakfast out on the terrace, Greek Nescafe with evaporated milk, fresh bread and butter and honey. Stefan wants to walk up to the church after breakfast, to look for motifs to paint. "What do you want to do?" he says.

"I wanted to show you the village at the tip of the island. It's very beautiful. Completely different from this one. I thought we could walk there."

"I don't want to lose another day of work," he says.

"Then maybe I'll walk up to the church with you."

"I have to go by myself. Otherwise it will be too hard for me to concentrate. Why don't you walk to the village yourself? Or go over to Hans' for your things? Or just explore."

"Yes," she says, avoiding his eyes. "Maybe I'll read. Or write some letters. There are some letters I really should write. Yes, that's what I'll do. I'll write some letters."

They go back into the house. The beds are no longer on opposite sides of the room. They have been pushed close together. Lola begins to cover them with the maroon-and-orange spread.

"Let's move them first," Stefan says.

"Move them?"

"Yes. To where they were."

"Why should we move them to where they were?"

"Because of Thalassa. You saw her expression yesterday when you said we were engaged and not married."

"You mean you want to move the beds apart every morning for Thalassa's sake?"

"Why not? She has to come in here every day to clean. Why force her to face the fact that we sleep together?"

"There's nothing wrong with it," Lola says. "I don't care if she knows. And besides, our bedspread fits over both beds."

"I know you don't care if she knows," Stefan says. "But she cares if she knows."

Lola sits down on the bed. A look of strain is sharpening

around her eyes, moving in long ripples upward from her chin to her eyes to her forehead. She is holding the bedspread in her arms the way children hold teddy bears and security blankets. "If we pretend," she says, looking at him with a strangely wounded expression, "it's as if we're agreeing that it's wrong."

He is suddenly uncomfortable, as if, while making a simple practical statement about staying out of lions' dens, he has been tossed into one. "Everything doesn't have to be a crusade," he says, trying to avoid the precariousness of what he feels underneath the conversation. "You're not going to change her mind, and she's not going to change yours."

"That's not the point," she says. "I just don't need to be reminded every morning of the need to accommodate her perceptions. I don't want to feel cheap."

"Who is she to you, though?" he insists, still trying to stay away from what is happening. "Why should her opinion matter so much that you need her approval?"

"Why should you be afraid of her disapproval?"

"I'm not afraid," he says, sitting down next to her and lighting a cigarette. "It's a question of consideration. We're not adolescents who have to prove our defiance. We could make love in the middle of the road, too . . ."

She stands up. Her eyes have become large and fierce. "Stefan," she says. "Stop that. You know the one thing has nothing to do with the other. This is a matter of principle."

"As I recall, Lola," he says, looking for an ashtray and not finding one. "You said yesterday that you were going to try not to be difficult . . ."

"That's not it," she says, her expression beginning to waver.

"What is it then?" he says, reduced finally to flicking the ashes into the sink. "First you get so upset, because Hans thinks you're rich, that you have to tell him half your life's history in order to defend yourself. Then you get upset because a woman you don't even know who comes from a culture completely different from your own doesn't believe that unmarried people should live together."

"It's not a culture completely different from my own," she says, walking up and down now in front of the door, reaching out her hand to touch the handle each time she passes it.

"Lola, don't be silly," he says.

"I'm not being silly. And besides, not only are we not married, but you're married to someone else. Imagine what Thalassa would think if she knew about that?"

"Again?" he says. "Is that it?"

"No, that's not it," she says, turning the door handle back and forth. She cannot seem to continue.

"What?"

"Nothing. Forget it."

"How can I forget it when you dangle half a sentence in front of me and stand there looking stricken?"

"All right," she says, abandoning the door handle and coming back to sit next to him on the bed. "There was a letter from my mother the day we left. It was filled with questions about you. All I had written was that I had met a painter I enjoyed talking with. But she knows me. She knows that I never just 'mention' anyone. Who were you? she wanted to know. What were you doing here? What kind of relationship do we have? Now I have to answer that letter. It may be true that Thalassa and I come from completely different cultures, but my mother would have exactly the same reaction to the idea of our living together as Thalassa has. Except my mother doesn't go to confession. So I have a choice between lying to my mother, and not, as you say, 'forcing things on her,' or telling her the truth and making her miserable. There is no way that she is going to believe the truth anyway. And besides, at this point I don't even know what the truth is. The truth that will matter to her, though, is that you're Austrian and married. A married man is a married man. A German is a German. That's not the same truth that matters to me, but . . ."

"I'm not so sure of that," Stefan says, lighting another cigarette.

"It's different, Stefan," she says. "I'm living this day by day. She'll have to live it in one chunk, through one letter. And what about my father? It will upset him even more. Or maybe she won't tell him because she wants to save *him* from knowing what he doesn't want to know. Well, everyone wants not to know *something*. So where do you draw the line?"

This time it is Stefan who moves toward the door. He had not expected that things would become so complicated, so difficult. And yet, how could he have thought that? He goes back to the sink, turns on the water and lets the cigarette sputter out. Then he tosses the butt out the door.

"It isn't the first time, though," he says, deliberately ignoring what she has said about his being Austrian and married. "I mean it's not as if you're a virgin."

Lola hesitates for a long time and looks away from him again. "But it is the first time I've lived with someone," she says very quietly.

"Oh," he says. And does not know what else to say. He would like to go over to her and say that everything will be fine, except he's not sure that would be true, and besides, something stalls in him, something . . . "I didn't realize," he says. "You never told me. And I assumed . . ."

"I know you assumed," she says. "And I let you assume. Because I thought the truth would make you uncomfortable."

"Is that why you were so strange in the beginning?"

"No," she says. "That's not why. And anyway, there are different problems now."

"The problem is," he says, "that there are always problems."

"Well, I didn't make them up."

"I know you didn't. Let's forget it."

"I can't forget it. I still have to write to my mother."

"I know. So what do you want to say?"

142

"I guess I'll tell her. I might as well face the music."

He thinks of the letter he mailed last week to Franz, telling him that he was in love with Lola. "Please don't tell Marianna," he had written. "But I must talk about it with someone. And you . . ."

"But you said that you don't love me," he says.

"I know," she says, her face flushing.

"Then why write to your mother about us?"

"Because . . ." She sits down on the floor with her back to the door and lowers her head to her knees. Her shoulders are trembling. Her voice is muffled. "I don't know why," she says. "I don't know, I don't know, I don't know."

He stoops down next to her, stroking the back of her neck. "I think we should go for a walk," he says. "Come on, let's go for a walk."

The next morning, when Thalassa comes to clean the room, she finds a maroon-and-orange bedspread covering the two beds, pushed together so you can hardly tell them apart.

*T*HERE ARE things I can do, she thinks. There were always things to do. So why is it that now, suddenly, there is nothing I want to do except walk up to the church with him, have a picnic with him, drink retsina with him and make love with him? The cafe was always fine. Going to buy tomatoes was fine. Reading a book and writing a letter, that was fine too. Why should it be lopsided now, nothing fine in itself anymore? Everything is scrambled again, she thinks. Just when it seemed to be unscrambled. The days for a while had stopped lurching and stalling. Every little thing counted. Vasilios stroking his mustache counted, and Christos with his stamps counted. But now she walks into the cafe and hardly even *sees* Christos or Vasilios. All she can think is that Stefan will be back in an hour or two hours or three. The light is all focused on him: brilliant in one spot, completely dim in the others. "But I don't love him," she thinks. "That's the problem. I don't even love him." She is startled at the vehemence with which she says that to herself.

What she wants to write is so simple, so painfully simple that she can hardly say it out loud to herself, let alone make that great leap into the unstable world of her mother's confidence. Dear Mother, . . . I have stopped having nightmares every night. I have fewer headaches. I am living with Stefan. He is a painter. He is married. I don't love him, yet. Maybe I will. I am scared sometimes, and less scared other times. Do you remember when you used to sing me that Russian lullaby? For a few minutes the

144

world seemed safe. But it's not. And I have to learn to live with that. Stefan is very patient with me. He loves me. I am difficult and regret it. I watch myself and say "stop," but often I can't. He tolerates far more than he should. I have no idea what will happen with his marriage.

She stops composing the letter in her mind. There is no point in writing it. After all, she never mentioned having nightmares or headaches, never mentioned being afraid. I can't live my life based on your fears, Mother, she thinks. There has to be a way to survive without feeling perpetually doomed to disaster. There has to be some joy in life, even if you have to risk everything to find it. We haven't had much joy yet, she thinks. I haven't let go yet. It's all been jumping over hurdles. I want to let go, Mother. I want to be able to shout my head off and make love all afternoon without this fear, this certainty that nothing will ever work out and I will be abandoned.

She realizes that she is talking out loud to herself. She has not written a word, but she feels like crying for all the wasted energy that goes into being afraid, never believing in herself, never believing that she is safe enough to drop the armor that clanks in her ears, thinking always, the bad old past will poison the future.

Whatever it is, she thinks, it's not a tragedy. Mother, listen to me. It is not a tragedy.

After all, she thinks, it is not as if we see each other from time to time when it's convenient. We're living together. It's not as if I can't reach him when I need him. All I have to do is walk up to the church. It's not as if this is wartime, and he's a Nazi and I'm a Jew. I was a baby during the war; he was a child. This is so much better than anything ever before, Mother. Character, Mother. That's what really matters. Character and the ability to . . . Well, what will that accomplish? Character isn't a "fact." Marianna will be here in a month . . . no . . . less than that. Lola's boat leaves for America in six. Those are facts. And then it will end. Except that is not a fact. That won't be it. All of a sudden, she knows that won't be it at all. Who are you fooling? she thinks. When has that ever been it? When have you ever jumped in and jumped out?

It's a lie about the headaches being better. She has one now. She sits out on the terrace with her head in her hands. "Dear Mother," she writes. "In answer to your last . . ."

No. That's not the way to begin. "Dear Mom and Dad." No. Not that either. It's better to leave him out of things for the time being. "Dear Mom. You asked me about my friend, and I've decided to tell you . . ."

She stops, feeling exhausted, as if the transfer of emotion from a hidden inner boiler, up to the page where the letters burn holes in her imagination, is an effort requiring the endurance of a professional firefighter. She goes into the house and lies down on the maroon-and-orange spread.

"Dear Mother. Dear Mother. Dear Mother."

• • •

She still has not written the letter. Shopping in the village for the shriveled vegetables that arrive twice a week from the mainland, she runs into the Australian who says to her, "Do you know when the last earthquake was?"

"Ten years ago," she says.

"And the next one?" he says. "Is there a pattern? Do you have any ideas about the next one?"

"We're about due," she says.

"Oh," he says. "I've been having dreams about it. Also about volcanos going off. And crippled children. Have you noticed that there are an unusual number of crippled children here?"

"Yes," she says. "Deformities are common on islands. Because of so much incest. But why think about it? Why be morbid?"

"Would you like to walk with me for a while?" he says. "I'm going to the other end of the island. Have you been there?"

"Yes, I've been there," she says. "But I'm busy now." She thinks of Stefan wandering up near the church, searching for motifs. There is really no reason not to go for a walk with the Australian. I have to do things on my own, she thinks. Without Stefan. Already it has begun, this desire to be with him all of the time, this sense of being severed from herself as well as from him when he goes off to work. I have to . . . She thinks suddenly of Marty, of the day on the beach. It seems so long ago, in another era, when her feelings for Stefan were composed of almost pure fear. The fear is still there, but now . . . there is a voice inside of her which keeps trying to speak, to say things like "I love you," but then she feels violent again, kicks at it until it rolls over, plays dead and is silent. But it isn't dead. It isn't. No matter how many times she kicks it, it refuses to die. And the words keep forming in her mouth, keep . . .

"I have a lot to do today," she says to the Australian.

"Perhaps tomorrow," he says.

"No," she says. "I really do have to go now."

She walks down the narrow path that leads out from the town, thinking that maybe what she will do is visit the two women anthropologists, maybe . . . anything to stop thinking about Stefan and the force, like a force of gravity, drawing her back toward where he is, even if only to watch him work . . . the force . . . her mother . . . the letter.

• • •

Lola walks along the spine of the island. Small orange flares of cactus blossoms pattern the horizon. The sunline shifts over ridges and terraces, picking out the curve of a monastery, the shadow of an earth-packed wall. A row of eucalyptus edges the sea. The fine edges of froth burst against the pebbles of black sand, spitting them back and swallowing them again while the sand flies hop in frenzy.

In a square on the periphery of town, the mules are unloading wooden crates filled with sucked orange peels, fish bones and refuse onto the great mound of debris that is the town dump. The long cry of the mule drivers mingles with the sound of hammering coming from the new hotel where Ioannis' father, the pope, is sitting on a slab of stone facing the sun with his hands folded across his belly.

The two women live near the arch-walled monastery now being built by the Pappas family. Already there is a ten-pronged star with a great P cut in marble in the center, placed before the monastery door like a godly doormat that assures the Pappas family's continued presence in the prayers of the village.

At the bottom of a flight of whitewashed stairs, there is nothing but the rise of terraces to mark the division of property; the houses are glued edge to edge like a continuous cubist sculpture. Some boys playing under a grape arbor never heard of the foreigners. The sloped maze of the town leans toward the sea. There is no sign at all of foreigners. At the end of a lane that branches off, one branch going back toward the town, the other moving even farther down the cliff, she gives up. As she is climbing up the stairs again, she hears a low hum of voices coming from an invisible window. The words are indistinguishable, but their rhythm has the bony angularity of English.

"*Kalimera*," she calls out. "Is someone there?"

The conversation stops.

"*Ne?*" says a cautious woman's voice. "*Pios ine?*"

"My name is Lola. I live in the next village. Hans told me about you."

"Oh," says the voice. "One moment."

The woman who comes to the door is not the same woman

who spoke. Her face is broad and flat, with a slight feeling of distortion around the edges of the features, as if the face had been formed through the vision of a wide-angle lens. The eyes, too, verge outward, stretching themselves as much as humanly possible toward the back of the head, as if more interested in what might be going on behind her than in what she can see straight ahead. She is wearing blue jeans and a red bandana tied around her breasts into a kind of halter. There are red splotches on her throat.

"Yes?" the woman says. "Is there something you want?"

Lola hesitates. Putting things that way makes it difficult. "Nothing in particular," she says. "It's just that we both live on the island and . . ."

"I see," the woman says. "What did you say your name was?"

"Lola. Lola Bogan."

"Yes, I see," the woman says again, but without offering her own name. "Well, I suppose you might come in for a few minutes."

The inside of the house is very dark. The shutters of the single high window are closed. There are pieces of pottery piled up on the sill and photographs of Greek faces and Greek houses tacked up on the whitewashed walls. A whitewash-covered broom stands in a whitewashed corner. There are stacks of books on the floor and sheets of paper strewn about the room.

The woman whose voice Lola first heard is stretched out on a cot with her back against a pile of pillows. She is wearing a white terry cloth robe.

"My name is Leila," she says. "How do you do?" Her accent has that strange precision acquired by foreigners who spend years studying the language before they ever speak it. Her hair is long, heavy, black, perfumed with musk. It stands out several inches from her head. She is smoking a thin, black, gold-tipped cigar.

She reaches out a hand to shake Lola's, but her handshake is so desultory that the grip seems to vanish.

149

"Do you mind my asking where you're from?" Lola says, sitting down on the floor.

"Egypt," Leila says.

"Oh. I know nothing about Egypt. Except Durrell's Egypt, which is mostly Alexandria and mostly imaginary."

Leila lifts her head slowly. "That's what most tourists know about Egypt," she says. "It's romanticized and facile."

"Yes," Lola says. "Of course."

"We're anthropologists," Leila says.

"I know."

"And when we came here we were the only foreigners. It was a culture which had remained intact. We have been witnessing its rape. What are you doing here? Junior year abroad?"

"No," Lola says. And does not know what to add. She has never known precisely what she was doing here. Until she met Stefan. She thinks that, although Leila is Egyptian, her question is very American. Europeans never ask what anyone does.

"Are you researching something here?" Lola asks.

"Yes," Leila says. "I am doing my thesis on the cognitive process as related to Hegelian dialectics."

Lola thinks of Christos drawing a map of Asia, of Thalassa standing in the doorway. Hegelian dialectics. The words are like a thick hedge designed to prevent entry. "I've been reading Engels on *The Origin of the Family*," she says and instantly regrets the attempt to prove herself.

"Ah," Leila says.

Lola suddenly remembers the words of a British Tory M.P. speaking on television to coal miners and saying, "Of course, something must be done about your problems. What you need is someone with quiet dignity." And then the M.P. vanished. She is not sure of the exact connection between Leila and the M.P., only that they remind her of each other.

"Darling, please pass me a cigarette," says the woman who

still has not mentioned her name. Leila leans forward, letting her bathrobe fall open. She runs the nail of her little finger across the upper lip of her friend and says, "Perspiration. Tiny drops all along your lip." She passes a gold-tipped cigarette, lights a match and cups her hand over it.

"I like your house," Lola says. "How long have you been here?"

"Two years," says Leila. The unnamed woman smiles at Lola and says, "Would you care for some mint tea?"

"No thank you," Lola says. "I have to go soon."

"How very American," Leila says. "Always rushing somewhere."

"If not tea, then how about a cigarette or some hashish?" the unnamed woman says.

"I don't smoke," Lola says.

"Which? Hashish or cigarettes?"

"Cigarettes occasionally, but never any hashish."

"You should try the hashish."

"I can't. It makes me hallucinate."

Leila laughs. "It's supposed to."

"Yes, but I have enough difficulty with what's really there."

"Just try one or two puffs. And wait. Allow it to happen slowly."

"All right," Lola says. She breathes in the cigarette, feeling the smoke singe her lungs. "That was fine," she says. "Just one puff was fine."

"An innocent," Leila says. "Are you sure you're American, that you weren't raised in a Skinner Box?"

"No," Lola says and takes a second puff. The room has begun to rise around her like the sun coming up over the rim of her eyelids. The lit cigarette is throwing sparks into the air. Leila's smile wobbles like a drop of water falling slowly from a cup. Both women are smiling; their fingernails are trailing through the air.

151

Leila's bathrobe is still open. The unnamed woman is stroking her hair. Lola watches them lazily. "You look very beautiful together," she says.

Leila laughs. "That's because we are," she says.

The unnamed woman has begun drawing designs with a feather on Leila's body in the space between the open bathrobe. The feather moves up and down so slowly that it seems to have been dropped by a bird in flight and caught up by the wind. Lola imagines that the feather has a will of its own, traveling about the enclosed universe of Leila's body, up over her face, her shoulders, down across her breasts and belly, sinking in a slow stroke between her legs, and then again downward across knees and thighs and ankles and toes.

She shuts her eyes. The feather travels across a dozen disembodied human forms. Sometimes the feather floats. Sometimes the bodies float. There are musical notes rising up out of pores. Honey flows from a breast onto a belly, where the feather comes to sweep it away. She feels a toe sliding across her leg. A delicate barely perceptible toe.

Then she is dreaming. She is in a whirlpool bath, and the water is swirling around her and inside of her. Colored lights are floating across a screen. The drops of water break into flowers. Everything is opening.

The dream goes on for a very long time. She is in a revolving door turning around and around. There is a gingerbread house. She is a child. She is in the woods with her sister. They are holding hands. They are covered with feathers. All over, everywhere, the feathers are stroking, lovely warm feathers, lovely warm, lovely warm. And Leila is smiling and Lola is smiling and the unnamed woman is smiling, and everything is beautiful, everything so beautiful.

The room is dark when she wakes up, even darker than when she arrived. The unnamed woman is lying in Leila's arms. Lola gets up. Her head feels very heavy.

"I have to go," she says. Leila doesn't seem to hear her. Neither does the unnamed woman. She walks back out into the light, where everything seems gilded, and then back up through the maze of the village, past the arch-walled monastery of the Pappas family. Stefan is already at the house, waiting for her.

"Where have you been?" he says.

"With the two women anthropologists."

"It must have been interesting," Stefan says, "if you stayed with them that long. What were they like?"

"Interesting," Lola says. And feels relieved to be home. She runs the nail of her little finger along the edge of Stefan's upper lip and sighs.

• • •

"I didn't write the letter yet," she says.

"It's not an easy letter to write," he says. "I thought about it while I was walking up near the church. I also considered the possibility of writing to her myself. If you wouldn't mind."

"You?" Lola says, her face coming into sudden sharp focus, as if he had handed her a present which she suspected of being a bomb. "Are you out of your mind?"

"I don't think so," he says. "I just thought it might help . . ."

"Help with what?"

"Help to reassure her."

"You are married, Stefan. Don't you remember that? How could you possibly reassure her?"

"I don't know," he says. "I haven't decided 'how' to reassure her. I just decided that I want to."

"Oh," she says. "Oh." Her face has gone completely white. There is an expression in her eyes which he has never seen before, something utterly yielding, utterly compliant. She sees him seeing

153

her, as if his perception of her is a mirror in which she herself is revealed. She turns away. "Excuse me," she says, rushing to the door. "I'll be right back."

He does not go after her. Today, while walking up the road to the church, he noticed a curve in the path which reminded him of the line of her body from ankle to breast. A few ruins on either side of the road. A single tree. He wants to paint her, hidden in the landscape. Why not write to her mother? Why not face things now?

After a while he walks out on the terrace. Lola is standing there, looking up at the sky. It is a Toledan sky, pale, greenish, with clouds blowing across it lit by the moon and the bank of houses tumbling jagged down the side of the mountain. "It's a beautiful night," he says. She doesn't answer.

"If you don't want me to write to her, I won't," he says. "I'm sorry if it upset you."

She turns to face him. Her eyes are blurry. "It's not that," she says. "I do want you to. It's just that I have never in my life heard of a man doing such a thing. You're so honorable, it shocks me. But no matter what you say, she'll still think what she thinks. No letter is going to make any difference. But it is sweet of you. It really is."

Her voice has a different timbre in it, a timbre which matches the expression in her eyes before she left the room. You do too love me, he thinks. You do too.

• • •

Stefan sits with a pad on his knees looking out at the volcano, mentally composing a letter to Lola's mother. Now that he has decided to write it, the "how" has begun to seem more significant than he realized when the idea first occurred to him. There are three main issues to tackle—his marriage, his nationality and his plans—and each involves an assault, in its own way, on the person he has decided to reassure. Each involves not only the past, but the future. What should have been clear to him before he suggested writing to Lola's mother strikes him now with exaggerated clarity: there is only one thing which could possibly reassure Mrs. Bogan: a flat statement of his intentions . . . though it is exactly that flat statement which he wants to avoid making. He feels a momentary flash of irritation at Lola for putting him into this position, as if she had devised a preposterous scheme for trapping him, even as he realizes that he is the one who proposed writing the letter in the first place.

Maybe, he thinks, it would be best to begin with the subject of his being Austrian. That at least has the advantage of being clearcut. True, he was Austrian, is Austrian and will be Austrian. But he is not and never has been a Nazi. If anything, it is his sympathy for the Jews, his knowledge that it was his people who caused hers so much pain, a sympathy which has invisibly carried over into his relations with Lola, that reinforces his decision to write at all and lends him a sense of strength. Here, he can defend himself without ambiguity. Here, his feelings form a natural empathetic bond, which applies as much to the fact of his being, generationally, somewhere between Lola and her mother as to anything else. He begins to write. "Dear Mrs. Bogan, I am writing to you on this occasion . . ." He stops, scratches out the sentence and begins again. "Dear Mrs. Bogan. Your daughter has already written to you about me, and I am writing now in the hope that I might add my opinion to hers. I understand how you, as a mother, must feel about me. I am a member of that race . . ."

The words come slowly but with regularity. He writes of his own mother, of his childhood, of his awareness that there are still many Nazis in Austria. He writes that in some ways he feels more Jewish than Austrian. He writes that he hopes for her tolerance. And yet . . . even in this, even at the height of his empathetic capacities, he feels a peculiar emotional undertow, which draws him away from time to time from what he is trying to say, an obscure sense that logic and sensitivity, even when pursued in combination, may be insufficient tools for dealing with hatred, fear and grief. He concentrates on staying away from that patch of water where the pattern of currents so visibly alters and becomes a whirlpool. When the undertow approaches him, despite his efforts to stay away from it, he stops to get his bearings, and shifts a little bit in another direction. If he is truthful, he thinks, truthful and fair, it will . . . it will have to . . . help.

When he has finished writing about his being Austrian, he stops to think again, though, just as he is closing off the first part, a flash recollection of a Margaret Bourke-White photograph of Jews at Buchenwald goes through his mind. Those faces behind the barbed wire: dazed, passive faces, gaunt, almost insensible, as if, unable any longer to experience their own feelings, they were trying to look at themselves from a distance through a barbed wire fence. What to do about those faces? It occurs to him that this is an odd way to begin a letter that is also an introduction, with talk about himself and the Nazis. And yet, what else can he do?

An hour passes before he is able to begin tackling the subject of his marriage. About this, he can write clearly only in terms of the past. The future, as yet, is unknown. And Lola's mother will care, certainly, only about the future. I'm sorry, he says to himself, experiencing again his earlier irritation, combined now with a flash of claustrophobia, I'm sorry, but I can't make any promises. And then . . . what do you both want of me?

What he writes finally contains only the merest shadow of a reassurance. "I, like you, want to take good care of your daughter. I, like you, love her. As you know, I am married and cannot set your mind at rest about the future . . ."

He stops again. What is the point of writing at all if he cannot set her mind at rest? He finds himself thinking, though, that

Lola has never been easy to get along with, never been all that decisive in her behavior. If Lola's mother would consider the problem of her daughter's character, instead of caring only about promises, she might . . .

He stops one more time, feeling sobered. This letter seems, even to him, to be weak and indecisive, an awkward compromise with his original intentions. Yet, it is something. And something is better than nothing. If it contains no promises, it at least does contain his willingness to face her honestly and seriously. If she has any sympathy at all, she will respond . . .

He does not know how she will respond. It is impossible to know. And pointless to think about. He has done his best. If his best is not good enough, well . . . He rereads what he has written, feeling a gnawing dissatisfaction with its tone, and in particular with the part about his marriage. Something is missing. Something essential. He knows it but can't help it. After some time, he reluctantly pens an insert just after the sentence about "not making any promises." "Though I cannot predict the future," he writes, "I will do my best to make things easier for us." "Us," he thinks. That is the key word, the word which makes him nervous. Not him. Not Lola. But "us."

He looks at that sentence for a long time, divided between his own resistance to including it and his sense of its necessity. Then he recopies the letter, leaving in the "us," puts it in an envelope, seals it, addresses it in his careful, even handwriting, and takes it down to the post office. There, he thinks, with a certain sense of relief. There, it is done. Though the "us" reverberates in his mind long after the letter has passed out of his hands.

. . .

157

For three days now, Lola has been writing her letter.

"Dear Mother," she has written, "I dread writing this letter. I do not know what to say to you. Nothing I might write could change anything in your feelings. Except if I were to say that I am getting married. I am not, however, getting married . . ."

"Dear Mother, The first thing you must understand is that we are of different generations, that times have changed . . ."

"Dear Mother, The first night in bed with him I was so terrified that I tortured him. For the first month that we knew each other, I was impossible to get along with. It is only now that I am beginning to . . ."

"Dear Mother, Regardless of what will happen between us, I have very strong feelings for this man. I don't know what he is going to do . . ."

"Dear Mother, I wish I could confide in you. I wish I could hear you say, 'Tell me about it. Are you happy?' I wish . . ."

•

This is my MOTHER, she thinks. Why should it be so difficult to write to my own mother? These letters, or rather, these attempts at a letter, are all replies in advance of a response, instead of that yielding exchange of confidences for which she longs, the attempt, within some newly resilient context, to take the chance of self-revelation. Defensiveness in the face of anticipated disapproval. The familiar and artificial postures of independence. She knows they are artificial but doesn't know how to relinquish them. It is what she has always felt obliged to simulate, as if the entire series of possible exchanges between her and her mother had become encapsulated into a single exchange, as if every attempt at communication was forced to contend with the presence of the capsule which could (and probably would) explode at any second. Off limits, the capsule said. Off limits for confidences. Off limits for need and fear. Off limits, most profoundly, for that tender vulnerability which lurked right beneath the surface of things and was in fact what she knew to be the capacity for love.

The capacity for love. Mother, she thinks. I have to write you a real letter. But I don't know how to do it. I have to, and I can't.

She looks at the pages covered with her own handwriting, at the dozens of aborted beginnings. Her breathing is shallow. The harder she tries, the more her headache intensifies. She rests, again, for an hour, then gets up and without stopping to think anymore, begins to write.

"Dear Mother, In your last letter, you asked me about the Austrian painter. I am writing now to tell you something about him, and maybe something about myself too. I can only hope that you will try to understand before judging.

It has always been difficult for me to talk with you about my private life. You always said that you wanted me to be happy. Yet, your definition of happiness excluded all of those moments which *I* considered happy. Stefan is one of the most decent men I have ever known. He has been patient with me when my behavior called for impatience. He has understood me even when I insisted upon being misunderstood. It is true that he is Austrian and married. It is also true that we are living together. For now, I am grateful for whatever happiness I can find . . . whenever I can find it. I know that in this, I am taking a chance. I know you consider that I should think more carefully before I act. What you do not know is that I think too much already. I can only try to use my best feelings as a guide. What I need most is to be free to love. Try, please, to explain all this to Dad. Love, Lola."

She does not read over what she has written. She is afraid to, afraid that if she does, she will never send it. I know, she thinks again, that in this I am taking a chance. By the time she seals the envelope, she can no longer even remember what she has written.

159

She walks into town to mail the letter, feeling a moment of acute dread as it passes from her hand into the hand of the postman. What a long thread, this umbilical cord. What an impossibly long thread.

She shuts her eyes as she turns away from the post office, thinking, I will not ask him to give it back to me. I will not.

"*W*HY DON'T WE spend the day exploring together?" Lola says. "We could rent mules from Andreas and pack a picnic or else stop at the taverna on the beach. You remember which taverna I mean, the small one with the grape arbor and the two tables, the one where they have keftedes and stuffed tomatoes and turtle steaks. Or else we could have a picnic for lunch and go to the taverna for dinner. I'm tired of being so serious. Every day I invent expeditions for us. And then we don't go on them. I just keep wanting to run or dance or sing or shout instead of being so restrained all of the time. Please, Stefan. Just this once. A whole day for ourselves with no purpose whatsoever other than our own pleasure.

"Maybe later," he says. "After I finish painting."

"By then the whole day will be gone," she says.

"If not today, then tomorrow."

"Do you promise?" she says.

"I can't promise. It depends . . ."

"Then let's do it today."

"I don't see what the rush is, Lola."

"You don't? You don't see?"

"No."

"You're leaving in three weeks, and you don't see what the rush is?"

"We'll see each other again," he says. "I'll come to America."

"What about the time in between?"

"We'll write to each other."

"Write to each other," she says, looking at him strangely. "And to you that would be the same?"

"Not the same but . . ."

"It won't be anywhere near the same. Ever."

"Why make it sound so final?"

"Because things change so quickly. They change even more quickly when you're separated from someone. Letters take weeks. You write one and by the time you have an answer, everything is different. As far as I'm concerned what we have is today. Maybe if today were miserable, I would place my faith in tomorrow. But today is . . ." She stops and quickly climbs out of bed.

"Today is what?" he says.

"Beautiful."

"And tomorrow will be, too."

"No," she says. "It's funny. I'm the one who wants this to last forever. And the one who can believe only in today. You believe in tomorrow and think not at all about the future. Sometimes . . . I don't know."

"What?"

"Sometimes I feel this urge to punish you, just for making me care about the future, making me worry that . . . And then I want to do something to destroy even the illusion of possibilities."

"The illusion of possibilities," he says. "Lola, listen to me. I wrote to Marianna yesterday. But there was also a letter from Franz. All he could say was that, of course, I was in love with you, hadn't I always been in love with someone? Just what you're saying now. He could see only the past. And he kept referring to what he called my 'one-year infatuations' instead of trying to . . ."

"Wait a minute," she says. "What one-year infatuations?"

"Oh," he says, looking away from her. "I didn't realize . . ."

"Didn't realize what?"

"That I hadn't . . . that we hadn't . . ."

"Would you stop it, Stefan? Would you just tell me what you're talking about?"

"A pattern," he says reluctantly, feeling the heat rise up around the back of his neck.

"What kind of pattern?" she says.

"Of things lasting a year," he says.

Her face is suddenly frozen, immobile. "A year," she says stiffly. "Was it always a year?"

"Yes, more or less," he says, attempting a casualness which even he can see rings false.

"I see," she says.

"I don't think you do," he says, wondering how on earth he managed to get himself into this and remembering suddenly what they had begun with. "We were talking about the illusion of possibilities," he says. "And I was telling you that I didn't think Franz understood. What I want you to know is that I wrote to him saying that this was different . . ."

"How do you know that it's different?" she says, beginning to twist a strand of hair around her finger and looking away from him. "How will you know until after a year? A year?" she says. "It's always been a year?"

Stefan stands up. "Lola, I explained to you just now that I had written to him . . ."

"We don't even have a year," she says. "So far as I can tell, what we have is three weeks. Of course, for three weeks it will be different. It's easy for things to be different when you only have three weeks."

"We don't have just three weeks," he says. "I started to tell you that I also wrote to Marianna. I asked for a separation."

"You asked for a separation?"

"Yes. I did it for you."

"You did it for me?" she says. "But, Stefan, you can't do it for me. Things like that never work if you do them for someone else. You have to do them for yourself. I'm not just being capricious."

She feels suddenly a kind of despair which appears to her as something infinitely circular. One portion of her mind has seized on the word "separation" while another portion has seized on the words "a year." The two thoughts have begun to chase each other around in a circle like a tiger chasing its tail. There is no way to reconcile them. Which one is it? she thinks. Which one is it really? What shall I believe?

"Lola," he says, grabbing her shoulders. "Did you hear what I said? I said that I asked Marianna for a separation."

"You said two things, Stefan," she says. "I heard both of them."

"Don't you think that one of them is just a little bit more important than the other?"

"I don't know," she says. "I think both of them are important."

"You know, Lola," he says. "Sometimes you make me furious. Here I am telling you that I want to get a separation from my wife, and you can't even hear what I'm saying, even though you've been talking of practically nothing else for months."

"I have not been talking about 'nothing else,'" she says. "I haven't even mentioned it in over a month. All I said was that you shouldn't do it for me, that you had to do it for yourself. Otherwise I'm your life preserver, and it will end in a year. Don't you understand? I don't want it to end in a year."

"Two minutes ago you were upset that it was going to end in three weeks. Now you're upset that it's going to end in a year."

"It will," she says.

"It is not going to end in a year," he shouts at her. "Would you please get that crazy idea out of your head?"

"I can't," she says. And bursts into tears.

He walks out, slamming the door.

•

She stands out on the terrace for a long time, looking out at the volcano. She is paralyzed with fear. She realizes suddenly that despite her protestations about the future, she has always assumed its existence, has told herself one thing while believing another. "Don't count on it," she has said to herself, while feeling always that inevitable drift in the direction of counting on it, counting on it more and more from one day to the next until . . .

A year, she thinks. Just a year. This morning, she counted, again. Just to be sure. Her period is almost ten days late. For a week she has been chasing the thought from her mind. But now it looms suddenly before her: a reality with which she must, somehow, contend. In a year, she thinks, if she really is pregnant, she will have a four-month-old child. And Stefan will leave. But he wouldn't, she thinks. He wouldn't leave if I had a child. But if I didn't, her mind argues back, he would. He would stay for a child . . . but not for me. The thought fills her with a kind of anxiety more profound than anything she has ever known before. This morning, she was thinking that she wanted more than anything to have a child, and that somehow, strangely, she was not at all afraid. Now, all she can think about is this fear. What can I tell him? she thinks.

She walks back into the house and lies down on the bed. It's crazy to have a baby, she thinks. It's absolutely crazy. She sees herself nursing the child, sees it playing in the back yard (what back yard?) sees it . . . him, her . . . a girl, she thinks, I want a girl . . . coming home from school, sitting at the kitchen table eating chocolate chip cookies or in her arms in front of a fire while she sings the Russian lullaby. But what about? Her mind stalls. I'm completely unprepared for this, she thinks. And then, but there really is no way to be prepared. The preparation is all in that change of perspective which took place inside of her only this morning when the child began to seem a real possibility, when her life suddenly assumed a new dimension, a different specific gravity, a sense of implicit reordering around that future she had struggled for so long to hold at bay. In that moment, she even saw Stefan differently, as if, until then, no matter how much of life he had experienced and thought about, no matter how committed he was to his work, in some way he was still a boy. And her mother too. Suddenly she saw her mother differently as well. She thinks of the letter she has mailed. Please, Mother, she thinks. Please try. And wonders what her mother's reaction would have been if she had included in the letter something about the baby, the maybe baby.

I'm tired of being free, she thinks. I don't like it anymore. I want the responsibility. Without that, everything seems all passion and no purpose. Without that it could be a year or six months or two years. Without that . . . But what about us? she thinks. What about just being together, the two of us? There will be other chances. But what if there aren't? What if it never happens again, and I have to say later on that I made a mistake, a disastrous, terrible mistake?

She sits up in bed again. I have to tell him, she thinks. I absolutely must tell him. He said he would get a separation. He said . . . but what if I'm not pregnant, what about a year? What about his wife? It would be nice to have his child. It would be terrible. What if this ends in a year, and I'm left with nothing . . . what if . . . I would manage, she thinks, somehow I would manage. Who are you kidding, Lola, . . . how would you manage? Somehow, she thinks, somehow I would manage. The child . . . would it look like him or like her? A child is a way of preserving something even if it does end in a year . . . I couldn't handle an abortion, it would give me a nervous breakdown . . . now wait a minute, you're not even sure . . . it's only been less than two weeks . . . I would regret it, regret what? . . . having a child or not having it? . . . either way probably . . . he said, he did say that he would get a separation. . . . WHAT ABOUT A YEAR? . . . the thing is . . . I'm getting hysterical, she thinks. Stop getting hysterical. I want to be a mother. I want to be married . . . I am getting hysterical. I really do want to be a mother, now when we love each other. She uses the word without even noticing it now, though all along she has avoided it. *I want to be a mother.* I do I do I do.

I'm exhausted, she thinks. I really am exhausted. She presses her face into the pillow. "But I want to be a child too. Still, I do I do I do I do."

•

An hour later, she gets up and walks to the cafe. She does not know where Stefan has gone. Probably up to the church. I have to tell him, she thinks. I have to tell him.

She walks up the path, and finds him sitting on a rock below the church.

"I'm sorry," she says. "I'm sorry I got so upset."

"You should be sorry," he says.

"There were reasons," she says. "Good reasons."

"I doubt that anything could be good enough."

"I think I may be pregnant," she says. "And I'm afraid that in a year . . ."

"You think you're pregnant," he says.

"Maybe," she says.

"Oh," he says.

"And I spent the last hour at the house feeling hysterical about it."

"I'm sorry," he says.

"About what?" she says. "About a year or about the baby?"

"I'm sorry you didn't tell me before."

"Well, I'm telling you now," she says, beginning to cry again. He stands up, comes over to her, and puts his arms around her. "There, baby," he says. "I think it's time to go home."

• • •

Lola and Stefan are in bed. It is eight AM. Thalassa opens the door. The sun enters the room before her, a ray of light that stretches across the entire room and in an instant envelopes the bed.

"I brought you a baby chick," Thalassa says. The single shape of double thickness in the middle of the bed separates with a rush. The springs creak; the bed threatens to collapse. Stefan's body is suspended over the widening space between the illusory double bed.

I knew it, Thalassa thinks. It is true what Vianoula said, that the tourists had sex together in the morning, in broad daylight. What would the pope think? What would her husband think? For a moment her mind floats off into imaginings of what it would be like if she and Leonidas were to have sex in the morning, not in the middle of the night when she was tired and Leonidas smelled and snorted over her and fell dead asleep five seconds after he was done, what it would be like to have breakfast together on the terrace and hold hands. Well, she thinks, stopping herself. It is perfectly clear that these are the sins the pope has talked about in church, the sins against which her daughters must be protected, the reason why her daughters should not even be allowed to talk to the foreigners. It was everywhere, the pope said, corruption and immorality, throughout the civilized world. And Thalassa agreed, which was why she brought over the baby chick so early in the morning and came in without knocking, just to see, just to find out if it was true. Well it was, everything Vianoula said, and God only knew what else.

She mentally crosses herself and says, "*Kalimera.*"

"*Kalimera,*" Lola says, drawing the covers up over herself and trying at the same time to move them so that they will cover Stefan as well.

"The baby chicks hatched just this morning," Thalassa says.

"Oh, yes?" says Lola.

"Yes. I thought you might like to see them."

"We would," Lola says, "after we put our clothes on. Do you always come in this early without knocking?"

Thalassa laughs. "Early?" she says. "This is not early." Her mind is swimming with the new and unexpected information: not only do they have sex in the morning, but they do it without any clothes on. The thought makes her dizzy.

"For us it is early," Lola says.

"Oh yes. For you," Thalassa says, in her distraction forgetting altogether the formalities of exchange between foreigners and herself. "For you who do not have to work . . . for you who are on vacation . . . for you who can . . ." She almost says, "do this in the morning," but recovers herself just in time. "Well, yes," she says. "No . . . I mean no. I just wanted for you to see the baby chick. You see," she says, walking toward the bed. "Here." She places it on top of the maroon-and-orange bedspread. "I will leave it with you. When you are ready, come to see the rest of them."

Walking close to the bed, she is able to see that Lola's shoulders are bare, the white upper curve of her breast, also bare. She cannot help herself: she stares.

Lola stares back.

"Thank you," she says, as if they are talking at an afternoon tea party. "Thank you very much. We will see you later on then."

"Yes," Thalassa says. "Yes, of course." And rushes out the

door, with the bare bodies tumbling through her mind like acrobats, bare bodies, bare breasts, bare bodies. When she reaches the chicken coop, the baby chicks, all but one, are all tucked beneath the mother. Christos is holding the other in his hand, throwing it up in the air and catching it, a blond puff like dandelion wisp.

"Didn't I tell you . . ." she says, and then forgets what it was she wanted to say. "Go and play," she says.

Christos looks at her uncomprehendingly.

"But I am playing," he says.

"Somewhere else," she says. And then adds, "And I'm warning you, if I catch you talking to the guests . . . Do you hear me? I forbid you to talk to the guests."

"Yes, Mama," he says. She slaps him on the head, and he begins to run off, jumping from the terrace to the ground, wondering, "Why is her face so red, so red, so red?" wondering, "Which chick will be mine?"

• • •

Stefan puts his head under the covers, rests it against Lola's belly for a minute and comes out again.

"What were you doing?" she says.

"I was listening," he says. "To be sure."

She laughs. "It's a little bit early for that, don't you think?"

"It's never too early," he says.

"Are you sure?" she says.

"Yes."

"I'm surprised at you." "You don't even like children."

"Well, I've never had any before. Have you?"

"Are you serious? How could you ask me such a thing? Don't you know?"

"I wouldn't assume anything with you."

"Even something like that? Don't you think I would have told you?"

"No."

"Because I'm secretive?"

"Not exactly. Just very private."

"Oh, darling," she says and is startled at herself for having used the word. She has never said it out loud before in her life, and the fact that she does now escapes Stefan's attention entirely. It is to her one of those words that can pass in a conversation for chatter while still retaining its authenticity, and she has hoarded it up as something all the more precious for its being a cliché. It pleases her now that she has been able to extend herself so far into the sphere of an acute intimacy without its taking on the proportions of a confession, though for her, silently, it is precisely that.

"You really would want for me to have it?" she says.

"Yes," he says.

"But what about a year?"

"This is different," he says. "I would marry you."

"Marry me?" she says.

"Yes," he says, surprised at his sudden feeling of certainty, and wondering, even as he says it, about his own sincerity. Something sinks in him and something else rises, though he cannot tell what the "something's" are. The "yes" is a purely spontaneous thing . . . the product of a strange euphoria, fused with a sense of renewal that he has had since yesterday. And yet, it leaves a trace of something sticky behind it, as if in the midst of being utterly serious, he is also being utterly frivolous.

"Anyway," he says, trying to grapple with the collision of emotional forces inside of himself. "Anyway, we don't really know yet."

"No," she says, looking at him carefully, as if trying to determine how much weight to give his words.

He looks away from her. "We'll just have to see," he says.

"I guess we will," she says and feels a sudden shift into de-

171

pression, as if imagination were being forced now to contend with reality, the passage of time, the passage of certainties and uncertainties.

"Rest," he says. "The baby needs rest."

He turns his back to her and draws her arms around him so that she is holding him in the hollow inner curve of her body, like the baby, which in her mind has already come to life.

"Stefan," she says softly.

"What?"

"You don't want it, do you?"

He doesn't answer for a moment.

"Tell me the truth," she says.

"I can't," he says. "Because I don't know myself."

Again, the thoughts start going through Lola's mind. What if . . . a baby . . . a back yard. I'm not going to think about it anymore, she tells herself. I am not going to get worked up again. She curls up against him and lies awake thinking.

"I can't rest," she says.

"Why not?" he says.

"Because."

"Because what?"

"Because of the baby."

He sits up and looks at her. "Don't worry," he says. "There's nothing to worry about."

She gets up out of bed and walks over to the sink. She washes her face, her hands, under her arms and between her legs. "Will you do my back?" she says after several minutes.

He comes over, folds the washcloth in quarter, rubs the bar of soap over it and slowly begins with small circular strokes to wash her back. Then he rinses out the cloth, and beginning at the base of her neck, wipes away the soap, kissing each vertebra as the soapy film vanishes from the top to the base of her backbone. She stands, without moving, her head tipped back, shivering slightly.

"That's instead of a towel," he says. He has reached to just below the curve of her waist, and has gotten down on his knees. The washcloth in one hand, the other hand on her hip, the soap on the floor.

"Like a cat," she whispers and turns her body slowly around against his mouth until she is facing him. He kisses her belly twice. "One for you and one for the baby," he says. She holds his head close to her and says, with a tremolo in her voice, "You know, Stefan. I think I love you. I really do think I love you."

"I know," he says, kissing the innermost corner of her thigh. A reflex jumps beneath her skin, like a heartbeat. "I love you too."

"Can we still go on the picnic today?"

"Yes, we can," he says.

Both of their voices have become slightly muffled.

"And make love on the beach?"

"Yes. We can make love wherever you want."

"Here?"

"Yes."

"Now?"

"Yes."

•   •   •

It is noon before they start out for the other side of the island. They take two mules with them, plus Andreas riding his own. Andreas has agreed to leave with all of the mules when they reach the beach.

"We will walk from there," Stefan says.

"Yes, I understand," Andreas says, half winking at Stefan.

"We are going on a picnic, Andreas," Lola says, emphasizing the word "picnic" and looking at him coldly.

173

"Of course, yes of course," Andreas says. Already this morning, Thalassa told his wife and his wife told him about finding them in bed together naked in the morning.

He looks at her breasts and half closes his eyes. I'd like to myself, he thinks. Just a few minutes that's all. These foreign girls. They all do it. Down around the monastery where the trees are thick and no one can see. She'd never tell. That's for sure. They never tell, these foreign girls. Because they know it's what they want. See it in the way they always show everything, the way they look at you. It's in their eyes, short skirts right up there so you can see it all practically, like to get in there myself, like to . . .

"Andreas," she says, "How long will it take us to get over to the other side of the island?"

"One hours, maybe less, *kiria*," he says formally, politely, emphasizing the "madame."

"Good," she says. "Just in time for lunch and a swim."

"Yes," he says. "Is nice to swim there." He himself has never gone swimming in his life and does not know how to swim.

"I'm sure it is," she says and smiles. The smile is a little bit less warm than usual, cautious almost. "Well, let's go," she says.

He reaches to help her up onto the mule. "No," she says stiffly. "No thank you. I can manage by myself."

Too bad, he thinks, imagining the feel of her skin as he lifts her up. In a loud voice he says to the mule, "*Helas, helas. Delop, delop.*"

And the mule sways forward.

$\mathcal{T}$HE MULES JOG unevenly down the road. Stefan's camera bounces against his body. Lola watches his profile; he has not cut his hair since they met, and it has grown down over his ears and collar and forehead, like an enlarged Buster Brown, concealing the nape of his neck. He stops to photograph a herd of horses and mules in the distance, then wants to make a detour in order to take closeups of one dappled horse, larger and leaner than the others, which remains on the outer edge of the herd.

Andreas leads them down through the meadow to where the animals are grazing among the daisies and sorrel and anemones, which have already begun to turn brown from the sun. The dappled horse moves first, separating itself entirely now from the others, flicking its tail and turning its angular face toward them. The hollows of its haunches and neck make a dark accent against the lightness of its body. Its mane is tangled. It squints. Stefan drops to his knees and photographs the horse from several angles, as it first glances in his direction, then turns away, lowering its head to the ground. When he has finished photographing the dappled horse, Stefan returns to the herd again, snapping them in groups, with the horses hovering high above the mules, which in contrast seem small, rugged and innocent.

They make one more stop en route to the beach, after passing along a dusty row of eucalyptus and through a village in which there are no signs of life. On the outskirts of the village, they pass a small boy wearing a blue cap and brown-and-white checked shirt. In one hand, he is carrying a baby chick cushioned with straw. "*Hierete. Thelete na parete afto?*" he says, pointing to the chick.

"What is he saying?" Stefan asks.

"He wants to sell us the chick," Lola says, laughing. She climbs off the mule to talk to the boy, gives him ten drachmas and takes the chick, carrying it the rest of the way in her shoulder bag. "I'll give it to Christos when we get back," she says. "He can add it to his brood." During the course of the day, she often takes the chick out of her bag, holds it to her face and nuzzles it. Each time she does that, he is reminded that maybe she is pregnant, maybe she will have a child.

It is almost two-thirty by the time they reach the other side of the island. Andreas leaves as he has promised, and they climb over the volcanic rocks to a cove just out of sight of the main beach. They leave the food in a cool spot between two rocks, spread their towels on the black sand, then strip to their bathing suits and swim far out into the water.

"I'll race you back to the beach," Lola shouts. "One two three go!" She swims quickly and precisely with high strokes and her head above water. He swims with low, choppy strokes, his head under water. She almost keeps even with him, but as soon as she falls slightly behind, she abruptly stops, turns on her back and floats back out. When he reaches the shore, he stands up, shakes the water out of his eyes and looks to see where she is. She is drifting lazily, eagle spread, rising and falling with the movement of the waves. "Lola," he shouts. "You cheated!" She pretends not to hear him and keeps on drifting. "Lola!" he yells again.

"Wha-at?" she says in a slow singsong.

"You know what," he says.

"I'm sorry, I can't hear you. If there's something you want to tell me, you'll have to come out here."

He swims out to her. She is still floating on her back. When he is a few yards away from her he changes to a breaststroke, then glides out to her on his stomach. He puts his arm around her waist and tries to hold her up so that both of them are half floating together, body to body, making small kicking movements with their legs. "You cheated," he whispers into her mouth. "I know," she whispers back. "Because I was sure I would win." She laughs. "It was out of consideration for your weakness. I didn't want you to look bad."

"Oh yes?" he says.

"Yes," she says, still laughing.

He kisses her and their mouths are full of seawater. He keeps his eyes open; she keeps hers closed. Afterward Lola separates from him and says, "I have to tell you something."

"What?" he says.

"I can only tell you under water. Duck your head and open your eyes."

He ducks, opens his eyes and sees her face floating close to his, her eyes blurry with seawater, her hair fanning out around her head in long ripples. She mouths the words slowly, "I love you."

He mouths them back. "I love you too."

When they come back to the surface, she says, "I just wanted to make sure that it was still true."

"It's still true," he says.

"Then I can say it again?"

"Yes."

"You're sure?"

"I'm sure."

She draws in her breath. "I love you I love you I love you I love you," she says. Her voice crescendos with each repetition, until the last time she says it, the sound echoes out over the water. She stops and seems to be listening to her own voice as if it is the voice of someone she is meeting for the first time. Her eyes are glittering. There is something so passionate, so absolute in her face that for a moment, at the center of his most acute exhilaration, pride and expanding sense of sureness, there is a flash of panic. He has never seen her like this before, with this near to excessive purity surrounding her like a cape of fire. For an instant he feels outstripped and is afraid.

She puts her arm around his neck and treads water, moving her body back and forth against his, skin gliding against skin, the currents of water moving against them like hundreds of small undulating hands. He holds her very close to him and with one hand undoes the top of her bathing suit. She breaks away from him and dives into the water. Her legs disappear in a trail of foam until, an instant later, he feels her arms encircling his knees. She reaches up for his trunks with one hand and pulls them down to his ankles. He kicks his feet until he is free of them. When she comes back up to the surface, she is carrying them between her teeth. She grins and swims back to him again. He reaches his hand down to the upper edge of her bikini bottoms, pushing them down, while she, with her one free hand, helps him.

Then suddenly, she turns away from him and starts swimming with rapid strokes toward the shore, carrying his trunks in her mouth like a retriever with a prize stick. He chases after her, overtakes her and tries to recapture his trunks. She holds on, and pulls away from him, clenching her teeth around her trophy. There is a tug of war, then the sound of something beginning to tear. She looks startled, and surrenders, though in an instant, she has ducked her head under water again and come up, spitting water into his face. He spits it back. She dives, grabs his foot and surfaces with it in her hands, dumping him backward so that his arms thrash in the air for balance and his head goes under. He grabs her around the waist and throws her into the air. She comes down splashing and climbs onto his shoulders. He balances her, naked, as she tries to stand up, holding on to his hands. For a

178

moment, she succeeds, but then skids and topples back into the water.

They swim out into deep water together once more, meeting under water with their eyes open, making faces at each other, kissing and swallowing water, blowing bubbles, touching each other with an almost careless yet acutely aware sense of intimacy, the familiarities of possession becoming a binding playful affection. Underwater, it is impossible to remain immobile. Just staying in one place requires the most rapid and subtle motion: wavings, flickerings, scullings, flexing of ankles, flexing of wrists, undulating of torsos, fingers plucking at the water, toes wriggling. When they swim back into shallow water, it is with her riding naked on his naked back, floating above him like a bicycle streamer in the wind.

Standing in water up to their shoulders, their hands shape the curves of water against each other's bodies in slow motion.

"Have you ever made love under water?" she says.

"No, have you?"

"No. Do you want to try?"

"Yes."

He raises her body through the water, lifting but not lifting her, guiding her weightless through an ether of expectation. He slips into her, rests, moves, rests again, moves with the movement of the water itself, a perpetual whirlpool surrounding them and blending with them until they stand together in absolute stillness with the water itself the only motion, a motion so subtle and pervasive and encompassing that it surpasses the gentlest gesture that could be made by human hands or human bodies.

She takes a deep breath and sighs into his mouth. "I have to say it again," she whispers. "I love you." And then, "Are you hungry?"

He laughs. "Yes," he says.

"Let's eat then."

They walk together back toward the shore, holding hands,

with the water dripping from their bodies and a small V forming in the water, like the wake of a motorboat, where their hands, joined, trail out behind them.

• • •

They lie on the beach for a few minutes with arms and legs entangled like seaweed washed up on the shore. The sun dries the salt on their bodies, sticky and abrasive now. The skin around Lola's mouth is reddened and chafed. Her breasts are sore. Salt burns in the corners of her eyes and between her legs. The sun moves behind the mountain. The air cools. They dress slowly, then spread out the picnic on her beach towel; feta and kaseri cheeses, black bread, tomatoes, olives and retsina. The faint taste of turpentine from the retsina blankets the walls of their mouths. The baby chick is let out of the bag; Lola feeds it crumbs, then holds it between her breasts, looking down at it.

She cannot stop thinking about her body. The changes inside of her, though physically still unconfirmed, seem so total nonetheless that it is as if she has passed into some other dimension of existence. And when they were making love under water . . . then it had been even more compelling, as if she had become part of something so much larger than herself, part of an entire generational process. There was her womb with life inside of it, and also the water a womb which she was inside of, and also Stefan inside of her. It felt suddenly as if everything was inside of everything else, like an endless series of Chinese boxes, as if human souls could be passed on as a breath of life from one Chinese box into another.

She lies on the beach, looking up at the sky, moving inside of the Chinese boxes.

"What are you thinking about?" Stefan asks.

"Chinese boxes," Lola says.

"Chinese boxes?"

"Yes," she says. "The baby, you, me, the water. Chinese boxes."

"I see," he says, though he's not sure that he does.

"You don't," she says. "But maybe it doesn't matter. And besides, it's hard to explain. The thing is, Stefan, that I know that for all of the sensible and practical reasons, I should be hoping that I'm not pregnant. And yet, no matter what I tell myself, I keep hoping that I am. Yesterday, it suddenly occurred to me that I was part of something so much larger than myself, part of a process that had been going on since human beings first appeared on the earth, that regardless of wars or famines or plagues, regardless of changes in governments and ideologies, women keep on giving birth to children. There is always a new generation that springs to life. Even during the war, when millions of people were being exterminated, someone refused to cooperate, and despite everything, had a child, or two children. My father's family was destroyed, but then I was born, and my brother was born, and a new family was created. Always, so long as the world continues to exist, that process will keep on going. Always there will be someone saying, 'I'm going to have a child.'

"Maybe I would be a terrible mother. Maybe I would hand down to my child the same weaknesses that my mother handed down to me. On the other hand, maybe I won't. Imagine . . . a living creature just waiting to be shaped. I love you, and I want things to last forever. I can't make them last forever. I can't even believe that they might. And yet . . . there's this child . . . this maybe child. I won't last forever; the child won't last forever. But the process . . . the process will.

"I know that what I'm feeling is nothing new. But what difference does that make? It feels new to me because I'm the one who's experiencing it. It's as if there has been some totally unexpected explosion of knowledge inside of me, the sense of an entire invisible universe opening up, a universe that I was never aware even existed. Do you understand what I mean, Stefan? Do you understand at all?"

"Yes," he says. "I think I do." He is finding it difficult to look at her now. Again her face has that purity and absoluteness which he saw in it when they were swimming together, though now the look seems to have expanded beyond her into some realm which he cannot even touch. He has a quick recollection of *la jeune fille*, of her pregnancy less than a year ago, of her rapid decision to have an abortion. It had never been a question. He didn't want a child. She didn't want a child. A child made no sense whatsoever. So the child had been eliminated. He had never even thought of it as a child. He had thought of it as an accident. Yet here was Lola talking not only of a child, but of some global experience, some dimension which he has never even considered, let alone attempted to apply to his own life. He himself does not have any of these feelings, yet he cannot help being at once shaken and moved by what he sees in Lola. Certainly she is no longer that woman who lay silently in bed next to him and refused to be touched, nor is she the woman who insisted that he tell her about Marianna, nor even the woman who stood on the road with Hans defending herself with rhetorical flourish and embarrassing assertion. She is all of those things, but also, she is something else, something new.

It is as if, in these last two months, she has been giving slow birth to herself, and has arrived now at a point where she wants to expand outward, without restriction. There is a peculiar dignity about her now, a kind of spiritual enlargement. He recognizes the Lola of those first days as merely the shadow of what she could be, of her own potential. And he . . . a thought has suddenly jarred inside of his mind. But I am intermingled with all this, he thinks. I have not made her into who she is, but I have helped bring her out. I am responsible. The thought terrifies him. It implies something so permanent, so rooted in life's processes and its consequences that he cannot contend with it. He feels a surge of love for her, and alongside of it, another surge of fear so acute that it leaves his body weak. It is as if he is being sucked into some immense whirlpool, which will never let him go, which will just spin him around and around, never stopping. Inexorably, he is being drawn into her world, her terms. Marriage, children, permanence, commitments: all of the things that he does not want but that seem to be such strong forces in her life that they act as an undertow for his. What he feels toward the idea of a child is only a dim glimmering alongside of what she feels, and yet, even that dim echo has a power that goes beyond anything familiar to him.

He suddenly wants to paint her as she is now, paint a series which would make visible the transformations that have been taking place in her. That expression: there is something about that expression. When he closes his eyes, he can see it before him as a sharp image. Though alongside of it, there is the other image which has never left him, which he cannot shake, of the child he carried on his back in the dream. The two images blend together, distorting each other, each making the other become grotesque. He doesn't know which one is right, or whether right and wrong even enters into it.

He remembers Franz's letter again, the letter written almost two months ago . . . "Your work has grown static." Static. Static. Static. Thirty-six. And then forty. And then forty-five and then fifty. And still static. Unless he can make something change. Marianna will be here in less than a week. Lola will perhaps have a baby in eight months. An image of blue paint, and of a child on his back. How exhausting it all is. And Lola makes it more exhausting, almost insists on it . . . not just exhaustion for its own sake, but for the sake of something larger. There is something about the way she moves through life that has become for him a part of the natural rhythm of things. Her emotions are all extreme, sequential and transforming. She lives through each stage with an absolute intensity, unable to compromise for the sake of some immediate comfort, some more palatable way of experiencing things. And she is transforming him along with herself.

Again he feels the sweep of terror and of love.

"I want to take some photographs of you," he says, "of the way you look now. So that I can paint from them later on."

"Why don't we go for a walk first?" she says. "I feel tired from all this thinking."

"That's fine with me," he says. "But let me take a few shots now, before your face changes."

"I'm sure it's changed already," she says, laughing.

He looks at her. She is right. Already, it is as if the feelings which only a moment ago were drawn full upon her face are receding back into her, being gathered in so that only their reflection will remain visible by the end of the day.

"That's all the more reason for me to take them now," he says.

"I'm all yours," she says quietly.

He picks up his camera and begins to photograph her. In the first frame she is grinning so widely that her eyes become narrow slits; her face is engulfed with laughter. In another, her face is sober but glowing, the smile vague, inward. In a third, she has covered her head with her arms, so that only her eyes are visible. In the fourth she is tying her sandals, getting ready for the walk.

It is the third one that stays with him, because of the seriousness and intensity of her eyes. The image is welded together in his imagination with the image from his dream, and the image of her expression as she talked about the baby. Locked together, they become part of his permanent store of thoughts, feelings, memories.

He closes his eyes, fusing the images together and separating them. Then he opens them and says, "Let's walk."

• • •

When they have climbed over the rocks to the meadow foot-path that leads along the cliff's edge, he says to her, "Tell me about the first man in your life."

"I don't know what to tell," she says. "It lasted much too long, it was painful and after many years I realized that it had never amounted to very much. I used to think that it had destroyed me."

"When was that?" he says.

"It started when I was sixteen. He was forty-seven when we met, married, with five children, a New York boy who grew up on the Lower East Side and wound up in Great Neck running a company that made junior lingerie. He was tough, vulgar and out-spoken. Once, in a restaurant on Allen Street, he cried when a woman sang 'Yiddishe Mama.' It was the only time I ever saw him express any deep emotion. He wisecracked constantly, told dirty jokes and said to me that I analyzed things too much, that I should quit it, because he couldn't understand what I was saying anyway. He said that one night when we were making love in his office."

"So you slept with him when you were sixteen?"

"Not exactly. He had a very precise, technical sense of what was appropriate: as far as he was concerned it was all right to do anything except interfere with my virginity. Sometimes he tried to romanticize it and said that he was protecting me for the right man. It was his rather distorted way of 'acting in my interests,' although . . ."

"Although what?"

"I just realized that I have never talked about this to any-one before. I can feel all of the old emotions rushing to the

185

surface again. It's hard to reconcile the person I was then with the person I am now.

"Will you tell me what happened?"

"We hadn't seen each other in months. I kept coming to New York and calling him the minute I arrived. He always said, 'Lola, make sure to call me as soon as you get here.' And I did. Then he would say that he was busy but that I should make sure to call the next time. 'Hey kitten, you won't forget about your old Marvin, will you?' That's what he would say. And that was all I needed. Instantly, I was under his power again. He once told me that everyone thought he slept around, but he didn't. What counted, he said, was affection. And I thought, well everyone else may believe that they know what he's like, but they don't. And I do. I know the truth. I thought that knowing the truth would help me to bring out the good side of him. I believed in the saving power of my own purity, that it would transform him. In fact, I didn't change him at all. And he practically ruined me. I thought that my vulnerability would triumph over his invulnerability. I was wrong. I suffered terribly, but I kept coming back for more. It sickens me to think about it. Do you mind if we sit in the meadow for a while?"

"That's fine," he says. There is a terrible tension in her face now, as if talking about this is wearing her out physically. She lies back in the sorrel and starts to cry. "I don't know why I'm so upset," she says. "It was almost ten years ago. I'll tell you about it in a few minutes. I promise I will."

He looks at her crying and thinks that somehow, though he does not know how, he will have to make things up to her. He wants to hold her but hesitates. Instead, he covers her eyes with his fingertips, like a protective blanket, and waits for her to speak.

Lying in the field, she remembers. She was eighteen. It was summertime and they were going to spend their first night together. She would stay with a friend in the city for a few days and would arrange to spend one night with him. It would be like a honeymoon trip. That was the way she tried to think of it, as a honeymoon trip. Though at the same time, without knowing why, she left half a dozen notes around her parents' house, intended for him, but carelessly forgotten in obvious places.

•

Her mother is and always has been scrupulous about not reading things that aren't intended for her. She says, "Lola, I'm sorry, I found this note you left on the kitchen table by mistake." And, "Lola, I found this piece of paper in the bathroom." And, "Lola, would you please try to keep your writings in your own room?"

Her mother knows, Lola thinks. She may even know who it is. But she can't bring herself to face the truth, can't bring herself to intervene.

At the train station, when Lola is leaving for the city, her father hugs her. There are tears in his eyes. She wants to cry too, but instead, she pulls away from him. "I love you," he says. "Please take care of yourself."

"Sure, Dad," she says. And runs away from him.

For safety's sake, she spends the first night at Jean's. Jean's parents are away, and no one will ever know. Lola's parents call in the evening. "We just wanted to make sure you were all right," her father says. "You know we worry about you, baby. You take so many chances. It's not that we don't trust you. It's just that we don't want you to be hurt."

"There's nothing to worry about," she says. "I don't know why you're making such a fuss. When are you going to realize that I'm old enough to take care of myself?"

"We're not making a fuss, angel," her mother says. "It's just that to me you'll always be my baby. Will you promise us one thing, that you won't do anything you'll be sorry for?"

"Don't be silly, Mom. Why would I do something I'd be sorry for?"

"We're glad to hear that," her father says.

"We kiss you and love you," her mother says.

The day she and Marvin are supposed to go to the Magic Mountain Motel together, Lola gets her period. She calls him and says, "Marvin, there's something I have to tell you."

He says, "I have a customer with me. I'll call you back."

"But I have my period," she blurts out. "What are we going to do?"

"Do?" he says. "Listen, let me call you back."

"Marvin, I just want to know . . . I mean . . . do you still want to go?"

"Yes, of course," he says. "What difference does it make?"

She has brought only one dress with her to Jean's house. It is white. She wanted to wear a white dress, like a celebration, like a wedding. She puts Chanel Number 5 between her legs. It burns and smells strange. She is afraid of bleeding through. She puts in two Tampax for safety.

He picks her up in his car. They drive out on the highway toward the edge of the city, past the playgrounds of Harlem and the water hydrants turned on full, kids bicycling along the walkways of the river, someone with a fishing pole leaning out over the water catching eels. Neither of them says anything. Lola wonders if he's nervous too. He turns on the car radio.

> There's a bridal suite
> One room nice and neat
> Complete for us to share
> Together.

"Small Hotel," she thinks. From *Pal Joey*. She has the record at home. With Rita Hayworth singing the strip song,

Zip . . . I was reading Schopenhauer last night
Zip . . . and I think that Schopenhauer was right.
Sigmund Freud has often stated
Dreams and drives are all related,
Zip . . . I'm a firm believer
Dorothy Dix' daily column
Tells that love is dear and solemn
Zip . . . I can take or leave her . . .

And then there was "Joey the Heel" and "Bewitched" and "Lady
Is a Tramp." What a great show.

She thinks about the white dress and hopes that she won't
bleed through, then says, "Marvin, did you have a good day at
work?"

"No," he says.

"Oh, so that's why you're in a bad mood."

"I'm not in a bad mood. Just a little edgy. There's nothing
wrong with being edgy."

"I don't mind if you're edgy," she says. "I love you."

"I know," he says.

The sun has set. The car is sealed in darkness. She thinks
about what they will have for dinner, about the waiter's being
charmed by them, about the room. She wonders if Marvin has
brought flowers and is saving them for the room. Then she thinks
about her mother.

"Marvin, there's something else I have to tell you."

"What?" he says.

"I think my mother knows about us."

"Knows what?" he says. "What the hell is there to know?"

Something contracts inside of her. She doesn't know exactly
what it is, only that it has something to do with sensing all of a
sudden what another person is really like, and not being able to
bear what you see, but seeing it anyway.

189

"I don't know what she knows. She just knows. You know how mothers are. They know everything." She is trying to sound mature, like his equal, but she is feeling frightened.

"I think we should go back to the city, Lola," he says. "And that you should go home like a good little girl."

"Marvin, please," she says. "Don't be upset. I can convince her it isn't true. You know I can."

"I thought you said she knows."

"Not knows, Marvin. Just *thinks* she knows." She has a sudden recollection of her father's driving up to visit her in camp one day driving an old, well-preserved Lincoln Continental and of her being so proud of the impression he made on everyone, even though they were broke that year, and of his saying, "Things will be better now. Just you wait and see. Things will be better."

She looks out the window. There are black trees along the edge of the highway, and trucks passing them. There are a few lights near the road where families live, families having supper maybe or getting ready for bed or watching TV.

"Marvin," she says, grabbing his arm. "We just passed it. We passed the exit."

"I know," he says. "I changed my mind. I don't want to go there. I want to keep driving for a while. I want to think."

"I'll take care of everything," Lola says. "I told you I'll take care of everything." She is even more frightened now than before. She's afraid that he's going to leave her, that he will never want to see her again. Maybe he'll just keep driving around all night. Maybe . . .

She reaches out her hand, takes a deep breath and puts her hand on the zipper of his fly. She has never done anything like that before, and it makes her queasy.

He laughs and says, "I have to admit, for a kid your age, you're quite something."

He unzips his fly, holding the steering wheel with one hand. She doesn't know what to do next. He takes her hand in his and puts it inside of his trousers. She feels the damp warm flesh, the cold edge of the zipper and the sheer overwhelming size of him. She thinks that maybe she is going to vomit.

"Here's a motel," he says. "We can stop here."

It is a Howard Johnson's motel, just like the ones all over the country, just like the one where she stayed last month with her parents.

"We can't stay here," she says. "We just can't."

"What's wrong with it?"

"Nothing . . . I . . . Please, Marvin, we just can't." All she can think about is her parents and his children and his wife. Doesn't he know anything about Howard Johnson's motels? They're for families, Marvin, for fried chicken and double-dip ice cream and Coke and Ho-Jo's.

"It's ten o'clock already, baby," he says. "And there isn't another motel for at least thirty miles. I have to work tomorrow. I can't spend the whole night looking for the perfect atmosphere."

Already he has driven off the exit ramp and into the parking lot. They are surrounded by cars and bright, friendly, impersonal lights.

"Come on, Lola," he says. "We can get something to eat and then go to bed. That was what you wanted, wasn't it, to go to bed?"

She flinches and says, putting all of the energy of desperation and love into the words, "I won't. We can go back to the Magic Mountain Motel. We can go anywhere. But I won't stay here."

"You're being hysterical," he says. "You're being hysterical over nothing."

"It's not nothing," she says.

"It is," he says. "But I'm not going to sit out here in the car discussing it with you. I'm going to check in, so that we can *enjoy the evening.*"

"All right," she says, feeling suddenly exhausted, feeling the blood flowing inside of her again. If only she could stop making him feel guilty, she thinks, then he would stop trying to hurt her. But she doesn't know how to stop making him feel guilty. "We can stay here if you want. I don't care."

When he comes back, he says, "All taken care of. We can just move right in."

She doesn't know why she feels this need to keep on saying things, the wrong things, the things that make him feel bad, but she does it again now. "How did you sign the register?" she asks. "Did you put Mr. and Mrs.?"

"Mr. and Mrs.! Don't be childish, Lola. I put my brother's name. And guest."

"Why didn't you use your own name?" she asks.

"Because I never do."

"Never?"

"Lola, please cut it out. I don't want to discuss this. It's a very simple thing, and there's no reason to start attaching all this significance to a simple thing."

She feels as if her insides are caught in a paper shredder, spinning her around, tearing her to bits. She can't move. She can't go in. She just can't. But she wants to. She wants to get this over with, wants to . . .

There are no personal details in the room, just a double bed and a nightstand on each side and a fiberglass chair and a TV. He walks straight to the bed and turns down the bedspread.

"Now you see," he says. "It isn't as bad as you thought. There's a shower right in there." He puts his arms around her and holds her. She keeps wanting to cry but keeps wanting also not to be hysterical, so she just stays where she is while he rubs her back and shoulders, rubs and keeps rubbing until all of the fighting muscles in her have softened and she stops caring about anything at all except the fact that he is holding her, and if she can only stay calm, everything will be fine, everything will be fine, everything will be fine.

"Do you want to wash up?" he says. She nods, remembering again that she has her period. In the bathroom, there is a baby blue bathtub and a baby blue shower curtain and baby blue soap and baby blue hexagonal tiles on the floor.

She takes down her underpants to see if she has bled through. She has. There is a small red stain on the back of the white dress, like a tiny danger flag in a field of snow. If she washes the dress, they won't be able to go downstairs to eat. If she doesn't wash it, she'll have to go downstairs with a stain on her dress. She sits on the toilet and puts her head in her hands. She wishes that she were at home in her own bed, wishes that the whole place would disappear and Marvin along with it. Everything is spinning around inside of her. She can't think straight anymore. We're just going to bed. Just going to bed. No flowers. No honeymoon. No anything. Not even brownies. She starts to sob. When she has finished sobbing, she washes out her underpants and washes out the stain in the dress. She comes out of the bathroom naked with a small towel wrapped around her, tucked in at the side.

"There's blood on my dress," she says. "We can't go downstairs for dinner."

"Then we'll just have to stay here for a while I guess," he says.

She sits down next to him on the bed, holding on to the top edge of the towel.

"You know, Lola," he says, "that's what I like about you. You're shy and sweet. Not like the tough broads you see around, the ones that just want to get into bed. No feelings, nothing. I like a woman who has feelings."

He kisses her fingers and tugs the towel away. It falls around her hips. Instinctively, she covers herself with her hand, even though she has just put in a new Tampax.

"You're worried about your period?" he whispers.

"Yes," she says. "I'm sorry, Marvin, I really am. I wish . . ."

"You don't have to be sorry, sweets. Just relax. Take it easy and enjoy yourself. You know old Marvin wouldn't hurt you. Don't you know that?"

"Sure, Marvin. Sure I know it."

"Okay," he says. "Why don't you just climb under the covers so you don't catch cold? We wouldn't want you to catch cold, would we?"

"No," she says. "I guess we wouldn't."

She crawls under the covers and waits while he goes into the bathroom. She hears the toilet flush and the lights being switched off. Marvin walks into the room. He still has his underpants on, the kind that hold tight to his body and curve up along the line of his thighs. They look strange now, with his penis standing up inside of them, pushing out the material like a tent. He comes over to the bed, climbs in next to her, pulls the covers around both of them and shuts off the light. He rubs his face against hers. He hasn't shaved since the morning, and his beard grates against her until the skin around her mouth and chin are sore. He begins to touch her, here, there, moving from one place to another until she almost can't tell anymore where, just feels as if her whole body is aching with wanting, wanting for him to do it finally, just do it, please do it. Then slowly, she feels his hand pushing against her head, pushing it down down under the covers. It is a long time before she realizes what is happening, realizes what he is doing, and then suddenly her face is right up against it, and he is telling her to . . . he is telling her to . . . he is telling her to . . .

Her mind goes blank. She remembers nothing. Except the terrible bitter taste in her mouth, and the stuff all over her face and his mouth on her, and the feeling that she is going to smother under the covers, and that she is going to die, just die of shame.

"Did you like it?" he says, when it is finished.

She can't answer.

"Come on, baby," he says. "Tell me you liked it. You see I told you it didn't matter about your period. Didn't I tell you?"

194

He lights a match and looks at her face. "You're upset," he says. "Now what's there to be upset about? There's nothing wrong with doing that. Don't you know there's nothing wrong?"

She tries to nod and can't. "Have a cigarette," he says. "It will make you feel better."

She shakes her head no. "I have to go to the bathroom," she says and climbs out of bed. In the bathroom, she washes out her mouth and gargles. She avoids looking at herself in the mirror. She wants to take a bath but decides against it. Suddenly she knows that she is going to throw up. She walks over to the toilet, and retches. But there is nothing inside of her stomach. Then she sits on the edge of the bathtub, rocking herself like a baby and singing to herself, singing the song her mother used to sing and saying to herself, over and over again, "It's all right. It's all right. Nothing wrong with it. Nothing wrong with it."

When she comes back into the room, he is already asleep. She climbs in next to him and curls up against the bulk of him. He doesn't move, doesn't reach out for her, doesn't even seem to know that she's there. After a long time, she falls asleep.

During the night, she wakes up with her back to him, curled into the hollow of his body. His arms are circling her waist. She lies there thinking, I love you. No matter what, even so, I love you, thinking simultaneously, leave me alone, don't touch me, don't touch me, don't touch me. He stirs in his sleep, but then suddenly he's not in his sleep anymore, and there is a strange pressure against the back of her, and she is in a panic thinking, but Marvin, this is a mistake, you're making a mistake, and the pressure is still against her and then hard inside of her and he is silent the whole time until she screams. Then he stops and she is crying, crying, crying and saying, "Oh God, why did you do that? Why did you do that?" until finally he gets up out of bed and says, "Lola, would you cut it out? Would you please cut it out?" But she can't cut it out, and she is breathing in and out so fast and hard that she thinks she is going to faint, screaming and screaming and screaming until finally he slaps her hard. And there is nothing anymore. Nothing. Nothing at all.

In the morning he doesn't look at her. When she looks at him, she sees his face covered with stubble; there is a bald spot in the middle of his head where his hair is usually combed over, and the rest of his hair flies around his head in thin wisps.

They walk out of the room together, leaving blood on the sheets. There is bright sunlight outside. There are children playing in front of one of the doors. She can't bear to look at them. She thinks . . . the children, the children, the children. And wants to cover up her face so that they won't have to see her, won't ever have to know.

They ride back through the morning rush hour traffic. In every car, there is a man in a business suit, alone. He drops her off at Grand Central. She is going back home. "I don't want to be late to work," he says. "I have a lot to do. But give me a call the next time you come into the city, and we'll do something nice. Okay, sweets?"

She doesn't answer.

During the ride home, she thinks, the only thing that counts is doing it for love. It doesn't matter so long as you do it for love. She writes a poem called "The Tree of Life," in a style sort of like Emily Dickinson. It is romantic and philosophical. She cries while she is writing it, and thinks again, it wasn't so bad. Really it wasn't so bad.

•

"It actually happened that way?" Stefan says.

"Yes."

"What an awful beginning."

"I used to think that I would never be clean again, never be good enough for anyone. I thought it was all my fault, because I had allowed it to happen. I could have prevented it. I didn't have to be with him, then or ever. And if I was, it was because something was wrong with me, because deep down I was just like him, no better, no better at all."

"But you were young, Lola. There was nothing unusual about your getting involved with him. The only thing that's out of the ordinary is his getting involved with you."

"I tried thinking of it that way, but I couldn't. There had been other things when I was younger . . ."

"What?"

"Haven't you had enough for one day?"

"No."

"Well, I have. I'm exhausted. I'll tell you another time. Besides, there isn't much to say. It has to do with hexagons, with a nightmare about hexagons, and someone doing something when I was small. But I don't remember what. And maybe I never will. There are hexagons everywhere and . . ." She stops speaking suddenly; her face pales. "Even at the Howard Johnson's motel," she says in a whisper. "But that wasn't it . . . that wasn't . . . I don't think . . . there was something else too, another time, I . . . " She stops again in confusion.

"I don't remember," she says firmly as if willing herself not to remember. "But I didn't make it up."

"Why didn't you ever tell me about any of that before? I would have understood," Stefan says.

"I don't think I wanted to be understood," she says. "I wanted to be loved."

"So you took your chances and hoped I would stick with you?"

"I took my chances and hoped you would stick with me."

He kisses her. "Do you want to start walking back?" he says.

"Yes."

They stop along the way for a cup of Greek coffee. They are the only ones in the cafe. They drink the coffee outside, under the shadow of a grape arbor. They scarcely talk during the meal. Two children are chasing chickens in the back. Afterward, she photographs him along the route to town. In profile, with a cigarette in his hand and a sweater draped over his shoulders. Then, full face with an intent, serious, almost worried expression on his face. Then smiling. There is no one to photograph them together. What they are left with are photographs of each other, completely separate, smiling at each other across the barrier of a frame of film.

*I*T IS a very quiet, almost unobtrusive coup, as coups often are for those who are cut off from the center of communications and can see only as far as their eyes permit: to the nearest corner, the nearest face, the nearest table. The university radio station is the first thing the colonels aim for; the students are on Easter vacation; Mikis Theodorakis is interrupted mid-phrase. In the morning, the world is one way; in the afternoon, it is another.

When Lola and Stefan come back into town, they find it strangely quiet. A crudely lettered cardboard CLOSED sign dangles from the handle of the post office door. All the shops are closed, but the metal gates that the shopkeepers slide down like garage doors at the end of the day have been left open and unlocked. Crates of food are still out on the street. A crate of oranges has been tipped over and the oranges have rolled into the path like miniature bowling balls flung down an alley by a small child in a fit of random energy. No one is there to collect them. The streets are completely empty.

Lola goes into the cafe to give Christos the baby chicks. The cafe is deserted except for Thalassa.

"Where is everyone?" Lola says.

"*Politiki*," Thalassa says. She shrugs and lifts her hands, palms up, in the air. "*Communisti. Kako. Militario.*" Then she makes rapid rat-a-tat-tat noises, aiming an imaginary machine gun around the room. "*Poli kako*," she says. "*Parapoli kako.*" She shakes her index finger, and makes a sound as if she is trying to shoo away squawking chickens.

Lola runs back to the house. "Turn on the radio," she says. "Something has happened with the government. All Thalassa can say is that it has to do with the Communists and the military, and that it's something bad."

Stefan turns on the small transistor radio which he has brought with him from Austria. At first he gets nothing but static. And then finally a station playing military music.

Lola sits with her eyes fixed on the radio, rubbing the center of her open palm back and forth against her mouth. "And we were on a picnic," she says. "A picnic! Spending the whole day making love. We should go back to Athens right away."

"There isn't a boat until Thursday, Lola. Today is Friday."

"Then we should at least call Hans. He's at the King George in Athens."

"The only phone is at the post office and the post office is closed."

"Well, we can't just sit here and accept this."

"That's exactly what we'll have to do."

"While there's a revolution going on, we're just going to sit here?"

"First of all, you don't know if it's a revolution, and second of all, yes."

"But I want to know what's happening. I want to do something."

"You'll find out when everyone else finds out, Lola. There's nothing you can do. You're learning what it's like to be in the middle of something and not know anything about it."

"Spare me the bourgeois wisdom, Stefan."

"I'm just stating a fact."

"I understand. Please keep trying the radio."

It is almost midnight when the radio finally yields up an English language broadcast, transmitted via Belgrade: "There is a news blackout in Athens today. Sources say that a military coup has taken place. Leaders of the coup have not yet been identified. The capitol is ringed by tanks."

They remove the orange-and-maroon bedspread after that and lie silently for a long time holding hands. She is thinking of her mother, of the letter suspended now somewhere over the Atlantic, of Marvin, of the baby which either does or does not exist, of the regime which either will or will not succeed in taking over all of Greece, of her father and the sepia photograph of his family on top of his dresser. He is thinking of the elections which were scheduled to take place next week, of what it is like to be in the middle of something and not know anything about it, of the photographs he took of Lola, of Marianna and the phone call which has not yet been made, the arrangements which have not yet been made.

All communications have been severed.

They lie in bed and wait.

•

In the morning, there are planes flying overhead. It seems as if the island is being bombed. The children run through the streets while the white rain falls from the sky, a white rain of leaflets drifting out over the Mediterranean, over the volcano, showering the churches like wedding rice, catching in the crevices of buildings, landing on crates of vegetables, in the center of vineyards, in the middle of fishing nets, grazing the edge of the chairs set out in front of the cafes.

The leaflets say: "For motherhood, for Greece, for patriotism, for the love of our country." The leaflets say (even though they do not say), . . . you see, we have an eye on you, on everything and everyone. There is no place to hide.

People appear in the streets, strangers wearing combat fatigues and military uniforms. Later in the day, more people appear. They are not strangers, but they are also wearing uniforms: Ioannis with his lame leg, Andreas with his mules, Michaelis the mason. Suddenly they are soldiers patrolling the island, carrying bayonets in their arms, their faces frozen into blandness.

Lola walks out of the house and up to the road. For half an hour she stands there glaring at the soldiers, wanting to find someone to blame, someone to call the enemy. But these soldiers are not the enemy. They are her neighbors. She wants to stop them and speak to them. But what could she say? And to whom could she talk? To Thalassa? To Ioannis? To Andreas? They are as helpless as she is. It has not ever before occurred to them that they could be anything but helpless, and it will not occur to them now. They have always been helpless. In order not to be helpless, they would have to coordinate their minds as if their single wish could be one wish, would have to articulate beliefs, expectations desires which all these years they have been trained out of having. They would have to reverse patterns of life so deeply ingrained that they have become automatic: they would have to first acknowledge and then rebel against the fact of their own poverty. They would have to fight, in some fashion that was unknown to them, the fact of their own ignorance. It is their destiny to get up at the first sign of light and slap cement onto the walls of houses that foreigners live in. It is their destiny to assemble their mules and drive up and down the steps for thirty drachmas. The coming of the regime is an act of God.

The man who runs the hotel in town passes by. He is not wearing a uniform. She stops him. "What do you think of all this?" she says. "Isn't it awful?"

He shrugs. "All governments are the same," he says.

She goes back into the house. "I can't stand it," she says. "I can't stand this passive acceptance. I can't stand doing nothing."

"There's one thing you have to understand, Lola. This isn't a toy takeover. The bayonets aren't toy bayonets. And the soldiers are here for a reason. You don't walk up to bayonets and start carrying on conversations with them. Even if the person who's holding one was your neighbor yesterday, he's a soldier today. And he has to do what he's told."

"Stefan," she yells, "I am not a German. I am not a good soldier. I don't believe in doing what you're told. 'Following orders.' They're just 'following orders.' My father's family was massacred by people who believed in following orders."

"Lola," he says very quietly. "Not everyone who tries to survive a dictatorship is a Nazi. Fighting back isn't always so simple and clearcut."

"It is," she says. "All you have to do is say, 'No, I won't cooperate.' "

"You've never lived through a war, Lola. Or a revolution. Or a takeover. You don't know a damn thing about raw power."

"You don't have to live through a war to know that you would resist."

"I'm afraid you do," he says. "You can protest or argue or demonstrate all you want in a democracy. It may not change anything, but at least you can stand up for what you believe in without risking your life. It's a different thing when there's a gun pointed at your head, or when you're supposed to be a soldier. Of all the Americans who have protested against the war in Vietnam, there has not been one who has had to die for his disagreement. It's easy to be heroic when you're running very few risks and when the government pampers you the way it pampers students. It's not so easy when your life is at stake."

"It may not be easy, Stefan, but people do it. There have always been resistances. It's just a matter of finding the people who are resisting. If I had lived in the Warsaw Ghetto . . ."

"If you had lived in the Warsaw Ghetto, Lola, you would have had nothing to lose. Either way you were going to die. And it was better to die fighting than to die like a sheep. In any other situation, where you might have been given a choice of living or dying, fighting or surviving, you have no idea what you would have done. I do not think that this is the moment in which to test your capacity for romantic heroism. If there's a resistance, you can be sure it's an organized one. And they don't need impulsive foreigners who don't know how to keep their mouths shut. If you really care about what happens to the people on this island, the best thing you can do is try not to jeopardize them. Whether you believe or don't believe in following orders, for the time being, at least, you are going to follow orders just like everyone else. Because there's nothing else that you can do."

She bursts into tears and rushes out the door, slamming it behind her. He follows her and catches her on the terrace. He seizes her shoulders, begins to shake her and then stops in mid-gesture. "You have to stop this," he says in the same even voice that he has used all along. "I'm telling you, you have to stop it."

She is sobbing. "I can't," she says. "Don't you see that I can't?"

"Yes, you can," he says softly. And takes her back into the house where she sits on the floor for a long time with her head in her hands, crying.

He sits on the bed watching her and remembering: the mountains, the soldiers, the digging of trenches. He feels suddenly very old and very alone, washed by a kind of diffuse pity for all the thwarted urgencies of life. It is not easy to act, he thinks. It is never easy. And yet . . . over and over again, there are memories which come back to haunt you. Over and over again, memories.

•

In the afternoon they go out for a walk. When they come back to the house, it is in a shambles: the bed turned upside down, the covers stripped off, Lola's suitcases emptied out, her clothes strewn all over the terrace. Stefan's palette box has been emptied out and his canvases knocked over. A crushed tube of vermilion lies on the floor, with the color squirting out around it, and vermilion footprints leading from the tube to the bed. Pages have been torn out of Lola's journal. Nothing has been taken except Lola's books: *Doctor Zhivago, The Origin of the Family, The Gambler, The Stranger,* and a book on the Spanish Civil War.

Lola's face is pale. "I want to leave," she says. "If there's nothing I can do, I want to leave. Will you come with me?"

"You can't flap your wings and fly away, Lola. I told you already. You have to wait for next week's boat."

"And if I wait for a boat, will you come with me?"

"I don't know. I have to talk with Marianna first."

"What does Marianna have to do with it?"

"She's supposed to meet me here next week."

"She won't come after what's happened."

"Probably, but that's for her to decide."

"Why does your decision have to depend on hers?"

"Because she is still my wife. And because I promised that we would meet. I have to stick to that promise. I can't just vanish. It's not my way of doing things. I know waiting isn't easy, Lola, but real life is filled with it. As soon as the phones are put back in service, I'll call her. But I promise that I'll stay with you here on the island or somewhere else until Marianna comes or I go to meet her. Is that good enough?"

"And after that?"

"After that I'll come to New York in the fall and start arranging a divorce."

"We're just getting used to each other, though. I don't want to leave now."

"There will be plenty of time for us to get used to each other. If it's worthwhile, it will still be worthwhile three months from now."

"What do you mean 'if'?"

"All I mean is that I don't think three months will make any difference."

"What if I'm pregnant?"

"We'll worry about that if you are."

"What if . . ." her voice trails off.

"What if what?"

"I don't know. Just what if everything changes between now and then? The government has changed. It could change again. Your feelings could change. My feelings could change. I could turn out not to be pregnant. You could change your mind about wanting to marry me, or even about getting a divorce."

"It's true that the government could change and you could turn out not to be pregnant, but I'm not that capricious."

"I know, but I can't help being afraid anyway. I'll go back to America and wait for you. That's what I'm afraid of: waiting for you."

"You don't have to wait. I'll just come."

"Yes, I do have to wait. You said it yourself: for the boat on Thursday, for the government to change, for the divorce to take place, for the baby to decide whether or not it wants to be born. For everything. It's hard being obliged to wait, and obliged in the meantime to live with so much uncertainty."

"I know it is, Lola. But I'm living with it too. I'm taking exactly the same risk."

"I know."

Later in the evening, walking up to the cafe, she passes the postman. He pauses in the road, seems to be making up his mind whether or not to stop, takes two steps forward and one step back, wipes his palms on his trouser legs and then propels himself forward with his arms swinging, as if determined to maintain the momentum of his decision to keep on walking. After going twenty paces, he abruptly turns back and runs toward her.

"*Kali spera*," he says.

"*Kali spera*," she says. He clears his throat, then clears it again. A small choking sound rises up out of his chest and is caught before it completely escapes. His eyes are feverish.

"What is the matter?" Lola says. "Are you all right?"

He looks at her mutely. Tears begin to fill his eyes. They roll down his cheeks. He does not wipe them away. And still he is silent.

Finally he clears his throat once more, seems almost to strangle and whispers, *"Democratia!"* He looks at her anxiously, as if he has staked himself on a game of Russian roulette after five of the chambers have been emptied.

Lola reaches for his hand, presses it and says softly, *"Democratia."*

He shakes his head up and down slowly several times. Then he turns and walks away.

When Lola comes back to the house, she says, "I think maybe there are reasons to stay." For the second time today, there are tears in her eyes.

*T*HE GOVERNMENT DOES NOT change. On Monday the newspapers appear with blank white spaces all over the front page and paternal photographs of the colonels who have saved Greece from a Communist takeover. The post office is open again, people sit in the cafes again, the stores are open again. Everything is as usual. Except no one says a word about politics. Ioannis and Andreas and Michaelis say that it is tiring to be a soldier patrolling the village all night and then getting up at five in the morning to start driving mules, installing sinks and plastering walls. Andreas does not come to the house for grappa. He says, "One must make sacrifices for the good of the country."

There is a swarm of people in the post office, all of them waiting to use a single telephone. The foreigners, particularly the Americans, stand out from the crowd like birds of paradise among a flock of crows. The two women anthropologists are there; the Australian is there, anxiously muttering to himself and looking balefully at the women in black who have come by mule from the villages, as their bodies surge and sway against his and their voices escalate in a high-pitched chorus. The honeymoon couple is there. Lola hears him say to her, "Please, sweetie, this isn't the end of our honeymoon. We'll just go somewhere else that's all. Believe me, it isn't the end."

The postman lowers his eyes when he sees Lola. People keep shouting across the room. The women in black recede from the crowd and sit quietly, almost invisibly, on the benches around the edge of the room, pretending to a patience so habitual it would appear to be natural, except for the extraordinary rapidity with which it can be replaced by a violent impatience mobilized quickly, anonymously, en masse.

For six hours they sit waiting. Finally, a free line to America opens up. The postman signals to Lola that her call is ready. Three minutes is the limit that anyone is allowed. Lola stands in the phone booth, conscious of an invisible presence on the line: the occasional, scarcely perceptible sound of someone breathing.

"We were worried sick," her mother says. "How are you? Are you safe?"

"I'm fine," Lola says. "Things are very quiet here. You would never know that the country had just been taken over by fascists."

"What?" her mother says. "I couldn't hear the end of what you said."

"I said that I can't stand the fascists," Lola says.

"I'm sorry dear. There must be something wrong with our connection."

Stefan watches Lola from the bench at the far end of the post office. With one hand she holds the handle of the phone booth's folding door, folding and unfolding it, so that fragments of sentences wildly disparate in tone drift through the opening and closing space, at one moment filled with a taut, guarded restraint, then veering off to a staccato of annoyance which winds rapidly back down again to an apparently resigned quietude and stays there while her face gradually assumes the expression of a wild animal trapped finally in the forest after a long chase in which it has been forced to muster, one by one, all of its accumulated instincts for survival. She looks out of the booth once, seeming to search for some reference point against which to measure herself, but the moment her eye catches his, she turns away, slams the door shut and presses her forehead against the back wall of the phone booth, cradling the receiver with her entire body as if to shield it from the impact of anything external.

"This German man . . . ," her mother says.

"Stefan," Lola says. "He's Austrian."

"Well, this man . . . please, dear, you have to be sensible. We wrote to you before all of these things happened with the government and . . ."

"He's getting a divorce, Mother. Stefan is getting a divorce."

"Please, dear. Don't be naive. Let's not discuss . . . Just try not to be too upset when you get the letter. You know how your father is . . ."

"What was in the letter, Mother? What did he say?"

"Nothing, dear. You'll see when . . . just don't be upset. Promise me you won't be upset. Because we love you and care about you, and . . ."

"Mom, for God's sake, would you just *tell* me what he said?"

"I can't, Lola. It's very hard on the telephone. You have to be realistic, Lola. This is very difficult for him."

"I know it's difficult," she says. "But . . ."

"Just promise me you won't get upset. Will you promise me that?"

Lola doesn't answer right away. Then she says faintly, "All right, I won't be upset. I just want you to know that he's a very good man. Please try to understand . . . he was just a child . . . and his wife . . ."

"Lola, sweetheart, of course I understand. Things will take care of themselves when you come home. You'll forget all about it. For now I'm just concerned about your safety. Your safety, sweetheart, that's the only thing that counts. Just don't be impulsive and don't get involved with the wrong people. I want you to promise me you'll be careful not to get into trouble."

"Who are the wrong people?"

"You know what I mean, Lola, the people who are always getting into trouble."

"*Mother.*"

"You sound upset sweetheart. Don't be upset."

"I'm not upset." The postman is signaling that her three minutes are up. "I have to hang up," she says.

"All right, dear. Please, sweetheart. Please keep in touch. And please be careful. And don't let anything upset you. Promise?"

"Yes, Mother, I promise."

"Goodbye, darling. I love you. And your father loves you, too."

"Goodbye, Mother."

Lola walks out of the phone booth slowly, like someone sleepwalking, or like a prizefighter after a second round knock-down struggling to regain his equilibrium and still preserve enough strength for the remaining thirteen rounds.

She sits on the bench next to Stefan, staring straight ahead of her and not speaking. The force of her entire body tends downward, as if only the intervention of the horizontal line of the bench prevents her from collapsing altogether. Her hands are absolutely still, her face immobile.

"What's the matter?" Stefan says. "What did she say?"

Lola doesn't answer. Her eyes seem to be fixed on some object inside of her mind from which she cannot separate herself.

"Come on, Lola. Talk about it. Tell me what she said. You'll feel better afterward."

She shakes her head back and forth very slowly, moving it only an inch or two in either direction. Still she is silent.

"All right," he says, taking her hand. It rests limply in his. She continues to stare straight ahead of her without speaking.

He watches the hands of the clock across the room as they inch downward toward the half hour and then upward again toward the hour. Although she seems not to be looking at the clock, there is a perceptible shift in her body when the hand passes the half-hour mark, as if the cadence of time bore a direct relation to the rhythms of her mind. Her face and hands remain immobile, but her body begins to gather itself together. When the clock passes the hour and begins to descend again, she says in a whisper, "She didn't understand. She didn't understand at all."

"Didn't understand what?"

"Anything. About you. About the government. Nothing. She thought I should leave the country right away and stay out of trouble. She thought I would get over this whole 'romance' when I came back to America, that I would forget it the instant we were separated. She didn't believe that you were going to get a divorce. She thought it was one of those things that 'men always say.' "

"In three minutes long distance over the phone you expected her to understand all that?"

"Yes."

"You shouldn't have."

"Except that in the same three minutes over the phone, she managed to make me doubt myself. And doubt you. Just when I was beginning to feel sure, she made me doubt."

"If you were really sure, I don't think she could have made you doubt."

"But she did."

"Then you weren't sure."

"How could I not be sure?"

"I don't know."

"I'm sorry, Stefan. I'm sorry I mentioned it. I'm not being fair to you. Please, let's forget it. I love you. I really do."

"There's no need to convince yourself."

"I'm not."

"Well, time will tell."

"That's what frightens me. Time can destroy anything. You don't know my mother, Stefan. Even when she's wrong, her opinions still have a power over me. I begin to see the world through her eyes instead of my own. If she doesn't trust people, that doesn't mean people aren't trustworthy. And yet, I have to fight against surrendering to her vision of the world. When I was a child I had to fight against it, and I still have to fight against it. It's like getting stuck in a blackberry patch and having to spend hours disentangling myself, hours picking out the thorns. I understand that she's had a difficult life, that her life has made her into what she is, just as mine has made me into what I am. But sometimes I get so tired of having to sever the umbilical cord, not once but hundreds of times, over and over and over again."

"So why do you try to tell her things?"

"Because I still care about having her approval. Ever since Marvin, I wasn't sure about having my own. I started to believe that I wasn't better than she thought; I was worse. And now, no matter how much I separate myself from my parents, no matter how much I change, I still keep wanting their approval, still feel the urge to make them accept me on my own terms. I don't like lying in order to make life easier. I lied over Marvin. I don't know what would have happened if I didn't lie. But I can't anymore. I won't.

"You know what I would love to do: I would love to present you to my family in the high old way. I would love to sit down over coffee with my mother and tell her about you. I would love for you and my father to go into the library together and 'discuss the future.' I would love to feel that there was a clean line of certainty, approval and security in my life. But there isn't. You aren't a nice Jewish boy who wants to marry me. You're a nice German boy who's married. Besides, my family never had a library.

"On the surface, I've come a long way from my mother: I've been living on my own for years, paying my way, posturing at independence, having love affairs . . . not so many as I let people assume, but certainly more than my mother ever had. Yet underneath I still share my mother's values, still have her needs. I'm living in the middle of the twentieth century, when people are supposed to pop in and out of love affairs as if it were nothing. But basically, I still feel like a Victorian. Though maybe that's

213

the point about the twentieth century; we're all a part of it, but no one belongs to it.

"She said that my father wrote me a letter. But she wouldn't tell me what was in it. She just kept saying not to be upset. 'Don't be upset, sweetheart.' That's what she repeated, over and over again, that I should promise not to be upset."

She is silent again, looking down at her hands, opening and closing them. "I have four long fingernails, now," she says. "My father used to tell me that it was important for a woman to have beautiful hands, that it made a big difference to a man. I've never had beautiful hands. But now, when I look at those four long fingernails, I'm proud. Though I can't help thinking, 'what about the other six?'

"I'm tired, Stefan. I'm so tired. And so scared. I want to go home. Please, let's go home."

"I know you're tired," he says. "I am too. But we can't go home. I haven't talked to Marianna yet."

"Sometimes I wish things could be simple," she says.

He smiles and looks sad. But he doesn't answer.

•

It is another hour before Stefan's call clears. By then the post office is almost empty; the two women anthropologists are gone, and so is the Australian. Only the honeymoon couple remains, she half-asleep with her head on his shoulder, he with his back stiffened artificially into a posture of manly strength denied by the anxious, tenderly adolescent expression on his face. Occasionally, he mouths words to himself in the widening silence, shakes his head and subsides back into quiet.

The postman signals Stefan to go into the booth. Lola watches him from the bench. He scarcely moves during the entire conversation, except to open the door once and stamp out his cigarette. His hand with its long fingers and squared nails rests on

214

the telephone counter. A vertical line in his forehead that starts at the inner edge of his eyebrow deepens and remains deepened. He is looking out of the booth in Lola's direction, but does not seem to see her. He bends his head to light a second cigarette, and leaves the door slightly ajar. After he has taken four puffs, he stamps the cigarette out again and lights another.

The postman motions that his time is up. He talks for another few seconds and hangs up but stays in the booth for several minutes, finishing up his third cigarette, with the door closed this time, and the smoke filling up the space around him like a cloud cushioning him against the impact of his return to Lola.

"Sometimes I agree with you," he says, when he comes out of the booth. His voice has a deliberate and artificial lightness.

"About what?" she says.

"Wishing that life could be simple."

"What did she say?"

"That she's coming here. She already has her train ticket to Athens. The train leaves from there tomorrow night and arrives in Athens in time for her to take Thursday's boat. She was going to cable from Athens if she didn't hear from me by tomorrow."

"Here! She wants to come here! On Thursday. That's crazy."

"Well, not exactly here. She's getting off at Eleuthera. And I'm supposed to take the same boat when it leaves from here on Friday morning on its way back to Athens. She wants me to meet her in Eleuthera."

"And you agreed to that? Stefan, that's three days from now. And that's the boat we were planning to leave on."

"I know."

"I don't understand why she wants to do that. Why torture herself? And why should you go along with it?"

"She imagines that I'm in love with you because we're on an island and life here is simple, romantic and idyllic. That's what she said. She thinks that if *we* spend two weeks on an island, things will be restored between us, and I'll realize that this 'fling'

I'm having has more to do with being on an island than it has to do with you personally. She forgets that our marriage was over before I met you. She even brought in 'Death in Venice' as an example of the 'sensual delirium' caused by excursions into presumably temperamental climates. You're supposed to be Tadzio, and I'm Aschenbach, suffering from a decadent tropical fever. Then she said that I had never taken *her* with me on one of my trips, that of course she wasn't very interesting when she was forced into leading a humdrum domestic life, coming home from work every day and washing my socks. She has never washed my socks. But her point was that I had never given her a chance to be the person she thought she could be. And she wanted me to give her that chance. She had obviously planned what she was going to say to me, and there wasn't time for me to think of an adequate answer. She seemed so absolutely determined that it was pointless to try to persuade her of anything else."

"But what about the government?"

"She said that we're living here and doing all right, so why shouldn't she?"

"Oh God," Lola says. "It's like the game we used to play as children: here we go round the mulberry bush. You and I are going to be obliged to leave this island next Friday. And you're going to get off the boat at Eleuthera. Am I supposed to stand at the railing blowing kisses to both of you and wishing you a happy voyage? Or do you stand on shore with her blowing me kisses? The whole thing is absurd."

"I know it is. I suggested meeting her in Yugoslavia, though I had no idea where. Or even on the Peloponnesus. But she insisted that it had to be an island, that if it wasn't an island like the one we've been on, she wouldn't be able to prove her point. She hasn't been in love with me for years. But now, all of a sudden, she's convinced that we can be happy together, as if we had been happy until I met you. She's afraid of being alone, that's all. She wants reassurance and doesn't know where to get it, so she decides that she's in love with me. Because if she isn't, then she doesn't know what to do."

"I wish I didn't understand how she feels, but I do."

"I understand, too. If I didn't, things would be a lot easier."

"What if she wants to make love?"

"What do you mean, 'What if she wants to make love?' "

"Just what I said. Would you make love with her?"

"She's not going to . . . oh for God's sake, Lola, this is ridiculous. She's my *wife*."

"I know. That's why I asked."

"Lola, I have no idea what's going to happen. All I know is that our marriage is over, that I love you, and that I'm coming to New York in the fall. We'll just have to get through the rest."

"I think she loves you, Stefan."

"You're wrong. She doesn't. She just thinks she does."

"Well," Lola says. And hesitates. "I suppose time will tell," she says finally.

He looks at her obliquely, and he says, "Let's go home."

*T*HERE IS blood on Lola's underpants. She sits in the bathroom for a long time looking at it, seeing a fetus take shape and fade away. A spot of blood and it is all over: the hope, the expectation, the fear, the hysteria, the desire that passes beyond the transience of mere desire and is imbedded in the subterranean physical knowledge that accompanies each month's release of blood. The moment she knows that she is not pregnant, it becomes impossible to find her way back to that state of mind in which the word "maybe" was infinite in its sense of unfolding possibilities. "I'm not pregnant," she says. And repeats it over and over again, the way children repeat certain words until the words themselves lose their meaning and become mere repetitions of sound. Not pregnant not pregnant not pregnant not pregnant not pregnant notpregnantnotpregnantnotpregnantnotpregnantnotpregnant. Not pregnant. There. It is dead.

She tells Stefan when she comes out of the bathroom. He watches her face, looking for a clue to his own appropriate response. Her face betrays nothing. There is nothing more to betray. "I'm sorry," he says. But there is no conviction in his voice. He is saying it for her sake.

"There's nothing to be sorry for," she says carefully. "It's probably for the best."

"Yes," he says, his face finally showing the relief which he has all along looked forward to, the relief which did not come to her even once during that spontaneous moment of discovery that, no, it was not true.

"If we're leaving in three days, we should get ready," she says.

"There's nothing to get ready. I need an hour to pack and so do you."

"I know," she says. "But I feel as if I have to get ready anyway. To prepare myself for the separation."

"You don't have to prepare yourself, Lola. It's just going to be temporary. Separations can be good for people. You see things more clearly afterward; there's a sense of renewal. Maybe we can arrange to spend a few days together before your boat leaves. And then we'll write. I'll miss you, but that's not so terrible."

"I swear, Stefan, you sound like a stock market analyst telling a little old lady that even if she loses her life's savings, there's still social security."

"And you sound like your mother."

She flinches visibly and takes a deep breath.

"I'm sorry," he says. "I'm just trying to see the positive side of things."

"I understand. But sometimes your way of expressing it . . ." She stops. "Listen, I don't think it has anything to do with missing," she says. "I see things as clearly now as I'll ever see them. And I don't need a sense of 'renewal.' I feel as if I'm attached to you with adhesive tape. If I try to tear myself away, you'll take my skin with you."

His voice is momentarily impatient. "Look, Lola," he says, "the point is that we love each other. We just won't be together for a while."

She looks at him carefully. There is a trace of fear in her face. "Just?" she says.

"Yes, just," he says firmly.

"We have different temperaments, Stefan," she says, struggling to keep the quaver out of her voice. "I love habits and familiarities and routines. I love certainty. You're better at making changes than I am. It's hard for me to start things and even harder for me to stop."

"I know," he says.

"Maybe I should pack for practice. So I can get used to it."

He laughs. "You're making it sound like major surgery instead of a Band-Aid. Don't be dramatic."

"You know," she says. "I can't help wishing that I had been pregnant."

"Why?"

"Because then I would be able to take it all with me."

"You can't ever take it all with you."

"That doesn't stop me from wishing that I could."

There is a small pocket of distance between them when they walk up to the crest of the hill together and sit there looking out at the volcano. She holds herself slightly aloof physically, as if she is walking into a heavy wind and fighting, by the stiff resistance of her body, against its force.

At night, for the first time in over a month, she lies apart from him in the darkness. When he touches her, he can feel the tension in her body between spontaneous response and strained withdrawal. She cries after they make love, and shifts away from him over to her side of the bed.

"I want to be by myself for a while," she says. He does not insist and they fall asleep separately, he becoming suddenly aware of how accustomed he has grown to the space that she usually occupies against his body. In her sleep her will dissolves and she returns to him. By morning they are once again entangled.

•   •   •

The letter arrives in Wednesday morning's mail. Lola stands in the post office reading it. Almost everything has been written by her mother, as if she were trying to create a protective cushion for what is to follow. *"You need someone who can take care of you, sweetheart, not a man who comes and goes when it's convenient. Married men always say . . . You didn't have to live through the war . . . the goyim . . . your father . . . not even a Volkswagen . . . you were on a long trip alone, of course you got lonely . . . his letter, well-intentioned, I realize . . . but what can that man possibly expect . . . your father."*

The letter is four long handwritten pages: explanations and explanations of explanations, cautionary advice, tender solicitude, the thread of ingrown fear that runs like an electric current beneath all of her words. And then the piercing but temporary flashes of pure perception which make it impossible to ignore all the rest, in the way that one might ignore the opinions of someone predictably insensitive. It is not so much that what she says is wrong; it is the way in which she arranges the evidence. The hors d'oeuvres may be perfect, but they are always too hot or too cold. Seeing so much, she is utterly blind in the places where sight might illuminate rather than darken the perspective.

And after her mother's signature, a brief postscript, a single sentence in her father's handwriting: *"As far as I am concerned, he does not exist."*

The words penetrate like a surgical incision. She feels a quick upsurge of pain, and then an absolute numbness, as if the knife, in the course of its passage through nerve, blood and tissue, had suddenly encountered a layer of stainless steel. Her vision blurs for an instant, and when she looks at the page again, the words have vanished, as if they had been written in invisible ink. She sees only the shadow of letters which refuse to shape themselves into anything comprehensible. She tries to focus on them again and cannot.

Stefan has gone to the upper part of the village to finish a painting. She walks back to the house alone, puts the letter on the bed, lies down next to it as if it were a human being, and looks at it in its plain white business envelope with its familiar handwriting. She realizes that she has been holding her breath after each intake, and letting it out only with difficulty. She tries to breathe regularly and cannot. She gets up from the bed, walks into the bathroom and vomits.

She is sick for the rest of the day, alternately feverish and chilled. When Stefan comes home he finds her in bed, with a small ravaged face, her voice reduced again to a whisper which seems to require, even in its minimal form, a maximum of effort. Her eyes are beyond tears, as if the tears had become part of the structure of the eye itself and no longer knew how to start or stop. He sits beside her, waiting for her to say something. She tries several times and fails. Finally she points to the envelope.

He lights a cigarette, opens the letter and reads. When he reaches her father's sentence, he grinds his cigarette into the ashtray.

"I can afford to be angry," he says. "And understand at the same time. It's different for you."

She nods mutely. He is struck by the way in which her face has become absolutely childlike, with the helplessness and bewilderment of a five-year-old.

He holds her for a long time, but she does not respond. Then he draws the covers up over her, lies down on top of them next to her and says, "Sleep, Lola, just try to sleep."

She looks at him and is silent, lying with her eyes wide open, feeling nothing.

Much later at night, when he is certain that she has already fallen asleep, she says in a very low voice, "It's too much for me, that's all. The letter, the government, Marianna coming, us separating, my not being pregnant. Everything in one week. I can't cope with all of it. I'll never try again," she says, with her voice catching. "I'll never try to explain to them again." Then she rolls over and buries her face in the pillow.

He lies next to her in the darkness, feeling in reduced form what she can scarcely tolerate to feel, lies and waits for that reduced form of things to transmit itself to her as well. Though he cannot help thinking that it probably never will.

THE HEAT HAS begun. It is Thursday morning. By six A.M. the air is thick and damp. The landscape has been drained of all color; the anemones have wilted and gone brown. All inner preparations dissolve in the heat. Even the coup dissolves, its sharp edges reduced to a vague blur in which nothing matters but hiding from the glare. It is difficult to stand up, difficult to walk. The sheets are wet rags. The skin, all pores, absorbs water and bloats. The dogs pant in the shade. It is the last day.

Lola lies on the bed with a wet facecloth covering her eyes. Stefan is up at the church finishing his final painting. The canvases have been removed from the walls, taken off their stretchers and thumbtacked, one on top of another, to a single stretcher on which they will all be transported, as if, having been painted singly, they have now become one canvas with feelings and forms superimposed upon each other. The room is stark, bare, returning once again to anonymity. It is too hot for the maroon-and-orange bedspread. Lola has folded it up and placed it in the bottom of her suitcase. Her clothes, too, are packed, with the exception of a towel, a bathing suit, a pair of shorts, a halter and a shift.

She gets up, splashes water on her face and under her arms and walks out on the terrace. The volcano burns in the white light of the bay. Thursday morning's boat lies on top of the water. From a distance it seems innocent, dimensionless, the steaminess of the hold invisible, the urine on the floors invisible, the lurching over the waves forgotten altogether. Like a painted set, it has been scrubbed clean of nuances of character, the mental baggage of departures and arrivals, expectations and disillusionments, the intransigence of enforced movement. Only the caïques move back and forth with their loads of passengers, like animated cartoons against a set backdrop which heat can never burn.

Already Lola has begun to compose in her mind the first letter that she will write to Stefan, as if the act of departure, separation and transformation could be passed over altogether, as if he could be held to her by an uninterrupted conversation of the mind which ignores the imperatives of distance and time. This afternoon he will stop painting and they will make a last expedition to the beach on the far side of the island. Tomorrow, the boat will lift anchor, stopping at Tipos, Eleuthera, Phraxo and Piraeus. Tomorrow, the world will turn itself inside out: from the deck of the boat, it is the island that will appear flat and one-dimensional, the island which will lose its detail. A simple exchange of unrealities, a sleight of hand, and it will be over.

At noon, Lola puts on her bathing suit and a shift, packs lunch and a bottle of retsina into a hemp sack and walks up to the church. By the time she reaches the top of the hill she is exhausted. Stefan is sitting in the shade, smoking. The canvas is done, the brushes cleaned, the paints packed away. There are rings of sweat under the arms of Stefan's shirt. His hair is damp.

"It's too hot to walk to the other side of the island," Lola says. "I could hardly come this far. We should go later when it's cooler and have lunch at the house now."

They walk back at a pace determined by the weight of the air. In the cafe they stop for cold water and a dish of rose jam. Thalassa gives them their bill, five hundred drachmas, seventeen dollars for the month.

At the house, food seems to curdle in the belly. It is too hot to sit out on the terrace, too hot to do anything but lie on the bed with a single sheet beneath them. Light scarcely penetrates the one small high window, and the room is cool and dark, though when they try to make love their skin instantly becomes slippery with sweat, and they move away from each other for the sake of the coolness of separation. Stefan gets up and splashes his body with water. Lola does the same.

By four o'clock the air has thinned. They dress and start up toward the cafe.

"There's a tourist sitting out in front," Lola says.

Stefan glances in the direction of the cafe and stops. "That's not a tourist," he says, with an unnatural stillness in his voice. "That's Marianna."

Suddenly it is no longer today anymore, but tomorrow. "I'm going back to the house," Lola says.

He hesitates for a moment, the alternatives arching through his mind like a series of acrobats. Then he says, "No. I want you to come with me."

"I won't," she says. "I'm not in the frame of mind for a confrontation."

"It won't be a confrontation."

"It has to be."

"Look, Lola, if she's here, she's here. As far as I'm concerned, you are staying with me and I am not going to let you hide in the house."

"Why?" Lola says. "If that's what I want to do?"

"Because I love you, that's why."

Lola reaches out and touches his face, brushing her hand across one cheek and then across the other, as if she is brushing away imaginary cobwebs. "I can't," she says. "I'm sorry, but I can't face her. It's going to be difficult enough saying goodbye tomorrow. I don't want to be obliged to let go a minute from now."

"You won't have to."

"Of course I will. I can't walk up to her and start a casual conversation as if she were an unknown quantity, someone who happened to wander off the boat with the rest of the tourists. I

226

understand why she came. But I don't want to be a hypocrite. It's better if I go back to the house."

"There's nothing to be gained by sacrificing yourself. If you go back to the house, you'll hate her and hate me."

Lola shuts her eyes for a minute and leans up against the whitewashed side of one of the houses. "You're right," she says. "But I can't find the boundaries between understanding her and feeling her feelings so strongly that they blot out my own. I don't know how to sympathize and still preserve myself. Give me a minute to think, please."

"All right, a minute," he says. "Because if it's more than that, you'll get trapped in the thought."

"I can do that in fifteen seconds."

"I know."

She is quiet for a while and then says gently, "Sometimes you amaze me. You're the most decent man I've ever known."

He doesn't say anything. He is looking up toward the cafe. The line formed in his forehead by the permanent cocking of a single eyebrow at the slightest sign of stress deepens. "I wish she hadn't needed to do that," he says.

"So do I," Lola says. "But it proves that she's human."

"Your time is up," he says. He leans over and kisses her hair. "Don't be frightened."

"I am."

"I know."

He takes her hand, but she pulls it away. "There's nothing to prove," she says.

He nods and they walk up to the cafe. The distance is only a hundred yards, but it is like a landscape traversed through the reverse end of a telescope in which the contractions of time impose mental markings on each millimeter of ground. In less than a minute, they are standing only a few feet away from the table where Marianna is sitting. She does not see them at first. Her head is bent over the cafe table. She is writing. Lola feels a quick pang of dismay: her hair is deep auburn, sleekly shaped around her head, a tonal complement to the blue of the sky which surrounds it. She's beautiful, Lola thinks.

"Marianna," Stefan says softly.

She looks up. The auburn hair descends in a flat fringe of bangs down to wraparound sunglasses. It is impossible to gauge the instinctive impact of their arrival; her eyes are completely hidden.

"Du!" she says quietly, and stands up. Stefan puts his hands on her shoulders and kisses her cheek. It is a brief, dry kiss. "*Ich will dir Lola verstellen*," he says.

"Ah," Marianna says and reaches out her hand. "Very pleased." Lola shakes her hand, noticing that their grips are about equal in firmness. Marianna's sunglasses are disconcerting; they prevent all possibility of visual contact, and Lola has the odd sense of being observed from behind an old-fashioned photographer's hood which conceals a highly precise hidden lens.

"She does not look the way I expected," Marianna says to Stefan. "She is less beautiful and more interesting. Why don't you both sit down."

"We were on our way to the beach," Stefan says.

"Don't let me stop you then."

There is a silence, in which the fragile equilibrium of emotional forces is temporarily suspended, as if a rush of wind had threatened to topple it altogether but succeeded only in momentarily endangering it. Lola finds it difficult to swallow, impossible to speak. Stefan lights a cigarette and says to Marianna "*Wie war die Fahrt?*"

"Don't speak in German, *Liebste*, your friend can't understand."

"Marianna!" Stefan says. "Enough."

The lens is broken. Marianna lifts her sunglasses. The eyes behind them are startling: great luminous blue globes awash with feeling, like twin pearls in an open shell seen from a glass-bottomed boat. It is understandable that she would want to conceal them. "I am sorry," she says. "It is not easy, you know."

Lola feels a rush of affection for her. "I don't think it's easy for any of us," she says.

"I will go back to the hotel now," Marianna says. "It was an accident that I came here. I was asleep when the boat stopped at Eleuthera. I didn't hear the call for debarkation. And then it was too late. So I got off here. I took a mule up the stairs and found a hotel room in the town. It was so hot that I fell asleep without having lunch. When it was cooler, I was no longer hungry, so I walked up in this direction, without knowing where I was going."

Stefan and Lola exchange glances. The lie is so blatant that it rings like crystal with a truth of its own.

"It doesn't matter, Marianna," Stefan says. "Maybe it's just as well."

"You should come to the beach with us," Lola says. "You shouldn't stay alone at the hotel."

Marianna looks at her. There is an instant of shared knowledge between them, a female knowledge which transcends circumstance, breaking through to a common condition.

Then Marianna looks away. "It is your last day together," she says. "I don't want to interfere with it."

The words cut both ways. Lola thinks that, yes, there is a shared knowledge, but also and inevitably, there is the rawness of that battle for ultimate control. It is a matter of maneuverability. Generosity is merely the other face of possessiveness.

Suddenly she is seized by an impulse to say something that will break through the structure of things. There is a pounding in her temples, like the mental beginnings of a volcano's quick release of steam.

She takes a deep breath and says, "If you come to the beach with us, maybe we will have a chance to talk with each other. I think that I like you, in spite of everything."

Marianna looks at her again. "I think I like you, too," she

229

says. "Also in spite of everything. I will go back to the hotel for my bathing suit. Is it far from the place where you go to swim?"

"About an hour's walk."

"Then I should wear walking shoes."

"Yes."

"Where shall I meet you?"

All through Marianna's and Lola's conversation, Stefan has been silent. Now he says, "We will come and meet you at the hotel."

Marianna and Lola both look at him. For now, at least, the decision has been made.

• • •

Stefan walks between the two women, surrounded by awkward silences and sidelong glances; he is the obstacle across which they are obliged to perceive each other. Over the last week, the landscape has altered entirely, singed by the heat. There is a breath of the meltemi in the air, playing across the nerve endings, a twelve-tonal scale blowing in from the Sahara. The nerves totter perpetually on the fine edge of hysteria like chalk screeching across a blackboard.

The road is all dust. It rises up around the ankles and dries out the nostrils. Tomorrow the meltemi will reach its full force; quarrels will escalate into murder, grief into suicide, irritation into mental collapse. It will be one of those glazed days in which the air becomes a razor-edged motionless second skin.

Stefan sees the beach in the distance with heat waves shimmering above it. He realizes suddenly that his memory of the beach is not really of the beach at all, but of the cove beyond it. And that the beach itself has been foreshortened in his imagination, telescoped toward the cove, as if the distance from the meadow across the beach and over the cove could be traversed in a matter of moments. In reality, the distance from the beach to the cove is almost a thousand meters.

En route, they pass the small village at the base of the hill which faces out onto the northern section of the beach. It was here that just a few weeks ago Stefan completed one of his paintings.

Marianna points toward a path which leads between the series of connected whitewashed cubes into the heart of the village.

"That reminds me of a painting you did three years ago in Morocco," she says. "Do you remember? The one the psychiatrist from Zurich analyzed?"

"Yes," Stefan says. "I remember."

Lola leans forward slightly in order to see Marianna. "He painted another one very much like it this month," she says.

"Oh yes? You know his paintings are often like that. The psychiatrist said . . ."

"She knows already," Stefan says.

"Oh," Marianna says, flushing, and draws her head back so that it is concealed again behind Stefan's profile.

"I'm sorry," Lola says, this time without leaning forward. "I shouldn't have done that. You've seen him work over many years, and . . ."

"Don't be sorry," Marianna says, though her voice is wavering. "And anyway, I'm sorry, too . . . though there's nothing to be sorry . . ." She stops, adjusts her sunglasses and says flatly, "None of this is necessary."

"It must be," Stefan says.

Marianna turns to face him, though her eyes remain hidden. "And you, Liebste?" she says. "You're merely observing?"

"Let me remind you, Marianna, that it was your decision to come here," he says.

"I wouldn't have had to come if . . ."

"Stop!" Lola says. "Please stop."

Marianna draws back from her combination of anguish and authority. The dust fills her nostrils. She feels afraid of her lack of control over what will happen, afraid of this woman who seems to occupy every inch of Stefan's interior space. She wants to say to him, "Please, Stefan, just tell me that everything will be fine. I'll go along with it if everything will be fine . . ." But of course that is impossible. Such reassurances are always necessary at the moments when they are obviously not to be had. For an instant her mind feels as if a glacier had descended upon it, trapping her emotions like a prehistoric animal caught in a single position, permanently preserved on the edge of doing, the edge of saying, the edge of becoming . . .

Without intending it, they have all begun to walk in step. They are at the end of the road. The black volcanic sand stretches northward to a series of cliffs and coves arching in a horseshoe curve that is visible for miles. To the south, the view is obstructed by the bluff protecting the cove where Lola and Stefan picnicked. It is impossible to see beyond that point.

"Ah hah," Marianna says, lifting her sunglasses and looking first right, then left. Her eyes stop at the bluff.

"Do you come here often?" she says.

"Fairly often," Stefan says. He has decided to protect the cove, to preserve it from her scrutiny. The beach itself, lacking in that quality of intimacy which is the defining characteristic of his life with Lola, is a false clue, and therefore easy to reveal. "It goes on for miles," he says, looking to the north.

"Yes," she says, without shifting her eyes from the bluff. "It is astonishing that such places still exist, that they have been untouched and unspoiled." Her voice is abstracted, vague, automatic. She shakes her head briefly, then turns back to them. "Are you going swimming?" she says.

"Yes," Stefan says, taking off his pants and shirt and walking toward the water.

Marianna unbuttons her shirt and removes it. Her skin is

very fair, untouched by the sun, a sharp contrast to the depth of Lola's and Stefan's tans. She and Lola observe each other covertly, looking for that illusory accumulation of qualities and defects which might translate into the language of anticipated success or failure. Marianna notices particularly how Lola's body inclines in the direction of exaggeration: extremely long-legged, extremely full-breasted, prone to movements which alternate between a strictly controlled almost balletic formality and grace, and a compensatory though equally self-conscious awkwardness. Gestures begun with complete fluidity end in complete disarray, as if she was embarrassed by her own ease and felt the need to apologize for it. She notes as well that Lola's weight, which is now simply sensual, could, after six months of carelessness, turn to fat, and that there are signs of a double tire around her midriff.

Lola, watching Marianna, is aware of her body as being narrower, less extreme in its contrasts than her own, a classical European body, which fits well into small cars and crowded compartments. It is an exercise in compactness: small-breasted, small-waisted, narrow in the shoulders, with a slight shortness in the length of the thighs and a fine fullness in the hips, the body for which millions of continental bikinis are designed, practical in its proportions, equipped to stand a good deal of wear and tear without being shored up from this angle or that. She does not need to work at it, Lola thinks. It is simply there, firm, lean, solid, and will be there most likely, in similar form, ten years from now, with only a slight softening of musculature.

This is terrible, she thinks. All this calculation, all this searching for clues. She turns away from Marianna and bends to remove her sandals, in the process revealing the white line of skin which the sun has left undarkened beneath her bikini bottoms.

"Do you ever swim nude here?" Marianna asks, trying to make up for her quick upsurge of relief over the discovery that there was at least a line.

"Occasionally," Lola says, without looking at her. She feels a sudden desire to protect Marianna against the compulsion to ask questions, the need to know details, as if by the slow exercise of her capacity for mastering the facts, she might ultimately triumph over Lola's and Stefan's being together at all.

"You mean no one ever comes here?" Marianna persists.

"Usually not," Lola says. Every word is so delicate and dangerous that each phrase threatens to upset the balance. She looks at Marianna, trying to gauge the strength of her reserves. It is impossible. She is no tougher and no more delicate than Lola. "Marianna," Lola says. "Don't make things harder for yourself."

There is a brief, sharp silence. Lola braces herself, guessing that Marianna is going to say something harsh or rude in reply, something to deflect the intrusion. Instead, she lifts her sunglasses again, looks directly at Lola and says, "I'm doing the best I can." She stops, as though surprised at the sound of her own voice. Lola feels a quick urge to ease her discomfort by broadening the channels of its possibilities, but her mind has gone suddenly, wildly blank. She can think of nothing at all to say.

By a common instinct, they both look out toward the water where Stefan has begun swimming.

"He seems to be enjoying himself," Marianna says finally. "Do you still want to go in?"

"Not really," Lola says. "I'd rather stay here." The wind has begun to scrape up against the raw edges of her mind. She wonders whether unfinished nightmares can be cured by compassion.

"So would I," Marianna says.

Instantly, they both lapse back into silence, as if the tacit admission of a desire to talk was in fact all they had to say to each other. Lola wants to cry but cannot help thinking it would be an insult to Marianna's efforts at self-control. The tides of hostility and empathy move in and out with frightening rapidity, rhythmic, precise, and extreme. I could be her, Lola thinks. At any moment, I could be her, and this could be happening to me.

They are scarcely able to look at each other. Marianna plays with her wedding ring, turning it around her finger, moving it up over her second knuckle and back into place, then up over the first knuckle. Once she removes it entirely, but then she returns it and continues carrying it along its restricted route back and forth, back and forth.

Lola is mesmerized by the gesture. She's his wife, she thinks, repeating the phrase over and over again in her mind, feeling it sink down into her like a stone. Marianna is his wife. No longer is Stefan "married." He is married to this woman sitting next to her, this woman who could just as easily be she. The idea explodes in her face. The shock of it, of a fact transforming itself into a felt reality, overwhelms her.

"He loves you," Marianna says suddenly. "And I want to hate you for it, but I can't. I hate you for ten minutes and it fades. I hate him for ten and that fades too. Why should I have to care about your being happy together? Why should I have to care about anyone but myself?"

The words seem to require an answer, though both of them know that there isn't one.

When Marianna speaks again, her voice sounds very tired, as if she has been rehearsing the lines in her imagination and has finally reached the point at which she can say them without a pause. "The trouble is that there's no one to blame. No villains. And without them, it's not even possible to be self-righteous. Everything turns into a precipice. I was supposed to meet you and know immediately that you were too trivial to be concerned about. But if you had been trivial, I would think less of him. Now there's no way to think less of anyone."

She looks out at the water again, at Stefan, swimming in the distance. "He's been unhappy for a long time, you know."

"What about you?" Lola says, struggling to keep her voice even. "Have you been unhappy, too?"

"Yes," Marianna says. "But differently. Because I . . ."

She stops and seems unable to continue.

Lola doesn't wait for the end of the sentence. She knows what it is and doesn't want to hear it. It is the only sentence that really matters.

"Maybe we should go swimming after all," Lola says.

"Yes," Marianna says. "Maybe we should."

In the water they all watch each other, carefully maintaining a physical distance from each other which denies the assertion of prerogatives. They are equally grateful for the cessation of contact. Lola does not swim toward Stefan, nor Stefan toward her. They remain three equidistant points of a triangle whose form is sustained entirely by the suspension of movement in any direction.

When they return to the beach, the moment of interlocked understanding has passed, along with its terrors and judgments. It has become an indulgence, to be retracted if possible, and regretted if not. Marianna keeps on her sunglasses and sits apart. Stefan says nothing. Neither does Lola. It seems to all of them that there is nothing more to say.

• • •

The walk back is steeped in silence. At Marianna's hotel, they all shake hands and separate, maintaining the uneasy cordiality which succeeded the momentary exchange of confidences. A semblance of egalitarianism has been tacitly accepted; it is Lola's time until the gangplank is lowered at Eleuthera, Marianna's time after that. The purely mechanical decision creates that illusion of fairness which can, at crucial moments, sustain circumstances otherwise intolerable. All boundary disputes are to be postponed.

Lola does not want to talk about the afternoon at the beach. Neither does Stefan. But later in the evening, Lola goes out for a walk alone, comes back and says, "I want you to go and stay with her."

"That's absurd," he says. "I won't. I've made my decision and . . ."

"Listen," she says. "Understand this. I have to protect her. Because if I were in her place . . ."

"You're not."

"The point is that I could be; two years from now, ten years from now, someday. It doesn't matter when. I don't like myself very well right now, and I have to make up for it. When you're on top of the mountain, you can afford to be generous. Otherwise you don't deserve to be on top of the mountain."

"Don't get carried away, Lola," he says. "You're not on top of the mountain. There's still a long way to go."

"I know," she says. "That's why I want to be generous now. I'm not sure that I'll get another chance. I'm very superstitious about these things, Stefan. She is not going to give you up. I know it. Because she loves you, or believes she does. It's all the same, isn't it? Eventually, things are going to be tooth and nail. And if I can't think well of myself now, I might not be able to live with myself at all later on."

He looks at her strangely, recollecting with a flash that jolts him the day when she insisted that he tell her about Marianna. But the flash instantly blends with another one, of the expression on her face when they made love together under water. It is as if the moments are being brought together now and encapsulated into one. Her face is glowing with something that blends the two seemingly disparate experiences: the same absoluteness, the same extension of herself into a realm where, conscious of her own power to affect, she is intoxicated with the awareness of unfolding possibility.

"All right," he says. "I'll go and have dinner with her. But I'll come back afterward. Is that good enough for you?"

"Yes," she says. "Yes, it's good enough."

She puts her arms around his neck and stands away from him, looking into his face.

He is overcome suddenly with something resembling fear, though it is not quite fear. He doesn't know what it is. Something surreal, as if life had become too microscopic and fragmentary to be encompassed by anything resembling his usual methods. For a second, he wonders whether or not she is really in love with him at all, whether she is not perhaps in love with these images of herself, in love with her own unfolding capacities. But then she says, "I love you," and kisses him.

The thought moves past him.

"I'll see you later," she says.

"Yes," he says. "I'll see you later."

•

When he comes back to the house after several hours, he finds her sitting on the edge of the bed, as if poised for flight.

"How was it?" she says.

"Fine," he says. And nothing more.

She does not ask for more, does not even seem to want it.

"Let's go to sleep," she says.

They undress slowly and carefully. He knows that they are not going to make love tonight, knows that yesterday was the last time for a long time. They lie in bed together quietly, she on her side, he on his. Neither of them knows how to say goodbye.

"I didn't do it to be good," she says suddenly. "I did it because I had to, because I don't know what I believe in anymore."

"I know," he says.

In the darkness they hold hands. And the night is an accumulation of every night, pocketed with memories.

. . .

They are on their way to the boat. Stefan carries his easel on his back. Lola carries a suitcase in each hand. They stop to say goodbye to Christos and Thalassa and Ioannis. The goodbyes are elaborate, but it is as if they have already left, already been forgotten. Thalassa is preparing for the new arrivals, a couple from France. Hans is in the cafe, talking to them about Athens.

"Awful," he says. "It was just awful."

Suddenly Lola is struck by it again. The coup. She has forgotten altogether about the coup, about the fascists. She has forgotten about everything but herself and Stefan and Marianna.

She tries to pretend it away, this lapse of concern so absolute that it makes her doubt whether she ever cared at all.

"We were wondering what happened," she says. "There was no news." She can hear the falseness in her own voice.

Hans looks at her sharply and then looks away. He speaks to the French couple. "There were tanks everywhere," he says. "People were rounded up and taken away. A woman was pushed through the plate glass window of the hotel. There was a young man who had just come from one of the islands with a group of Americans. I had dinner with them the night before. One of the girls was going back to Wisconsin to start a commune. The boy was very smart-mouthed, always saying, 'Fuck everyone.' He can't have been more than twenty. Suddenly, he went after the soldier who had pushed her. And right in front of us, they shot him. An American. A smart-mouthed twenty-year-old American. Killed just like that."

Lola has hardly been listening. She tries to focus on what he has been saying, but is too distracted. I should ask him whom to contact in Athens, she thinks. I should ask him what to do. She feels suddenly ashamed of herself for neglecting so completely to help. For a second she is transported back to the world that begins where she and Stefan and Marianna leave off. But then Stefan calls for her to hurry.

"Goodbye," she says.

Everyone shakes hands. Andreas loads up the mules with Lola's suitcases.

Together, they go down to the town.

• • •

Marianna is ready at the hotel with her things. Andreas has brought an extra mule. They descend in a caravan down to the boat. The caïques are loading up with passengers.

"Spectacular place," one man says. "Really quite spectacular."

Lola feels like saying, "We've been living here," feels like distinguishing herself from the people who have come for a day. But then she thinks, what difference does it make? And says nothing.

They stand at the boat's railing watching the other caïques moving back and forth from the dock. They are not the only ones leaving. It seems that, quietly, many of the foreigners have arrived at the same decision. The honeymoon couple is in the caïque that follows theirs. And the two women anthropologists are already on board.

The honeymoon couple smiles and waves to them and then walks over.

"Well, at least, we know someone on the boat," he says. "Are you two going home?"

There is a moment of chilled silence. Stefan makes a motion

with his head that is neither yes or no. Marianna says nothing. She stands slightly apart.

The gangplank lifts. The horn sounds several deep blasts. The boat moves out toward the water.

They reach Eleuthera early in the afternoon. Stefan spends the last half hour with Lola.

"I'll write every day," she says.

"Yes," he says.

They kiss goodbye. Marianna carries her suitcase. Stefan carries his easel. Together they walk down the gangplank.

No one waves goodbye.

The honeymoon couple stares.

Part Three

*A*LL SUMMER SHE WRITES to him, two, sometimes three, letters a day, strung end to end like a paper chain across the Atlantic. The moment she finishes one letter and brings it to the post office, she begins another, trying to create some seamless communication by which it would be impossible for him to slip through the net of an unshared experience. Her daily life is real to her only in the moments when she is describing it to him on the page. She weaves him tightly into the landscape of her imagination, constructing thick knots at the boundaries of her own world.

The letters cover page after page of white paper. She is withheld, released, withheld, released, like a dancer moving in and out of contractions. Yet the sheer number of letters gives her away, reveals a passion never visible when they were together, as if the mere fact of an unconquerable physical distance had created the space within which such a passion might expand, as if it were no longer forced to contend with any real obstruction. She cannot sleep without his body beside her: she stretches into the night for him, finding muscles and nerves never known before in full extension, fighting until dawn with the fear encountered at their ultimate point, the fear that he will never come. It's too much, she sometimes thinks. Already I need him too much.

He is stunned by her outpouring, even when it alternates with devices intended to dam it. Stunned, and a bit uneasy. He writes twice a week, steadily, consistently, letters which do not tumble over each other or become pell-mell, distracted by the sharp consciousness of physical separation. He writes that he is busy, that he is organizing a museum exhibition which is taking up most of his time. She interprets it as a veiled assertion that he has forgotten her. He writes that he has less money than he thought, and she is sure that he has decided against making the voyage. He writes that Marianna is suffering, that he has discovered new complexities in her, that he has come to feel a deep sympathy for her, and Lola is sure that his life with Marianna has reclaimed him totally. His every difficulty becomes part of a geometric progression of doubt's fevers. He is not there, and the proofs available are, by their very nature, merely verbal. As the volume of words increases, so does her feeling of the impossibility of ensuring anything at all.

"Do you love me?" she writes. "Yes," he writes. "Are you sure?" she writes. "Of course I'm sure," he writes. "Absolutely?" she writes. "Yes, absolutely," he writes.

She writes that she is afraid of losing him and then writes a second letter to contradict the effects of the first and a third to balance the influence of the second. It becomes a mania with her, the desire for an affirmation which seals off every possibility. She asks and asks, and drives herself into an exhaustion of uncertainty which cannot be cured by any reassurance.

At first, his letters are warm and encouraging. He reiterates, over and over again, that she has nothing to be afraid of, that he will come in the fall and everything will be fine. But her fear remains, and by July she has lost all sense of proportion.

In August, his letters begin to change. Initially, there creeps into them a slow sense of bewilderment, as if he is trying to resist a tidal wave by simply standing still in its presence, though, by the end of the month, his tone has become cooler, less filled with that aura of certainty which, even at its most certain, was never certain enough. The cooler his letters are, the more her desperation increases, until a gulf has opened up between them as wide as the ocean which separates them. It is happening, she thinks. What she all along has feared is actually happening.

She wakes up on the morning of her birthday with a simultaneous feeling of anticipation and apprehension. She has had a nightmare, of a woman wearing bright orange lipstick and a bright orange scarf tied around her throat, who sang while she pulled the knot of the scarf tighter and tighter, and then went down on her knees, with her voice still singing, beginning to sound choked and broken, while Lola yelled, "Stop, please stop," and the woman shrieked an unearthly wail, three times repeated.

The telephone rings. Lola reaches her hand out for it. "Happy birthday, sweetheart," her mother says. "The best of life, love and happiness."

"Oh," Lola says. "Thank you."

"Did I wake you?"

"No. I was just lying in bed."

"What are you doing for your birthday?"

"Going out."

"Oh. Well, enjoy yourself, sweetheart. And have a good day."

Lola puts down the receiver. She does not get out of bed. For a second she thought it was Stefan calling to surprise her on her birthday. For a second, she thought the woman really was going to strangle.

She showers, dresses, drinks a cup of Greek coffee and goes downstairs to check the mail. There is no sign of a letter, package or telegram from Stefan.

At five-thirty, she comes back to the apartment, goes to the kitchen cabinet and opens up a bottle of retsina. How different it is to buy retsina on Ninth Avenue, she thinks, than to buy it on the island. She pours out a glass. "Happy birthday," she says, lifting the glass in the air. "*Nazdarovnye!*" Then she goes to the refrigerator and takes out feta cheese, Greek olives, peppers, cucumbers and lettuce. Six o'clock. Seven o'clock.

247

The phone does not ring. By seven-thirty, the rivulet of panic which had begun to carve out a narrow channel inside of her has become a torrent. She climbs into bed, turning from her back to her stomach, her stomach to her back. She takes the phone off the nightstand and puts it next to her pillow. She stares at it, as if by the mere force of her will she could compel it to ring. It does not ring. I can't do it, she thinks. I can't.

In half an hour, she does. She picks up the phone, dials the operator and asks for overseas information. A voice with an Austrian accent gives her the phone number on Sommerstrasse. She closes her eyes, trying to imagine the house: the layout, where the phone is, who would be most likely to answer it. What if Marianna answers? she thinks. Then what would I do?

She looks at the number she has just written down. There is an expanding pressure in her lungs. It is reaching up into her throat, pressing against her rib cage. It is already twelve-thirty in Austria. If she waits any longer, it will be impossible.

She picks up the phone again and dials the operator. "How long will it take to get through to Austria?" she asks. "Very quickly," the operator says. "All right," she says. And hangs up. She has a sudden sense of fatality, as if she is dealing herself a death blow. But I have to, she thinks again. The sense of necessity, of absolute and indisputable imperative, overwhelms her.

She drinks another glass of retsina, while staring at the telephone. It does not ring. She lies down again. The image of him, riding across the island next to her on a donkey, floats through her mind. She shuts her eyes and dozes off. She is awakened by the sound of the telephone. "Ready on your call to Austria," the operator says.

She looks over at the clock. It is almost eight-thirty. She cannot seem to count. She just knows with a certainty bordering on terror that it is late, very late, over there in Austria.

She hears the phone ringing in his house. It rings once, twice, three times. Marianna picks it up. *"Ja,"* she says. Lola's mind goes blank. She can think of nothing to say. How can I have done this? she thinks. How on earth could I have done this? "Marianna," she says. "This is Lola. I'm in New York."

There is a silence on the other end. *"Ein moment,"* Marianna says. She walks into the living room where Stefan is asleep on the couch. *"Du,"* she says to Stefan. *"Telefon von Amerika."*

He is shocked into wakefulness. Something has happened, he thinks. Something dreadful. He follows Marianna into her bedroom and sits down on her bed. Marianna circles around, unable to decide where to go. "I'll be just a minute," she repeats over and over again. "I will. I'll go to the next room. I'll go to the kitchen. I'll . . ."

"Hello!" Stefan says. "What's the matter? Are you all right?"

There is a silence. "Lola," Stefan repeats. "Lola?"

The voice that comes over the telephone is small and stunned, the voice of someone who has been picked up by a tornado and thrown through the air, anticipating instant destruction, only to find herself back on the ground again, in the same place where the terrifying voyage began. "It's my birthday," Lola says.

"Your birthday?" Stefan says, astonishment for an instant outweighing all other emotions. "You called at three o'clock in the morning because it's your birthday?"

"Two," Lola says. "Not even two. I shouldn't have. I know I shouldn't have. But . . ."

At the same moment, Marianna is saying, "Her birthday? What in God's name is the matter with that girl?"

And Stefan is saying, "Marianna, please, do me one favor. Just go into the living room."

"But it's still my house, Stefan, and she can't do that . . ."

"I know she . . . Lola? Are you still there?"

"Yes," Lola says. "I'm still here. It really is my birthday, Stefan. And I can't stand it anymore. I can't stand being separated.

I feel as if I've made the whole thing up, as if it's an illusion. I can't touch you anymore, can't tell . . . Stefan, where is the telephone?"

"In the bedroom," he says. "Next to Marianna's bed."

"Next to *her* bed?" she says.

"Yes," he says.

"And where do you sleep?"

"In the living room. Lola, is that what you called to find out?"

"I'm going," Marianna says. "I'm going right this instant." Stefan nods, barely even hearing her.

"I'm sorry, Stefan. I'm so sorry. I didn't call for that. I called because, I called because . . ." She cannot seem to finish the sentence. "I called because I miss you, because I miss you terribly. I called because I want to come. Is that all right, Stefan, for me to just come?"

"Come?" he says. "How can you come? I told you, Lola. I'll be there in a month."

"But a month seems like such a long time, Stefan. I feel so confused and . . ."

"Your three minutes is up, New York."

"Thank you, operator," she says. "Stefan, please keep talking. I don't care what you say, but please keep talking."

"I don't have anything to say, Lola. Go to sleep. Do me a favor. Go to sleep. And I'll write to you tomorrow. I promise."

"Okay," she says. "Stefan, I'm sorry. Do you believe me that I'm sorry?"

"Yes," he says.

"And will you tell Marianna I'm sorry?"

He doesn't answer.

"Please tell her."

"Okay," he says. "Goodbye, Lola."

"Goodbye, Stefan."

When he hangs up, he sits on the edge of the bed for a long

time. He can hear Marianna moving around in the next room. "Marianna?" he calls.

She doesn't answer.

He walks into the living room. She is standing with her forehead pressed against the wall. "That girl doesn't care about anyone but herself," she says.

"She was lonely," he says. "It's her birthday."

"Yes, yes," she says. "But she has no sense of . . . no sense of anything, Stefan. What about me? I was alone the whole time you were with her. And I'm going to be alone again. I wish you would leave right away. I wish you would just go, and . . ."

He thinks suddenly that this is for now, for tonight, and that tomorrow it will be the same again, tomorrow she will say, "No, I don't want you to go. I don't want a divorce. You'll get over this affair, you will I'm sure, and . . ."

"You excuse her, Stefan. You really do. You should have refused to speak to her."

"I can't do that," he says.

"You don't love me," she says.

He doesn't answer.

"It'll end, Stefan. I swear to you. In a year it will be finished. And you'll come back. I know you will."

"Just go back to sleep, Marianna," he says. "Now go back to sleep . . ."

"Stefan," she says. "Would you mind . . ."

"Mind what?" he says.

"Would you mind sleeping in here tonight?"

"I can't," he says. And looks at her face, at the pained, restrained expression. "All right," he says. "If you want me to."

She climbs under the covers. He lies down next to her, on his back, without touching her. "Will you hold me?" she says.

"Yes, Marianna, I'll hold you," he says.

"Stefan, I love you," she says.

"Try to sleep, Marianna," he says. "Just try to sleep."

"Will you kiss me?" she says.

He doesn't answer.

"Please," she says.

He reaches over and kisses her cheek.

"How can you do that, Stefan? How can you do that?"

She is crying now, crying with all of the tears she has spent months on end storing up.

"Do you want me to go back to the living room?" he says.

"No, stay," she says.

"All right," he says.

"I hate her, Stefan. I do."

"I know. Go to sleep."

"Stefan?"

"What?"

"Nothing."

• • •

It is the middle of September when he arrives in New York. They walk up to her apartment: seven flights of stairs leading to four rooms. He looks around. There is no furniture yet, just a double mattress and a rocking chair she found discarded on the street. He stands by the window, scanning the landscape: the watertowers, the Shell station next door, the factory across the street with its huge billows of smoke settling over the sky like a parachute followed by other smokestacks all around in every direction, echoing each other contrapuntally as the air becomes grayer and grimier. On the next block is a firehouse. The fire engine comes screeching out, like a half-crazed creature bolting from an asylum.

"I had very little money," she says.

"Yes," he says.

"Without any money . . ."

"I understand," he says.

"It's not like Greece," she says.

"No, it isn't," he says.

She leads him through the three rooms to the fourth at the end of a corridor. It is completely empty.

"I thought you could use this for a studio," she says.

"A studio?" he says. "But this is a child's room."

"It was a child's room," she says. "Before I came here. I didn't change the wallpaper. I thought that when you arrived . . ."

He walks out of the room. "I think we should talk, Lola," he says.

"About what?" she says. "Don't you like it?"

He comes into the living room, looks for a place to sit, sees only the rocking chair and chooses the floor.

She moves to sit beside him, but he motions her away. "Take the chair," he says.

He lights a cigarette and looks around for an ashtray. She gets up, goes into the kitchen and comes back with the lid of a jar.

"I thought a lot while I was in Austria," he says.

"Oh," she says, afraid already to look at him, afraid to hear what he is going to say.

"I thought about you, about me, about Marianna. I must admit that your letters came as a surprise to me."

"I'm sorry," she says and then stops. She is ashamed of herself for needing to apologize for them.

"There's nothing to be sorry about. I just didn't realize. It was a side of you . . . it was unexpected."

"Yes," she says, nodding stiffly. "Yes, it was."

"I also thought about your mother," he says.

"My mother?" she says, looking startled. "What does this have to do with my mother?"

"Well," he says, "for your mother, it is a shocking thing, our living here together. It's not as if we're six thousand miles away. As I said, Lola, I gave this a great deal of thought. I would like to do a lot of work while I'm in New York. And a friend of mine from Austria gave me the name of someone to contact here, a woman who has a studio near Gramercy Park."

"A woman?" Lola says.

"Yes," he says. "A woman in her sixties. She has a studio which she sometimes rents out for a few months."

Lola's face contracts. She looks away from him. "But you have a studio here," she whispers.

He stands up and comes over to where she is sitting. He lifts his hand and strokes her hair. She does not turn or move. Her body is rigid.

"It would be better for us to live separately," he says. "Your mother will be less upset."

"Live?" she says with a wail. "You mean a place to *live*?"

"Yes," he says.

She is silent for a long time, as if she is standing with one foot in the air and doesn't know where to place it. The thought of his being alone in New York, separated from her, discovering a life for himself which does not fully intersect with hers and is not under her influence, horrifies her. She will not be able to track him mentally through his days. There will be huge gaps of uncertainty. Anything could happen. Anything at all.

"I don't care if my mother is upset," she says finally, still not looking at him.

"It would be better anyway," he says.

Again she is silent. "When did you make this decision?" she says after a while.

"In August," he says.

"After the phone call or before?"

"Before."

"Oh," she says, remembering now the change in his letters. "Did you meet someone else?"

"Why would I meet someone else?"

"I don't know," she says. "I have no idea."

"Lola," he says. "I just want to do what's best. I still love you. I just . . . want to do what's best."

She says nothing. But thinks that, no matter what he says, things will never be the same.

• • •

The studio, as it turns out, will not be available for another month. Stefan wants to begin painting; Lola wants to talk. They talk. They talk, it seems, for days. She cries, stops crying, turns to him in her sleep, stops turning to him.

He tells her about his summer, about Marianna, the changes which have taken place in her, her love for him. "It was a difficult thing," he says. "Saying goodbye at the airport to Marianna, and then right away starting all over again with you. There ought to be a period of . . . a decent interval. You don't leave someone just like that and . . ."

"Just like that?" she says. "Five months is not 'just like that.' "

"I know," he says. "But no matter how long it takes, in the end it always seems 'just like that.' She wanted a separation, she didn't want a separation. She didn't know what she wanted."

"And you?"

"Me? I don't know. I wanted to see New York. I wanted to be with you. And I wanted to paint."

"I see," she says.

"Do you want to lie down for a while, Lola?" he says. "You'll feel better."

"Better than what?" she says.

He doesn't answer.

255

In the afternoon, they go for a walk around the neighborhood. He is surprised that the buildings are red. He had expected everything to be gray and thirty stories tall. He is surprised at the neighborhood, surprised that she lives together with blacks and Puerto Ricans and Chinese and Ukrainians and Jews. He thought that white people lived in one part of the city, and black people lived in Harlem. He is surprised at the garbage on the streets. On her block there are burnt up mattresses, unstuffed skeletons of upholstered chairs, cars stripped of every useful part and then set on fire, a slaughterhouse with a gape-bellied whole pig being carried in from a truck, and a sewing cooperative followed by a Puerto Rican social club with a turquoise facade and yellow windowsills.

"All of New York isn't like this," she says. "Just the Lower East Side. Because it's a slum."

They walk uptown, past the fruit and vegetable stores with Ukrainian names, past the women wearing flowered babushkas, past a furniture store where an old man with payess down to his shoulders, wearing a black hat and long black coat, is dozing in a pink velour chair set out on the street.

Then they walk across town, to Sixth Avenue, where they take a bus to Riverside Drive.

"This is where I grew up," Lola says. "This is the park where I spent my childhood." They sit on a bench near the boat basin, where a Chinese junk is moored alongside a sleek houseboat. There is a metal guard railing between them and the river. Deep lavender light falls on the railing. Everything around it seems to be inked in.

"I love you," Lola says. "I can't help it. I still love you."

The line in his forehead deepens. "I love you, too," he says. "And I can't help it either."

Lola stretches out on the bench and puts her head in Stefan's lap. The pulse of him, the quick beating in his stomach when she turns and presses her head against it, the sense of him solid underneath her. This is what I want, she thinks. Exactly this. She abandons herself to the feeling for a moment . . . but then begins thinking about the studio again, about what she should do to persuade him against taking the studio.

"If you take that studio next month," she says, "you'll be obligated to it. If you live with me instead and save your money, you can see how things develop, see how you like the city. Then we can get a different apartment together."

"But I can't stay," he says. "I promised Marianna I would come back in three months. You knew that, Lola. I won't be divorced until the spring. Besides, I have an exhibition in January. You should get a job that you like and stick with it, instead of quitting as soon as I arrive, the way you did this time. I can't tell what is going to happen in these next months. All I know is that I can still make a living in Europe. I'm already established there. It takes a lot of effort to become known in America."

"Oh," she says. And then, "But Kokoschka did it."

"Did what?"

"Left Austria."

"But I'm not Kokoschka. And the circumstances were different in 1938. I don't have to leave. I have a choice."

"I thought you made your choice. Months ago."

"Lola," he says. "It's not only up to me. There are circumstances. I just told you . . ."

"A moment ago you were saying that Kokoschka left because of circumstances, but you had a choice. I don't believe in circumstances, Stefan. I never have."

"You can believe or not believe, Lola. They're still there."

"But you overcame those circumstances," she says. "We spent months in Greece discussing this, and now all of a sudden, you see your life as being controlled by circumstance. Is Marianna a 'circumstance'?"

"Listen, Lola," he says, ignoring her question. "Taking a job isn't irrevocable. You can always change your mind . . ."

That's the whole problem, she thinks. You can always change your mind.

· · ·

He gives in to her and temporarily abandons his plans for the studio. But he does not use the room at the end of the corridor. Instead, he does sketches and exercises around the neighborhood and two small canvases from the roof. At Lola's insistence, he comes back to the house every day for lunch.

In the morning, they get up together, shower, dress and drink American coffee. They do not linger in bed. Stefan prepares his paints and goes out of the house, while Lola takes the hemp bag she bought in Greece and spends the morning shopping for groceries.

She chooses food as much for its shape and color as for its taste. She designs still lifes on the table, patterns of vegetables in ochres, oranges and reds. She takes plates and glasses and cups, collected during her travels, out of a drawer. The plates are white in the center with an olive gray border, the cups low-slung ellipses, glazed in off-white with streaks of brown and brilliant turquoise on the inside that become even brighter when wet. The glasses are tall, slender, transparent, the color of brandy when it is held up in a bottle against firelight. They come from a small village outside of Mexico City. She carries everything to the table as if to a ceremonial, laying down the knives, forks and spoons, lining up the plates, admiring the patterns and thinking what an enormous difference there is between a table set for two, with each object having its counterpart, and a table set for one. She makes everything into a matter of aesthetic effect and decides that deep down she is really domestic.

Gradually this ritual of lunch together begins to take hold of her, begins to make her feel once more that perhaps she was mistaken about things' being over, perhaps it was just the strain of being separated for so long. Maybe now, she thinks, everything will be all right.

Though one morning he wakes up and says, "I've decided to go to Brooklyn today. To paint the Brooklyn Bridge."

"Can I go with you?" she says.

"No," he says. "I need to be alone."

"What about lunch?" she says.

"I'll be back for dinner," he says.

"Oh," she says.

"You look so stricken," he says. "I would never have expected you to become a hausfrau."

She flinches and laughs nervously. There is a barely perceptible edge of disdain in his voice. She suspects that he means it.

"Me?" she says. "A hausfrau?"

"Yes, you," he says. *"Ma petite Russienne.* A hausfrau."

He kisses her, gets out of bed, showers and leaves.

She puts the glasses and cups and plates back in the drawer. She doesn't go to the market. She sits in the house and waits.

• • •

At five-thirty in the afternoon, she is still in the house. The telephone rings. It is Stefan. "I'm calling from the Austrian Cultural Center," he says. "A friend of mine from Vienna is having an exhibition here. We are talking and having something to drink. They want to go out for dinner afterward."

"I thought you were in Brooklyn."

"I was," he says. "This morning. But at around lunchtime, I called my friend, and he told me about this exhibition. So I came back into the city, had lunch with him, and then came here."

"Oh," she says. She is having difficulty getting the air into and out of her lungs. All day she has been in a state of suspended animation, unable to go anywhere or do anything because of the thought, which she could not relinquish, that he might, despite everything, come home early. Even the trip to the employment agency had been canceled. I can't, she thought. I can't spend all day every day away from him. We have only three months together. For three months we can manage. Maybe a part-time job, maybe . . .

"Where is the Cultural Center?" she says. "I can meet you there."

There is a pause which arches through her mind like a rocket. "No," he says carefully. "You wouldn't enjoy it."

"How do you know?" she says, giving in finally to the desire, the desire and desperation. "I might. I could be there in an hour."

"No," he says, this time more firmly. "I'm sure you wouldn't. It's all Austrians. We'll be speaking German. And besides, my friend . . ."

"Yes," she says. "What about your friend?"

"He's a friend of Marianna's too. It would upset her. I . . ."

She takes the receiver away from her ear and slowly, cautiously lowers it onto the hook, so that there is almost no sound at all when the phone disconnects. She waits five minutes for it to ring again. It doesn't. She gets up, goes to the telephone book, looks up the number for the Austrian Cultural Center and starts to dial. At the last number, she stops, puts the receiver down again and walks to the closet. She takes out the only dress she owns, slips it over her head, brushes her hair and walks out the door.

In an hour she is at the Cultural Center, or rather, across the street from the Cultural Center. There are no lights on inside. She stands there as the cars pass by, obscuring again and again her view of the entrance. Once, she crosses the street, only to turn around and cross back again. After five minutes, she walks away, back to the subway, and goes home.

. . .

When he arrives at eleven o'clock, he finds her lying on the bed staring at the ceiling. She sits up when he walks in the door.

"What's the matter?" he says.

"What's the matter?" she says, her eyes widening with fury. "You've been gone the whole evening and you're asking me what's the matter?"

"You hung up on me," he says.

"Why didn't you call back?"

"Because I didn't have anything else to say."

"And why weren't you at the Cultural Center?"

"What do you mean?"

"I went," she says. "There was no one there."

"When?"

"After I spoke to you. I arrived at six-thirty."

"It was over by six. The Cultural Center closes. But why did you come when I told you . . ."

"Because I couldn't stand it," she says.

"Couldn't stand what?"

"The whole thing," she says. "I don't understand why you came here, Stefan. If you didn't want to be with me, then why did you bother?"

"I did want to be with you," he says, "but not every minute."

"In Greece . . . ," she says.

"This is not Greece. This is New York. There are *other* things to do besides be together. This is an interesting city. I want to get to know it."

261

"Why can't you do that *with* me?"

"I don't know. I just can't."

"You don't want to. That's the only reason."

"Maybe so," he says. He looks at her. Her face is pale and puffy. She seems to have gained weight. There is a kind of torpor in her body, the very opposite of that concealed languor which once so magnetized him. He feels a quick distaste for her stratagems and self-neglect. Your dignity, he wants to say to her. What about your dignity?

But instead he says, "I'm tired of this, Lola. I don't have any room to breathe. You put so much pressure on me . . ."

"What pressure?" she says, her face going white.

"I don't know what kind. Just pressure: to have lunch with you every day, to do this with you and that with you, to talk with you whenever you're in the mood for conversation . . ."

"But I love you," she says.

"What does that have to do with it?"

"People who love each other spend time with each other. They talk with each other and they do things with each other. I don't see what's so unusual about . . . And besides, Stefan. All we have is three months."

"That's what you're always saying, Lola. 'All we have is . . .' To me it doesn't make any difference how much time we have. That's your obsession. I live the way I live no matter whether I have three days or ten years."

"I don't believe you," she says.

"Well, you should," he says. "Because it's true. I can't stand all this 'talking' anymore. Talking on the telephone, talking in bed, talking through the mail. You never used to do that. You left it to me to figure out what was happening, instead of telling me every instant. You know, Lola, I have never talked about love so much in my life. For weeks we've been talking about nothing but love."

"I didn't think we were talking 'about' love," she says. "I was talking because I love you. What about you?"

"I don't know," he says. "I don't know anymore."

"Oh," she says. "I see. Well, maybe . . . we need time together, Stefan. Isn't that what we need?"

"We need sleep," he says. "Eight hours of sleep."

"Must you change the subject?" she says. Her voice is wavering.

"Yes," he says. "Yes yes yes."

She walks over to the window, looks down at the street, then turns around and comes back.

"I think I'll stay at a friend's house tonight," she says.

"If you want to be alone, I can go to a hotel."

"No, I'll go," she says, reaching for her shoes. When she looks up at him, there is a glint in her eyes of something he has not seen since the very first evening they spent at the restaurant in Greece when she went to sit with the Americans. It is something resembling hatred.

"Neither of us is going," he says.

"Oh no?" she says.

"No," he says.

He goes into the bathroom and puts on the pajamas which he has not worn since his arrival. The sight of him wearing them seems to affect her more deeply than anything else he has done. Her eyes fill with tears.

"You didn't have to do that," she says. "You didn't have to be so explicit."

He doesn't answer. He gets into bed, wraps the top sheet around him and moves over close to the wall, facing away from her.

She climbs in next to him. "Good night, Stefan," she says.

"Good night, Lola."

They lie in their separate places for a long time without speaking. Then Lola says, "Stefan, are you awake?"

"Yes," he says.

"Can't we just start over?" she says. "We could leave New York altogether. We could go back to the island. We were happy there. It was only when you came here. Do you remember . . ."

"Lola," he says, "there's no point in remembering."

"But there is," she says. "You have to understand. If things had been just a little bit different . . ."

"But they weren't."

"They could have been."

"Stop it, Lola."

"Stop what?"

"I don't know. Everything."

"I can't," she says. "I've been trying since . . ." She thinks back, trying to remember when . . . since the very beginning, trying . . . trying to stop . . .

Stop what? The Atlantic Ocean, the dental bills from coming, the mail that never arrived on time, the fact that he had been more critical of himself and at the same time more accepting, that he embraced contradictions without being torn apart by them, whereas she . . . that she couldn't stand to have him fall asleep first, that making love outdoors made sense to her, that he considered doing the dishes unmanly and got dysentery every time he sat down on the ground, that he disliked her need for "the freedom to vacillate" and she disliked the same need in him, that he also disliked the Expressionists, her housekeeping, long conversations, people whose passions were exaggerated, and managed, for a while, to love her nonetheless . . . that he was fifteen years older than she was and had stopped clawing at the world, that everything for her had a significance, that five days out of

264

seven when they were apart, she was miserable without him and the other two, indifferent, that he had been more patient with her than she thought she deserved, that she was mesmerized by his silences and memorized what he said, that she loves him, still loves him, in a peculiarly defiant, yet dependent way? STOP WHAT, STEFAN? WHAT DO YOU WANT ME TO STOP?

"I can't stop, Stefan," she says, crying now in earnest. "I can't stop any of it."

He doesn't answer.

"Stefan?" she says.

He still doesn't answer.

"I love you," she says, over and over and over again. "I love you, I love you, I love you. Can't stop. Why stop? Can't stop."

•

The lights from the street traffic cross and recross the ceiling, like the flashlight of a policeman looking for prowlers. There is the muffled sound of a horn on the avenue. The fire engine is still. Inside of Lola's mind, she hears it screeching. I'm not going to cry anymore she thinks. I'm not going to let things get the better of me. Besides, she thinks, she has cried too often already, cried her way straight into the meaninglessness of tears. A mosquito passes close to her face, then vanishes into the darkness. She swats at it and misses, feeling a surge of rage against a creature capable of catapulting her into a helpless agitation so intense that she is unable to resist it. She waits for the mosquito to pass again. Five minutes; ten minutes; she does not hear it. She turns over and presses her face into the pillow. The mosquito buzzes in her ear. She sits up in bed and looks into the darkness. Of course, she wouldn't be able to see it. She has no idea where it is. All she knows is that sooner or later it will come back, will torment her with its appearances and reappearances, the nerve-wracking insistence of its presence, and that she will lie awake ·for hours until finally she is able to aim just right and get it. It passes again, and again she misses. Each time she misses, her nervous system jerks spasmodically, like a puppet being flung about by some wild but inept puppeteer. She wants to turn on the light but is afraid to wake Stefan. He'll be annoyed, she thinks, we'll fight and then I won't sleep at all. We'll wind up going through the whole thing again: choosing our places, choosing our separateness. I wish we were in Greece, she thinks. If only we were back in Greece.

Suddenly, despite her resolve not to, she finds herself crying again, hoping that she won't wake Stefan, hoping at the same time that he will stir, wake, answer, deny, deny everything that with or without his denial still remains true. He doesn't love me anymore, she thinks. That's all there is to it. This time her mind does not race to intercept and filter the knowledge, to rearrange it and make it bearable. Thought comes too late to be of any use. She lies there beside him with only the dumb repetition of it rising up out of her, her body breathing it in and out, breathing and seeming to suffocate on it, repeating, he doesn't love me anymore, doesn't love me.

With no part of his body is he touching her. The top sheet is still wrapped around him, as if to enforce an added layer of distance. She reaches out and touches the nape of his neck with one finger, then draws back. The mosquito passes. At any moment, she is going to scream. She gets up out of bed and walks into the living room, thinking that what she really must do is leave in the morning, let him know nothing, no goodbyes, nothing that might alter her resolve. The thought inspires her with the power of something already accomplished; she feels uplifted by the rising belief that she will, by simply vanishing, earn his respect, his gratitude, and ultimately, though that is not to be thought of now, his love.

She sits in the rocking chair by the window, looking out at

the streetlights, until gradually she ceases to see New York at all and sees instead only the moonlight bonewhite bleached terrace of the house in Greece, the lemon trees with their whitewashed twisted trunks, the stone wall almost fluorescent beyond them, begins to hear the long-in-coming first rooster crow and the answering rooster crow down in the turning alleys of the town, begins to hear the first predawn sound of the first man on his donkey, its bells heard so clearly way up and around the invisible road, coming from the hills toward the town, increasing with the simultaneous increase of light until there is the beginning of a brightness in the air and the knowledge that it is only two, maybe less, hours until the bakery opens, with the man on the mule probably going down to put the bread in the ovens, in the dim whiteness of the dough-rich caverned rooms, where the opening up of possibility has already begun and all hysteria will end, where she can establish an early-morning independence, free of Stefan, allowing him his freedom by simply bringing back fresh early-morning bread from a bakery.

Yes, she thinks. In the morning, I'll go out to the bakery. First thing in the morning. It can be like Greece again. No reason why it can't.

It is settled then, she thinks, sure and settled. And within that sureness, there is a slow drowsiness, the fruit of imagination satisfied and conviction subverted. She watches the streetlights merge with the lemon predawn light and thinks: only two hours to wait, only two hours, must not fall asleep, no don't fall asleep, don't fall asleep, with the drowsiness growing, no don't sleep, no don't sleep.

•

In the morning, he finds her curled up in the rocking chair by the window. He shakes her shoulder and she wakes up. "Oh," she says. "I have to go to the bakery."

"Don't bother," he says. "I'm going out. I'll have breakfast on the corner."

"Please," she says. "Stay here for breakfast."

He shakes his head. "I thought about it last night," he says. "And as I said a month ago, I think it would be best if I went ahead and took the studio."

"The studio!" she says. "Oh no, don't take the studio. Please, Stefan, please don't take the studio."

But this time he is adamant. She cannot stop herself from pleading. She is sliding backward, back to that place where her life is his and not her own, where a night has simply passed and been swallowed up. She is sliding so rapidly that there isn't even enough time to jam on the brakes, to say, there was a mosquito, I sat up all night, it can be like Greece. No time to say anything.

"Please, Lola," he says, looking at her and seeing not her but the pool of desperation which surrounds her. "I can't stand to see you do this. Please, Lola."

She becomes suddenly quiet. She doesn't know what to do anymore. It doesn't matter about bakeries, memories, resolve. Nothing matters. She feels herself arching back into a web from which there is no possibility of disengagement. There is a schism in her system which seems to be irreparable. It is tearing her apart.

"Stop what?" she says. "What do you want me to stop?"

"What?"

"Nothing."